Katie In Love

CHLOE THURLOW

ACKNOWLEDGMENTS

Many thanks to Elizabeth W. for her suggestions and encouragement through the writing of this novel; and thank you Brian Rouley, surely one of , the best editors in the business

1
Midnight Kiss

If you add the shadow of death to a moment of passion you are in that instant free of all normal ties, your mind grows still and your body enters a state of non-being. Pleasure and pain, sex and death, *yin* and *yang* are mismatched twins, two fish each containing the eye of its opposite.

I wrote that sentence before my morning appointment with the doctor. It means nothing in isolation but I awoke with those words in my head and committed them to paper – the keyboard, the monitor. The winter is cold, bleak, colourless. There are no clouds, no sky, just a grey blanket like a shroud lowering over London.

The little finger on my right hand has a fracture. It is painful. The doctor spent a long time with my hand like a song bird nursed in his palm, his shirt cuff clipped with an onyx link, the gold face of his watch gripped by the strap nesting in a hairy wrist. Broken fingers are oddly intimate.

'You do look pale,' he said.

'Yes, I noticed in the mirror.'

'Are you sick?'

'Yes...'

He squeezed my good fingers. 'Do you want to tell me?'

I sighed. 'I write, you know, books...'

'Ah,' he replied.

He nodded wisely. He understood. Writing is a sickness, an ailment, an addiction. When I'm not writing, I'm thinking about what I have written that day and, when I do go to bed, I lie sleeplessly thinking about what I am going to write when I get up and start again the following day.

I am a night person, an insomniac, the girl at the bar who looks like she should have gone home and maybe has no home to go to. A false image I cultivate. I am thin, theoretically attractive, in an abstract sort of way. I have hollow cheeks, high cheekbones, long legs, perhaps too thin, lips dry with cold, clotted with gloss. I have stopped being promiscuous and compose my work in the dead hours between two and six while London sleeps and the night planes follow the Thames into Heathrow carrying businessmen and migrants hoping to make it in the greatest city on earth. When you are bored with London you are bored with life. That's what it says along the side of the number 19 bus Mother takes to Peter Jones.

When I do sleep, I sleep badly, in spite of the magnets under my mattress that are supposed to orientate my body north to south so the lay lines and dragon lines pass through the invisible portal at the top of my skull and down to my feet, my best feature, I would soon be told.

I have worked as a tutor, in marketing, and for a women's magazine, which involved writing captions for interiors and combat with photographers fixated on depth and apertures. Regular working doesn't suit me, it interferes with writing, and now I earn my rent as a waitress at corporate events where the high priests of the City banks congratulate themselves by drinking buckets of champagne and falling over. The change of job meant a dip in my salary, so I moved, from West London, where rents cost the earth, to East London, where the cost is broken streets, a fall and a fractured finger.

It was the finger that saved my life.

The story begins on New Year's Eve. Having dumped Julian, an actor with floppy hair and lots of good teeth, I went with a girlfriend I don't particularly like to a tartan-themed charity ball in a kilt too short and my little finger bound to its partner in blue tape. There is something oddly poignant going to a ball with another woman and she must have felt the same way, abandoning me, as she did, for the first hairy-kneed faux Scotsman to say *och aye the noo* over the long candle-lit table.

After dinner consisting of haggis, which I didn't eat, I danced alone on the fringes of the swaying crowd like a stray swallow chasing the migrating flock.

A man appeared.

They usually do.

Men in the 21st century are no longer hunter gatherers. They are game players, artists, sculptors. They see me across the

6

rainbow of fiesta lights as a blank canvas requiring their signature in a gooey splash of scribbled jism; a column of alabaster that needs to be reshaped, their sculpting hands eager to rid me of my clothes and go to work with their carving tools. I could be perfect, just perfect, if I only gave them the chance. The man, this shimmying shaking dancer, is wearing tartan socks, plus fours, like a lost golfer, and a Tam o'Shanter that gives him the earthy, intense look of Che Guevara.

'Dance?'

'I am dancing?' I answered.

'That's not dancing, it's just moving about.'

'I have a bad finger.'

'Not a very good kilt either.'

I liked him immediately. I can't stand men who say nice things as they push back their floppy hair.

'Drink?'

'That's very generous of you, seeing how the bar's free.'

We drank whisky.

'Twelve year old malt,' he said.

'You know about those things?'

'No. I'm just flirting with you.'

'Honesty can be very unattractive,' I said and he shrugged.

'I know, it's so hard to do the right thing.'

'Or know what it is.'

He tossed back his drink. So did I. He refilled the glasses. My eyes prickled as I swallowed the fiery fluid and the band silenced before a drum roll. A man leapt on the stage, the skirts of his kilt like a sail, and announced in a Highland accent...

'Twenty seconds...' He looked at his watch, paused, then counted backwards: 'Ten, nine, eight, seven, six, five, four, three, two, one...'

And we kissed.

It was at first a soft and tender kiss tasting of Johnnie Walker and garlic from the stuffed mushrooms that had accompanied the haggis. That lingering tang faded as I tasted his tongue and offered my tongue for him to sample. We kissed as if one of us, or both of us, needed mouth to mouth resuscitation. My heart was pounding in my chest and I wanted his hands that pressed against my shoulders to run down my back to my bottom that peeked out boldly when I bent from the shortness of the absurd kilt.

We joined a circle of people, crossed our arms and sang along as the band played *Auld Lang Syne*. I was wobbly on high heels. My finger hurt. My heart was popping in my chest like champagne bubbles. I took his arm and he held me steady, his hand running around my back and clinging to my side. He looked into my eyes. I love it when there is no need for words. I knew what he was thinking. I was thinking the same. If you are going to go to bed with a man it has to be right then, that night, that moment. The immediacy makes my pulse race, my underarms tingle, and it is just too sad to sleep alone on New Year's Eve.

'Your place?' he said, and took my elbow.

'Or yours?'

He smiled. 'I don't have one.'

'Lucky you met me, then.'

'Yes,' he said. 'I had a feeling my luck was going to change.'

The cab whizzed along the Embankment, the bridges lit like spaceships, the Thames a coiling sheet of silver steel. Our lips touched. My heart fluttered and I adored being in the back of a cab that black night with a stranger who knew nothing about me. I could be anyone – an artist, an actress, a Foreign Office analyst, a ballet dancer, recently retired, of course, more a choreographer. In the closet there are a thousand masks and every one fits.

He paid the driver and waved away the change.

'Happy New Year.'

I gave him the key to open the downstairs lock.

'It hurts with my bad finger.'

'Oh, yes, I'd forgotten that,' he said.

He dropped a kiss on my hand. We climbed the stairs and he opened the door to my flat without the fuss I always have, pulling in the door to a precise angle before turning the key. Men are always good at those things.

The lamp on my desk belongs to my grandmother. I had begged her to give it to me. It is an art-deco figure of a man in ivory-coloured porcelain. He wears a top hat and tails and stands below a Victorian lamppost lighting a cigarette. The woman he is waiting for has not turned up, perhaps her husband knows? But he perseveres. I like that. Men who persevere get there in the end and, while he waits, the lamp has a warm amber glow like an imagined sunset.

The living room, also my study, contains a cork board pinned with appointments, random phrases that weave their way into stories, a spare passport photo ready for when I lose my passport. There is a black leather sofa, a blue rug woven through with a Tibetan snow lion stolen from the loft at home, two tubular steel chairs from the 1960s and a table with extending sides. My laptop sits on a copy of Longman's *Chronicle of the 20th Century*, a gift from my uncle, a writer, because he is mentioned in 1985, the year I was born.

The ceiling rises to a peak, like an arrowhead. There is room to lay out my yoga mat at the entrance to the annex the landlord, Simon Singh, calls 'the kitchen.' The bathroom contains a tall arched window with a view of the grey slate rooftops and glass-walled City banks, hidden that starless and moonless night, although on sunny days I like to imagine men with binoculars watching as I step into my knickers.

On the floor there is a letter from NatWest containing three pages of threats. A loop of Christmas cards like a washing line is suspended at an angle between two walls and a sprig of mistletoe hangs serendipitously from the light fixture. I stabbed him in the chest with a good finger to get his attention.

'Excuse me.'

I pointed at the mistletoe and pointed at my lips. He grinned.

'Yes, they are beautiful.'

I ran my tongue over them. They felt cracked like flaking paint.

'Do you mean that?'

'I wouldn't say it if I didn't.'

'Mmm.'

Relationships are nine parts intuition, one part madness. The first part of the nine consists of physiognomy, and he was rather good-looking in that tousled hair, firm-jawed-needs-a-shave sort of way; big brown eyes full of secrets, wide shoulders in a white shirt.

He drew me to him, pressing his hands against my back. I was trapped, encircled, gathered up, protected. Our heads adjusted, and our lips moved in for a second tasting, slower, more ponderous, and I recalled something I had written, words that came into my head because they had been fiction and now they were fact: I kissed the stranger, this unshaved Che with sparkling eyes, and I thought, the kiss is the greatest of gifts, a miracle, uniquely human. A kiss beneath the mistletoe. A kiss after midnight. A kiss before dying. The devil's kiss. As a picture tells a thousand words, so a kiss says everything that's important. I am told prostitutes never kiss their clients. It is too personal, too human. We kiss to say I love you. We kiss the rings of the self-important. The feet of conquerors. The rich dark earth when we reach the promised land. We kiss our hands and wave as loved ones begin a journey. We kiss strangers before dawn in the first hours of a New Year because our wintry lips are incomplete until they are oiled by a kiss.

I enjoy the sway of two anxious bodies swirling about each other like a faltering gyroscope, like a whisky-soaked octopus. His hands slid under my short skirt, and the thing that went through my head was: oh, God, I wish I wasn't wearing tights. I wriggled free and dragged him towards the bedroom where I turned on the lamp. I have a big bed. I like big beds.

He gazed around at the clothes escaping from the wardrobe like fleeing ghosts, shoes too drunk to stay on their heels, the pillows like sand dunes on the beach of my saffron sheets.

'Messy clothes tidy prose,' I said.

'What?'

'I write.'

My first chance to lie and I blurt out the truth. It made him think.

'A journalist?'

'Novelist,' I replied, knowing the word sounds more boastful than the imprecise and unassuming 'writer,' which means close to nothing: copywriter, scriptwriter, underwriter, typewriter.

'Anything I may have read...?'

I sealed his lips with my finger.

'I hate questions.'

'So do I.'

He grabbed me. I liked being grabbed. I like wriggling free then being grabbed again. I like running away and being chased, being caught. We kissed and kissed, then paused for breath. He pressed his teeth against my neck, just gently, and I forgot to mention the kiss of the vampire and how that, too, is so wonderfully erotic. I could feel his cock swelling against my stomach, pushing at me like the head of a kitten pushing at a closed door. I ran my tongue over the bristles of his chin, his neck, his chest. He released my bottom as I slid down to my knees. I patiently unhooked his belt, unbuttoned the buttons on his plaid plus fours and tugged at his boxers – how sweet, I thought, they are tartan.

His cock was straight, firm and, in the dull light of the lamp, the head was pink like his lips. I sucked the head and ran my fingers over the quilted skin. He sighed. He relaxed. The stranger had met a girl at a ball and the girl had taken the stranger into her mouth, down, down, deeper and deeper; it was just so gloriously decadent being down on my knees like this and I wanted to swallow him whole like an oyster.

I came up for air and flicked my tongue like a feather up and down the warm flesh. He sighed and puffed. Time for the stranger was standing still. He wanted that moment to freeze and last forever. He had found a wicked girl, a promiscuous girl, a pleasant-enough-to-look-at-in-a-heroin-chic-sort-of-way girl and that New Year's Day in the early hours his cock was in her mouth. I sucked the head and rimmed the groove, teasing the nerve endings. I wet the fragile tissue of his testicles with a long stroke of my tongue and took his balls one at a time into my mouth.

His hands rested on the back of my head and he rocked slightly on his heels. I went back to sucking the soft cap of his penis. I ran my tongue down the shaft and up again, wetting the column. Many times I have found a boy's cock in my mouth and in the back of my mind a sense that this was so unfair, so one-sided, that true passion is give and take and this was a lot of give without a lot of get.

Sometimes, this time, it was different. His cock was a friendly creature massaging my gums, the inside of my cheeks, the bells of my tonsils. His pulsing cock vibrated over the membranes and tissues of my throat, touching my taste buds with its sultry perfume, the slap of flesh against flesh like the sound of the tree branch that tapped at night against my window. I was drunk on whisky, mesmerized, meditative. I sucked and kissed and nibbled and teased and he groaned and sighed and quivered and gasped. His cock was a wonderful toy, a drawbridge that sprang up when I pulled it down, that shook like a dancer when I teased the groove with the tip of my wet tongue. It was a magnet like the magnets beneath my mattress connecting the polar points of our passion and fusing them in an aura of completion.

I could feel his pleasure mounting. He was going to fill my mouth with his syrupy essence, spray his sperm across my face, my eyes, my nose. I imagined the taste of nougat and almonds as I took him deep into my throat, sucking hard, waiting for that moment, that sudden jerk, that first hint of pre-come. But just as the adventurer hesitates before claiming the prize, before the true king pulls the sword from the rock, he stopped himself and withdrew. I was ready for his orgasm, my throat gaping. I felt let down yet, instantly, immediately relieved.

He took my elbows and pulled me up so he could kiss me again, so he could taste himself on my lips. The way he expertly undid the buttons on my white blouse made me wonder where he could have acquired such skill. Did he take bad girls home every night? Was this handsome stranger Lothario, Don Juan, Patrick Bateman from *American Psycho;* so good, I read it twice.

He found the hook at the front of my bra, how clever, and weighed my breasts.

'They're small,' I murmured.

'Small is beautiful.'

'Not that small.'

'They are perfect,' he said and I purred.

He kissed my breasts in turn, left first, then right, taking my nipples into his mouth and biting down just hard enough to make them pop out, eager for more. At the same time his quick fingers found the zip on my kilt and the tartan fabric fell about my toes. He rolled down my tights and I hopped about from foot to foot as he expertly rid me of this clutter.

Just as I had gone down on my knees, like an echo, he did the same. He took the sides of my panties and pulled at the elastic. He ran the moist fabric down my legs and over my feet. He dropped down and adjusted his head so he could savour me. I adored the touch of his tongue and he drank from me as if from an upturned cup. I could smell my own scent. I pulled him up and we stumbled to the bed where, in a long kiss, I tasted warm salty seas with a fragrance as sweet as baby breath. I recalled vaguely a boyfriend saying once the stuff was 100 per cent protein and he wanted to try living on my liquids and nothing else for a week.

He slid up inside me, and time wasn't suspended. It was racing. He was going to come. I didn't want him to, not now, not yet. *La petite mort* is as often as not *la mort depuis longtemps*. The longer you wait, the more you delay, the more you reach the moment of release before receding, the greater the pleasure, the more wonder and mystery that wraps itself around the orgasm.

As he tensed, I let his cock slip from its warm cocoon and sewed kisses over the fine curly hair on his chest. I straddled his neck and lowered my drenched pussy over his mouth as if it were a saddle on a horse. He kissed and sucked, nudged my clitoris and wormed his tongue into the heart of my pulsating vagina. Liquids seeped from me in a continual stream, piquant and vital, the essence of sex. Tended the right way and in the right places, a girl is an eternal fount that just keeps giving, the milky fluid creaming over the walls of my pussy, over my spread lips, anointing the stranger in a fine spray that coated his face.

My heart was a little boat that had broken its moorings. My breath was trapped in my throat. I rolled to one side and slid across his body. I took his cock back into my mouth, completing the circle, his tongue pushing back into my vagina, my tongue wrapped about his shaft. We rocked to and fro like sunflowers in a field, deeper and deeper while the tree branch tapped like a metronome against the windowpane and we found perfect harmony.

My pussy continued to leak nectar into his mouth. Our bodies were slippery with perspiration. I could have remained in that position for the rest of my life, but the tempo changed, his body tensed and my throat filled with warm sperm that tasted like coconut milk. I gobbled it down, greedy for more. He kept pushing into me, I kept drawing at his cock and, as the last drips drained into my mouth, I grew rigid. I released his cock and gasped as his meaty tongue ignited an orgasm that made me scream. I cried out as if in pain but the pain was an intense, all-consuming pleasure.

My body was trembling as if in fever. I rolled to one side, arms wrapped around his legs, our bodies drenched, throbbing, electric. I was dizzy. He pulled me up and pushed his cock back inside me as if it were a jewel being placed back in a velvet box. We rocked gently like waves on an outgoing tide and, on that tide, the ship would soon be sailing.

We slept for an hour. We made love again and he slept again, staying hard inside me while I lay awake enjoying the feel of his weight pinning me down. Sometimes you have to picture what you wish for. I had pictured the stranger and willed him into being.

I must have drifted into sleep. I remember my eyes blinking open, a smile on my lips. There was dull light around the unclosed blinds. Morning had come. It was the first day of a New Year – a new beginning. He was dressing. He leaned over, kissed my forehead, and I watched as he left my bedroom. I heard the click of the front door. Then there was silence.

2
What Girls Really Think

Three times a week I go to the gym. I swim whenever I can and fast walk around the park listening to Bach. Coupled with flamenco, or rather *cante hondo,* which I also love, Bach inspired the Spanish poet Federico García Lorca when he was writing *Blood Wedding*, his most poetic and best-loved stage play.

Cyril Connolly, a biographer of George Orwell, said whenever you start writing a book you must set out to write a masterpiece. This counsel, both wise and haunting, is written out on a strip of card pinned to my cork board. There was a time when I read a lot of erotic writers, but not anymore. I don't want to be 'tainted' by styles other than my own and feel certain that you only find success writing when you are 100% you, original, identifiable, unique, on the edge of the crowd.

Writers I admire include Milan Kundera, Nikos Kuzanzakis, Camus, of course, Bret Easton Ellis, early Martin Amis, Stieg Larsson and Emily Brontë, who first caught my attention when I discovered the umlaut over the ë and fell in love at thirteen with Heathcliff, the archetypal romantic hero, beast and schoolgirl fantasy.

If all else perished, and he remained, I should still continue to be; and if all else remained, and he were annihilated, the universe would turn to a mighty stranger.

Thus spake Miss Brontë and I underscored those words in pencil.

At school, my skill at hockey and tennis was based on pace and anxiety more than talent. Reading was an escape; sex sublimation for girls trapped behind the walls of a convent clinging to the wuthering heights of the cliffs around the Kent coast. Writing I abhorred because it was formalised, regulated, imprisoned.

I was introduced at university to Anaïs Nin by Oliver Masters, my tutor, a lanky Heathcliff character who seduced my mind and encouraged me to write and submit a short story to an erotic magazine edited by a beautiful woman who had once been his student. All life is incestuous. The story was published. I was thrilled, terrified and at the beginning of a journey that has no end and no precise direction.

'Why erotica?' my friends ask; my mother, too.

And I tell them: erotica is an untapped well of human mystery and potential, the seam of gold hidden below the fault lines of a culture that imposes limitations on our true nature. If erotic writing is to be regarded as literature, the taste and cadence of the words must embrace the senses, ignite the passions. The emotion is integral to the story. Readers must be stripped naked and led to a warm bath perfumed by sex. They must feel as they dress the softness of silk and the chafe of leather. Each description is a portrait so fresh and vivid they can hear the adagio slap of flesh against flesh, the rattle of chains, the snap of the whip, the sound of one hand clapping against willing buttocks. Readers should be inspired to seek in their lovers new erogenous places, the enchantment of role play, masks, ball-gags and bonds. In the heat of the night, when you allow the brain to rest, the body lives a life of its own.

'Let go,' I tell my friends. 'Just let go.'

Erotica holds up the mirror to a society where those things damned and outlawed are secretly desired. The erotic explores human extremes, lost love, impossible love, innocence and purity mingled with decadence and debauchery. All human fears and hungers become clearer analysed under the microscope of erotica. As I keep telling Mother, erotica is about feeling, not fucking.

My head throbs. I swallow two Nurofen Plus with my Starbucks House Blend and stare across the rooftops at the fey grey watery sky. The night is still with me. I am wearing big comfy socks, a long tee-shirt, no knickers and a woolly cardigan with sleeves that swamp my hands. My finger hurts. My body is sticky and smells of the stranger. I don't want to wash away the smell. Not yet. My laptop is open but I can't focus on the little black words on the screen.

Daddy is home from his job in the Far East 'lying for England,' as Mother tells her friends. They are snug in their Chelsea terrace and will go out this New Year's Day to have lunch at the

Hurlingham Club. Perhaps I'll go, too. I haven't seen much of my father this holiday. I miss him when he's not there and rarely see him when he is. 'Daddy's little viper,' Mother said once, and I've never forgotten it.

I place my coffee cup beside the man standing under the Victorian lamppost and leaned over the laptop. I start typing out my thoughts on erotica for some future blog and my fingers freeze, all nine fractured like the tenth as if in solidarity. I hear the classic ring of my iPhone, but when I reach for the machine, it remains silent while the ringing continues.

Is this an Apple trick? Is my whisky-addled brain playing games with me? Is the codeine in the Nurofen finally working? I shook the thing. Nothing.

The time reads 11:47 and the weather app highlights a depressing minus two degrees, cloud and snow.

I call a friend to make sure the phone was working.

She answers immediately.

'Hi, Minnie, Happy New Year.'

'I don't like being Minnie any more. Anyway, I'm fat,' I said.

'I can't bear it when thin people say they're fat, it makes normal people feel obese.'

'I'm in love, Lizzie.'

'You've always been in love. With yourself.'

'I want to be coddled, not...not castigated.'

'I love that word. Who with?' she asked.

'I don't know.'

'Typical.'

I sniffed. 'I've got a headache as well.'

'Don't we all, dear. You're so spoiled.'

'No I'm not. You're not being very nice today.'

'Ah, poor Skinny Minnie, tell me everything.'

Lizzie is an old friend, someone I trust, a good ear to hear my New Year's Eve tale of love and woe. I told her everything.

'Then,' I said and sighed, 'he kissed me on the forehead and just left...'

'That's a good sign.'

'You think so?'

'It's a lovely story, really romantic. I'm going to write it down...'

'You'd better not.'

'I'm going to call it *The Little Red Kilt* and publish it with that picture of you in a mask, you know the one...'

'Elizabeth Elmwood, I'll murder you if you do.'

'According to Georges Bataille, even murder can be erotic.'

'I'm fed up with him, he ruined my life.'

'How's the writing going?'

'Slowly. You?'

'I am totally inspired by your story, in fact, I might turn you into a series.'

'I'm never going to tell you any of my secrets again,' I said and she laughed.

'And who else is going to listen?'

Again, I heard the ringing phone. I shook my machine.

'Can you hear that?'

'What?'

'Lizzie, gotta go.'

The sound was coming from the bedroom. I raced in, but the moment I crossed the threshold the ringing stopped. I searched through the bedclothes, under the pillows, under the bed.

There: an iPhone in a sensible black case.

So, the stranger had left behind something other than his smell on my skin, the stains on my bed sheets. I searched through the phone's settings and found his name. I looked at messages, search history, notes. I was tempted to check 'recents' and call back, but stopped myself.

I made fresh coffee. My headache was tapping away like an unlatched door in a far off room. A slice of light crossed my desk and I could see a helicopter, a giant insect against the sky, the roar making the windowpanes rattle.

Since giving Julian Rhodes the 'I don't think we should see each other for a while...' speech, I'd been *boyfriendless*, and that's not a wise place to be. Far better to be with a man you don't like, than to be setting off on New Year's Eve with another girl. Being single is an admission of failure, a lack of something. Was I too fussy, too demanding, too spoiled, as Lizzie always says?

No, I don't think so.

Most of the men I meet are more concerned with the picture than the meaning of the picture. They see the world as if from inside a *camera obscura*, a darkened box with a single hole letting in the light. They shoot snapshots that lack depth of field and capture a realism devoid of the surreal or sublime. They have an idealised view of glamour and beauty based on the air-brushed perfections of *Marie-Claire* and *Vogue*.

All girls compare themselves with every other girl. It is our nature; our tragedy. I can, with little effort, appear highbrow, with my hair in a pleat, demure at the country club in Barbour and tweed, a louche tart, who looks as if she has just thrown on her clothes and can't wait to tear them off again. The closet holds a cast of characters we explore every time we go out and sometimes it feels right to get it wrong, a subconscious signal that something else is wrong.

'You just don't bother do you?' as Julian remarked that night after he'd appeared in a fringe play at the King's Head and come off stage high on adrenaline to find me in jeans, All-Stars and a blue cagoule. It was the production's closing show. We went to The Ivy for dinner, a table booked, the girls in the gang dressed like butterflies. I was dressed like me.

Julian, when we got home, stripped off my jacket and jeans like wallpaper from the wall. He wasn't reaching for the me inside my clothes, but the me he had created in his mind, the shop store mannequin that he banged away at like he's hammering a nail, releasing the adrenaline and replacing it with the frail hope that the pub play would lead to the West End, a TV part, his photograph in the *Evening Standard* arriving at a premiere.

It was all about his needs. Men have so many. What he saw in *me,* was the girl behind *him,* in that photograph, stepping out of the back of a cab in a short skirt that showed her knickers. I was the accessory, the prize, the adjunct to his career. Julian always looked at me as if I were standing with my back to a mirror and what he saw was a reflection of himself. He had never bothered to read my books.

I finished my coffee and wandered through to the bathroom to comb the tangles from my hair. I could still smell him.

Tom, Tom, the Piper's son stole my heart and away did run.

I liked the stranger and liked him just as much now that he had a name. I liked the way he had danced at the ball, boldly, rhythmically, without showing off. I had felt a sudden rush of pleasure as we joined hands to sing in the New Year. 'Should auld acquaintance be forgot.' It is *such* wise counsel. When he said 'your place,' the way he had touched my elbow was with the confidence that anticipated my saying yes. A pact had been made by our bodies and we acted quickly enough not to allow our brains to step in and ruin everything.

Fireworks exploded in the sky as the taxi curved along the Thames. His kiss was a rare bird – the first sip of champagne. I loved the way he moved my body this way and that way, shaping me, turning me like a tailor with a bolt of cloth, lifting me by the hips so I could take him into my mouth while he sipped from my cup. He manoeuvred me on to my hands and knees so he could enter me from behind, his fingers gripping the handles of my hip bones, my breasts swinging like church bells, like udders, the position animal, feminine, deeply sensual.

I closed my eyes. I pretended there was a film crew in the shadows and now, in my morning memory, I watched the video, backside wriggling, mouth gaping as I gasped for air. He had been too polite to pierce my bottom, although he did in my fantasy footage, his long tongue oiling that inscrutable passage with my own juices before he pushed up into my core. I quivered with pleasure as he pumped out great gushes of hot sperm that filled my belly with a deep and abiding satisfaction.

My mouth had gone dry. I was holding on to the side of the sink panting and a faint moistness seeped from my sex.

Was it more exciting making love with a stranger? Without names, with our heads in the early hours drumming with music and our veins hot with whisky, we were lost to our primitive senses. We made love through the night like sun worshippers struck by the mystery of an eclipse. He was a considerate lover, a patient lover. You get by giving, you take through sharing. Men often see sex as combat, a battle to be won; a race to the finishing tape where the prize is orgasm. Tom wasn't like that.

The phone rang. His phone. I had taken it with me into the bathroom and sat on the loo to take a pee as I answered.

'Hello, Tom.'

'You found my phone?'

'Did you leave it behind as a device?'

'Subconsciously, I'm sure,' he replied. 'So, what about lunch?'

I thought for a moment. 'Is this an invitation for lunch or a need to retrieve your mobile? I can send it in a taxi.'

'How do you know my name?'

'I know everything about you, Doctor Bridge. Why didn't you look at my finger?'

'Not my field, I'm afraid, and I wouldn't want to interfere.'

This man named Tom who worked in Sri Lanka and sent messages that were never frivolous knew me as intimately as a man can know a woman and yet now, in the daylight, across the invisible wires, he sounded shy, sweet, a nice man in a world where girls, some girls, me, always fall in love with bastards.

'Do you remember the address?' I asked.

'Indelibly.'

'One o'clock.'

'I'm always on time.'

'I'm always late.'

We disconnected. I put my fingers to my lips. I do declare: I was smiling. The pulse of my headache ran slower. I flushed the loo, grabbed my own phone and called my parents. In turn I wished them a Happy New Year. I couldn't make the Hurlingham, I explained. Something had come up.

'Something interesting?' Daddy asked.

'Potentially.'

'Good. You deserve it.'

'Do you think so?'

'Absolutely, Katie, absolutely. How's your new flat?'

'A bit squalid. I stole the rug from the attic, the one from Tibet.'

'You're welcome to it, you know that.'

'Thank you, Daddy. When are you going back?'

'In a week or so. Will I see you before then?'

'Absolutely,' I replied; he loved that word. He lived in a world without absolutes and sought them wherever he could find them.

After taking off my clothes in the bedroom, I ambled back to the bathroom and stood in front of the mirror. I leaned forward and shook my head. Misty green eyes above pale blue half-moons tender to the touch. Cheeks hollow. Nose winter red. I sniffed. Three glasses of champagne, a big glass of red wine, two shots. Never again, I whispered. Never. New Year. New Regime. A New Year's Resolution.

'Work harder, worry less, be nice to Mother.'

There, I'd said it.

I stood back and continued the examination. Shoulders? Wide, clavicles defined above wells deep enough to gather coins in exchange for wishes. Breasts? Small but perky, fans of the uplift bra. I squeezed my nipples and a tingle raced up my spine that pressed boldly through the soft skin. Likewise my ribs, the keys of a harpsichord that tinkled with Bach's Concerto No. 1 in D Minor. I quite liked my hips, the way they jut out, the faint bulge of my belly that I stroked, wondering what it would be like to be pregnant. Long legs good for running away and revealing in short skirts; long feet with toes unembellished with varnish, long hands with a damaged finger. My pubes were matted. I stroked the hair and sniffed my fingertips. I adored being a girl.

I spent ages under the scorching spikes of the shower, ridding myself of those lovely smells, turning myself back into a virgin. I then stood in the window willing unseen eyes to be looking back. I brushed my hair, a long dark drape, brittle as kindling, in spite of the orange blossom conditioner. I stroked my tattoo. It has no depth, no response to my touch. But it is there, like a shadow, a memory.

When I was in my first year at university, I went one break with a friend to a tattoo parlour in Wardour Street, where she had two black butterflies engraved on the soft skin just above her left hip.

'Why do you want them?' I asked her.

'I don't know; it's just a bit of fun.'

She shrugged and looked away. There is something sad about England on spring days with the rain beating against the window and the people in the street hurrying by with umbrellas turned inside out. Alice went with the tattooist into the clinic and I studied the display as the electric needle buzzed through the open door.

It had never occurred to me to mark my body, but I suddenly understood why a tattoo made people feel as if they belonged to something they would find hard to explain or identify, a tribe, a mindset, a new era in which social media and marketing has sucked the marrow from our individuality.

Who was I and where did I belong?

I had no interest in ornamenting myself and knew girls who had been inked as a dare and then regretted it. My abrupt desire to have a tattoo wasn't to show that I belonged, but to remind myself that I didn't want to belong. The tattoo would be an aide memoire, a metaphor. To quote JG Ballard, another writer who belongs on my list of greats, I was living life as a bourgeois, but was secretly an anarchist.

My eyes ran over the designs on the wall and one of them jumped out at me like a dancer in a club picked out by a spotlight. The shape was like a dancer, a continuous swirling line a little over three centimetres wide at the base and vanishing to the point of an inverted spiral of the type calligraphers placed at the end of hand-written manuscripts.

I sat and watched the rain until Alice and the tattooist appeared, the job done, her hand nursing her hip through her skirt.

'Do you have time to do another?' I asked.

Alice looked at once shocked, then pleased. She wasn't alone. The tattooist was a Rastafarian, with dreadlocks down to his waist and the face of a saint. He smiled his laser-whitened teeth.

'I am so happy, and it will make you happy,' he said. 'You have chosen?'

'That one,' I said, pointing.

'Bit small,' Alice remarked.

'Small is beautiful,' I responded.

We went through to the clinic. I laid on a leather-topped massage bench, lifted my hair above my head and indicated the back on my neck at the point immediately below the hairline.

'There,' I said.

'No one will see it.'

'Yes, I know.'

'You won't be able to see it.'

'But it will be there.'

'You, you crazy girl...'

'Thank you,' I said.

Like my friends, I immediately regretted having the tattoo and it hurt for weeks. There were scabs, the skin was bright red and I laid in bed at night having imaginary discussions with my mother about life being a journey and if you take a wrong turn you can never get back on track again.

Then the scabs fell off, the red faded and in the three-way mirror I stared at the reflected spiral and changed my mind. I had at the time been reading a book about geishas in ancient Japan and discovered that these devotees of passion covered their bodies in heavy kimonos exposing only their hands, face and the nape of the neck, an intensely sensitive spot for women and one of those zones that can drive men into paroxysms of desire. It had not entered my mind when I had the tattoo inked into my skin that rainy day, but I had, in my first year at university, placed an extended foot on the road to the erotic.

3
Dressing & Undressing

Getting dressed is a daily battle in a war we are doomed to lose. That's why we keep buying new things. I run pictures from magazines through my mind, while I stand before the bathroom window applying Aloe Vera Gel to my arid skin, over and under my breasts, a bit small, although the stranger didn't think so. I stretch like a cat, pinch my nipples to shift the pain from my finger and smooth my palms down my sides, my legs, into the crease of my bottom.

My gaze passes over the alchemist's stash of unguents and creams, bottles and tubes, enough make-up to repaint my apartment when smart girls know that less is more and the artifice is to appear as if you aren't wearing any at all. Except lipstick, of course. I use repairwear under my eyes, some blush to plant winter roses in sallow cheeks, and a puff of powder, all from Clinique. If you pop into Harvey Nicks at tea time, svelte blondes from Eastern Europe hand the stuff out like it's Christmas every day. The whites of my eyes are bloodshot, but the green of the pupils are bright with...with what, exactly?

I'm not sure. No, I am sure. But not entirely sure. He'll be here in under an hour and I feel prickly with nerves, which isn't like me at all.

Or is it? I feel schizophrenic today, uncertain, hung over, the codeine making my teeth ache.

Wandering on tip toes to the bedroom, the word 'pink' slipped into my head and it is always a good idea to act on your intuitions, to leap before you look. We live at a time when we shield our eyes and gaze so deeply into the future we lose sight of the present. Mother, when I gave up my job describing interiors for the magazine, told me not to 'burn my bridges.' But is that really sound advice? Once burnt, there is no way back. You have crossed the Rubicon, the Styx, the Thames, for that matter. The landscape is new, terrifying. The only way is forward.

A friend of mine, who paints abstracts, lost all of her work in a fire. For months she walked around in a funk. Then, she rented a new studio. She started again and her paintings were fresher, freer, more layered, more interesting. I have files of unfinished short stories, notebooks of ideas, character descriptions. I keep going back to them, as if in the past we might find the future. But I have a feeling, a deeper instinct, that only when I find the courage to burn all these scribbled notes, will the universe reach down and lift me like a fiery phoenix from the ashes. You get trapped into repeating yourself, you plagiarise yourself, you become all those things you condemn in others. Sometimes, I pass a shop window and see my mother in the reflection.

I am naked still, the central heating pumping away, the sun through the leaded windows weak as a dying hand. My clothes are crammed so closely on the rail in the closet I start to sweat dragging things out and laying them in combinations on the bed. My underwear is packed like boneless fish in four wide drawers bursting with soft fabrics, fragile as spider thread, the latex and leather in the bottom drawer garlanded with rings that connect to buckles and straps. A mask, like an eyeless face, lays beside Louis Vuitton handcuffs and I recall Chekhov's law on foreshadowing that decrees if a gun is shown on stage in an early scene of a play, it must be fired in a later scene, or it should not be there at all. I run my fingers over the short chain connecting the black bracelets, and wonder, just wonder.

I dip now into the top drawer where the pink satin knickers and matching bra give headachy girls a bit of a lift. Next, skinny jeans, so tight under the crotch it's painful, that's the price we pay, and lace-up boots with two-inch heels of the poor little match girl variety. Tom must be six foot in bare feet and I thought by conceding a couple of inches we would both feel secure.

That's the bottom done. Tops are never as easy, not in winter. It is the clothes that cover us that stir desire for what lies beneath. The fig leaves Eve wore in the Garden of Eden were not designed to conceal, but to draw Adam's eye to what Eve had artfully hidden. Just as flowers come in infinite colours and put out sweet scents to attract the birds and butterflies that pollinate them, we paint our lips pink as an allusion to the moist flush of our sex and perfume our pulses to arouse the hunger in every stranger. A girl in primitive times was the victim of male lust and

26

the guile required to survive and flourish is the mask she subconsciously wears today. Love is war and clothes are our armour.

Half-dressed, as if posing for Helmut Newton, I stand before the open closet as if it is a sanctuary. Sometimes, when I am depressed, or facing a wall of silence, I creep inside and pull the doors closed behind me. I meditate in this dark silky womb. I tell myself to be positive. Writing is hard. Persevere. After each word, the next word has already burst from its cast and grown wings. All you have to do is catch it and pin it to the page. You find inspiration by writing, not by thinking about what you are going to write. For me, writing and dressing have become analogous. You select words as if picking glass from an injury with tweezers and each piece of clothing so that the ensemble makes an unequivocal statement.

I rifle through a field of blouses and tops before lighting on an ivory cashmere rollneck and a brown leather belt with a snake's head clasp. I reached for a military style jacket with two rows of brass buttons rising at an angle to wide shoulders with epaulettes. The jacket is cerulean, my favourite shade of blue, neither warm nor cold, the colour of the kingfisher. Most of my clothes are a pinch too small and I dress with the vague sense that someone else may later be undressing me. This doesn't happen very often. I am not *that* promiscuous. But a girl should always be ready, just in case.

As a painter stands back from the canvas, I stood back from the mirror to study the result. I looked serious, a shade severe, eyes puffy still, but it would have to do. I heard the buzzer, two short sharp presses. He was on time. I walked through to the narrow hall and waited for the third buzz before answering.

'Yes, yes, I'm here. Come up. The door's open. I'm not ready,' I said huffily.

I returned to the bedroom and bound my bad finger to its companion with three layers of surgical blue tape that matched the jacket, pure coincidence, and hooked dangly blue stone earrings to my ears. I played with my hair, killing time. I clipped it up with stray strands escaping the clip, tied a ponytail that would reveal the tattoo, which doesn't suit me, then brushed it straight down to my shoulders, which looks best. Hair. In the end, it's all about hair. I removed my jacket with the lines of buttons and

27

tried on a tweedy thing from Zara with red lapels and red elbow patches. No, no, no. What was I thinking? I put the other one back on, fixed a smile on my lips and whispered into the mirror.

'Be cool. Don't talk too much.'

He was staring out the window and turned, smiling. He looked different in daylight, deeply tanned, for one thing, a red and blue scarf wrapped around his neck, blue jeans, a reefer jacket with the collar turned up like a sailor home on leave. He was freshly shaved and his brown eyes were mischievous and vital. We brushed cheeks like old friends.

'Hi, you look different in the day time,' he said.

'I was just thinking the same about you – you're darker and I'm paler.'

'No, you look great...'

'Flatterer.'

His smiled broadened. 'I love this room,' he said, staring about. 'It's so you.'

'How would you know?'

He thought for a moment. 'You're dressed like your room,' he replied. 'Carefully careless.'

I wasn't sure how to respond. I followed his gaze and tried to see it all through his eyes. I had assembled things I liked, without trying to match anything together. The decor wasn't minimalist, but edited, a few bare adjectives like surf on a sea of simple nouns. My bedroom was a junk store, the closets brim-full, the plastic bags below the bed, ready for the charity shop. But my living area was my writing area and that was uncluttered, dust-free from regular passes of the wet wipes. My walls were pale cream, bare except for the print of the *Maja Nude,* which he approached for a closer look. The painting, thought to be the first by a European to show pubic hair, was a souvenir from a school trip to The Prado in Madrid. I had chosen it because I knew it would annoy Sister Theresa when it appeared in the dorm.

'Goya?' he asked, glancing back, and I felt ripples roll over my brow, something I was trying to stop doing.

'Ten out of ten,' I replied. 'Now, I thought you were going to take me out to lunch. I'm starving.'

'Me, too. Where shall we go?'

'I have no idea.'

'Isn't this your neck of the woods?'

I grabbed my coat from the back of the door. 'It is now,' I replied, and he glanced back as if I had given away a secret.

'I thought you were more Knightsbridge than Tower Bridge,' he said, like a line from a play, as he held my coat for me to shuffle into.

'Here.' I gave him his iPhone.

'Oh, great, thanks, my whole life's in there.'

'I know.'

Having devoted as much time as it takes to read a chapter of a book on dressing, my padded coat was like rusty scaffolding over an architecturally-pleasing building. I pulled on gloves and we descended the stairs into a crisp bitter day with fewer cars than usual. There was frost on the rooftops and a pair of plastic bags danced on the wind.

The grass crackled as we crossed Shoreditch Park. Birds had left arrow prints in lines across yesterday's snow. We watched men in black jackets exercising pugs and pit-bulls, and it suddenly occurred to me why they chose those particular breeds, it was not because they are tough and dangerous, but because those men and their dogs had a certain similarity in gait and manner. One of the men was yelling at a white dog with a long head and a pirate patch over one eye: 'Oi, you, get your arse over 'ere. You heard me. Get your arse over 'ere.'

I sneezed to muffle my laughter. No one laughs in this park. Laughter makes people think you are laughing at them, and, anyway, what's there to laugh about? I grabbed Tom's arm.

We passed another man with a pit-bull on a leather harness that strapped over its back and under its belly. The animal slobbered and strained at the leash. The man, head-shaved, tattoos on his knuckles and neck, was with a little girl of about five. She was wearing a pink sheepskin coat and matching boots, her blonde hair pulled back and her ears decorated with hoop earrings like wagon wheels on the carriage of her narrow face. She was breaking the ice on the puddles and her dad was alternatively dragging back the dog and shouting at his little girl.

'Come 'ere. Come 'ere. Oi, don't do that. Come 'ere. You listening to me, darlin'? You'll get all filthy.'

The dog kept pulling at the lead, trying to go for a run, the girl in her Christmas clothes kept jumping on the ice, and the man, who clearly adored his daughter, kept shouting, trying to prevent his dog from being a dog, his little girl from being a little girl. I glanced at Tom, but he was looking the other way. Pigeons scurried about our feet like a grey tide.

'Do you like pigeons?' I asked, trying to get his attention.

'They curry them in Sri Lanka.'

'They remind me of people...'

'Really?'

I'd got myself all worked up. 'They're greedy, aggressive, cowardly, all pumped up and pleased with themselves. Look, that one's too fat to fly.' I pointed. 'What happened to all the blackbirds and wrens and robins?'

'Posing on your Christmas cards,' he said.

'You shouldn't have looked, they're private.'

'I had to find out your name somehow.' He grinned. 'Is it Kate or Katie?'

'Catherine, I replied. 'Kate if I'm late and Katie if you're feeling affectionate.'

'Then it shall always be Katie,' he said, and I made an effort not to squeeze his arm any tighter.

'I get the feeling you are a spy, Dr Bridge!' I exclaimed, and he pulled his mobile from his pocket.

'Me a spy?'

'Touché,' I said and we laughed, breaking the convention, and I thought how rare it is to laugh. We smile, we grin, we smirk. But laughter is as rare as the robins. 'What do you do in Sri Lanka?'

'Doctoring, mainly. And other things.'

'Other things?'

'We run an orphanage. You know there was a civil war?' I nodded. 'A lot of Tamils died in the last months, the fighting was terrible. There are thousands of orphans getting older every day. We try to place them with families, but it's not easy.'

'I don't think it's very easy here, either, in England.'

'It's not the same. The Tamils are poor. They only take a child if they can make a contribution to the household expenses, if not straight away, at least in time,' he explained. 'What we have started doing is bringing volunteers from Europe and America to teach trades, carpentry, basket weaving, tailoring, pottery, English...'

'I could do that.'

'I bet you'd be good at it.'

I slowed again. It's not always easy to walk and think at the same time. Our breath made icy streams.

'You're a volunteer?'

'Not exactly. I get paid, I get expenses...'

'You're really doing something; something real. How does that happen?'

He shrugged. 'I was an intern in a hospital for a couple of years, in Southampton, then I was a locum for various GPs. Then, I was bored. Now, I'm not.'

We exited into Old Street. I led the way into *Pinchitos,* a tapas bar, and ordered in Spanish. I was showing off. I wasn't sure why, and felt ashamed worrying about words and pigeons when Tom worried about lives, about orphans.

'And two beers,' he said to the waiter.

Our knees touched below the table. He raised his glass when the drinks came and we clipped the rims.

'Happy New Year.'

'Yes, we live in hope,' I replied.

There was a lot to say and suddenly we were silent. We sipped our beers. His eyes were the same colour as the lager, golden in the dim light. He slipped his jacket on to the back of his chair and unwound his scarf. He was wearing an old-fashioned white fisherman's sweater, a checked shirt. He leaned forward and I knew before he spoke that he had spent that silent moment thinking about what he was going to say.

'So, do you, you know...have a boyfriend?'

'Now you ask?'

'Well...'

'I gave him the sack. I wouldn't have been on my own for New Year's if I hadn't.'

The food came and his face lit up as he stared at the dishes.

'Looks delicious. What are those?' He pointed at the deep-fried squid.

'Calamares,' I replied, and pointed in turn. 'Chorizo, croquetas, those are spinach, they're chicken. The patatas bravas are like chips, but they cook them in olive oil and slather them with big dollops of ketchup and mayonnaise.' I gave a little shake. 'Finally, the meatballs are called albóndigas, my favourite word in Spanish.'

31

He speared one of the albóndigas and held it to my lips. The restaurant appeared to go silent and I wondered if everyone had stopped to look. Our eyes were locked together and my instinct wasn't to take it from his fork, but then, as if I had lost my will, my head dipped forward, my mouth gaped open and I gobbled up the meatball whole. He wiped the corners of my lips with a paper napkin.

'Thank you, doctor.'

As I grazed over the dishes, he ate quickly, hungrily, with the nervous energy that sheds calories. He swigged his drink and I felt a certain tenderness when a splash of tomato from the patatas bravas landed on his fisherman's sweater. The waiter returned to the table with a basket of bread. Tom asked for another two beers.

'No, just a jug of tap water, please,' I said.

'Keeping a clear head?'

'New Year's Resolution.'

'I haven't thought of any yet. Well...maybe one.'

'And that's a secret, I suppose?'

'Oh, yes, they don't work if you blab about them.'

'That's why mine never work then.'

I watched out of the corner of my eye as he scoffed down all the calamares until there was only one left. He then performed the same trick.

'Try one of these, they're fantastic.'

I took the ring from his extended fork and I thought: I quite like being fed, and I remembered for some reason the plastic bags dancing on the wind.

'I was surprised when you just left this morning,' I said.

'Did you think you were ever going to see me again?'

'I thought you were Don Juan, or, what's his name, the character in the mask from *V for Vendetta*?'

'I never saw it.' He shrugged. 'Do you like masks?'

I was surprised by the question and wasn't sure whether or not to tell the truth. 'Yes,' I said finally. 'They allow you to be yourself.'

'Now I understand why surgeons are surgeons,' he said. He smiled. 'I always have breakfast New Year's Day with my sister and parents. It's a tradition. I had to race up to Richmond...'

'What if you hadn't forgotten your phone?'

'Well, I knew the address, and maybe I did leave it on purpose.' He produced the phone from his pocket.

'What's your surname?'

'I beg your pardon?'

He looked up and grinned. 'I only looked at the cards, not the envelopes in the wastepaper basket.'

'You were tempted though?'

He nodded. 'You got me.' He was holding the phone in his palm and tapped in some letters. 'Katie?' he said, and looked up expectantly.

'Boyd,' I replied. 'With a y.'

I watched him watch the spinning disc, then his brow went up. 'You're famous,' he declared, his eyes shiny as he looked back across the table.

I looked away, then back again. 'Just industrious,' I returned. 'FaceBook, Twitter, Goodreads, Pinterest, you name it, I'm on it.'

I'd lost him to the pull of the iPhone. The virus. Tap, tap, tap. He started reading to himself, looked back at me, then continued reading again.

'You've done heaps of interviews.'

'If you read them they're all different. I never say the same thing twice.'

'That makes you sound more interesting.'

'More interesting than I really am.'

'You do know, when someone says they are not interesting, it immediately makes them sound more interesting.'

'But it's true.'

He leaned forward across the table and took my hand, as if I needed reassurance. 'I don't believe that for one minute. Three books...'

'In five years.'

'It says here you live in Chelsea.'

'I lied.'

'Moved, I think you mean.'

'I decided to amount to something – in spite of my advantages.'

'I imagine East London's more inspirational?'

'The rents are cheaper,' I said, and he smiled, his teeth a gleaming arc against the darkness of his tan. 'I'm totally jealous of your tan. You look so healthy.'

'I get to swim every day, the sea's incredible...'

'Alright, alright, you made your point.'

He drained his beer. 'You haven't eaten very much,' he said.

'I had a huge breakfast.'

He finished the last albóndigas and wiped the dish clean with a piece of bread. He then took my right hand and unwound the blue tape. Like my doctor, he moved the little finger on its axis, the motion gentle but firm, the way he made love, and the memory film that flashed through my head brought the colour to my cheeks.

'It's what we call a boxer's fracture. The neck of the metacarpal bone has a hairline crack. You didn't punch anybody, did you?'

'Yes, my hand, on the ground.'

'You must have gone down with some force,' he said, his voice gentle, caring. 'It will get better.'

As he was reapplying the tape to my finger the waiter came.

'Algo más? Café, torta de almendra?'

'No, gracias. La cuenta.'

'No coffee? Tom asked.

'Not here,' I replied. 'Do you have plans? Are you dashing off?'

'If I had plans, Katie Boyd, I would cancel them.'

4
SNAP

Mother used to partner Peter Drew, from Drew Butler, the estate agent in Canterbury, when they played bridge in local tournaments. As they both have that killer instinct, they won every title that was going. Canterbury, the ancient city of Thomas Becket and Chaucer, is a short drive from our country house, and less than an hour from the coast, where I went to school in Broadstairs.

That unusually hot summer when I finished my exams, I planned to pass my days sunning in the garden reading novels, my nights drifting in and out of the student bars where there was live music, an air of anticipation and no holy sisters monitoring my every move, a fixation that began after an encounter with Bella in the showers.

Bella had been 'sent down,' a brilliant start to her musical career, and I had passed through the high gates of Saint Sebastian's with but one cloud in the sky. During the holidays, I always saw Simon Wells, who had thought of me as his girlfriend since that time when he slashed our thumbs with a penknife and mingled our blood with an oath of undying devotion, which I, at fourteen, never took seriously, even if he did. At Easter, after the last of his many battles in the war to remove my knickers, I had pledged to stop being 'a cock teaser,' as he put it, and allow his groping to take its conventional course. It seems astonishing, looking back, that at eighteen I was still *intacta*, a state I was anxious to rectify, although not necessarily with Simon Wells.

When we were nine and my brother was five, Simon locked Matt in the garden shed. Matt almost choked to death with an asthma attack and the memory of my brother's face turning purple as he gasped for breath always slipped into my mind as Simon's hands slipped into my clothes. Simon was late returning home that summer, he was retaking exams, but his emails, as if driven by a monomania, never failed to allude to my 'promise.'

I wasn't retaking exams. I had worked that last school year like a medieval scribe copying the Bible. I waited each morning for the post to see whether I had earned a place at Cambridge, an experience that had tied my tummy in knots, and spent my afternoons trying to relax on the sun-bed reading Yann Martel's perfectly silly *Life of Pi*. When it struck Mother that the gardener had butchered the hanging roses while gaping through the trellis at me in my yellow bikini, the tic on her temple began to dance and, when the gardener had finished for the day, she flew into a rage. She couldn't remove the gardener from the garden; they are as rare as ambergris in rural Kent, and decided to remove me instead.

'You've become such a little show off,' she began. 'Flaunting yourself.'

'I do recall you lying in the garden sunbathing, Mother.'

'What I do or do not do is none of your business. Hanging around doing nothing, with nothing on, wasting your time...'

'I've just finished my exams. I worked bloody hard...'

'Don't you dare use that language with me. You need a summer job, that's what girls do.'

I swallowed hard. My mouth had gone dry. 'A job?'

'You need...what's it called, work experience...'

'Like you'd know?'

'Katie, we live in different times. You have to find your niche...'

'Isn't a niche where they put dead people?'

She was about to continue but stopped herself. A smile came to her thin lips; she had once brought up the subject of Botox, and left the room with her fast step and usual determination. She spoke on the telephone for several minutes. I heard her voice rise and then she returned with that look people have when they fill in the last answer on a crossword puzzle.

[Crafty plot to arouse curiosity? 8 Letters.]

She had spoken to her bridge partner and arranged for me to work for a month as an intern in the office at Drew Butler. My heart dropped and I knew, knowing Mother, that she had, not one, but myriad motives in removing me from the earthy pleasures of the garden: the gardener's enjoyment at being in close proximity to a near naked girl and the near naked girl's fascination in being surreptitiously observed through the hanging roses.

36

Mother adored being at the heart of an intrigue, that 8 letter word, and made herself believe the whole world had an interest in her secrets. She was a beautiful woman crossing that trembling bridge from forty to fifty and needed, more than ever, to be admired; she dreamed of hand-written letters to tie in ribbon, and rushed on clicking heels to the door when the bell rang, as if expecting the florist with a dozen long-stemmed roses. When I was small and she made the occasional dash to Broadstairs to take me out for afternoon tea, she adored showing me off in my scarlet blazer and straw boater, but as my legs grew longer and my skirts got shorter, if the waiter fussed over me, it made her cross to even contemplate that she might be losing her life-long capacity to be the centre of attention.

Thus, the fling with Peter Drew, if that were the case, and curious that she would want to put me in his orbit, unless she were testing or tricking him in some way.

Before that particular summer, I had always been upset when my mother had a 'special friend,' but that promptly ended when Uncle Douglas showed me a photograph of Daddy with a young Chinese woman on the terrace at *Raffles*, the rather splendid colonial hotel in Singapore. As a writer, Douglas believes in show, not tell, and the nonchalant way in which he produced the photograph said a great deal more to me than the semi-truths compiled by his agent for Wikipedia.

My job started on a Monday. The gardener didn't work weekends. It gave the roses time to recover and me two long days in the sun without Mother bustling out every two minutes to make sure I hadn't taken off my top. Having to work was a 'negative,' and one thing the nuns at Saint Sebastian's taught was that we should, through the power of spiritual alchemy, turn every negative into a positive. I wasn't sure that the universe operated with such simplicity, but thought this might just be the answer to my prayers. As an intern at Drew Butler, I was not being paid, but had been promised a commission of a half of one percent if I sold a house – a sum that would amount to thousands of pounds and give me complete freedom at university.

My parents are not exactly impoverished, but belong to that generation that doesn't believe in mollycoddling their children – unlike my cousin Jayne, who has turned Guy, Daisy and Molly, aged six, four and three, into a fetish, with incessant Tweets, daily photographs on Facebook, and Christmas cards adorned with her offspring identically dressed and beaming with such boundless joy I am instantly reminded of pictures of African children with matchstick limbs and bloated empty bellies.

The first day in the office, I studied the property on the company books. Like all sensible people, Stuart Butler was on holiday, and I learned how to deal with clients accompanying Susanna Field, a plump chatty woman with school age children, on excursions to see various houses, none of which led to a sale.

Friday came, a scorching day, and I was dying for the weekend when I could climb back into my bikini and top up my tan. Susanna finished work at lunchtime. Mr Drew was locked in his cubby hole with a widow seeking advice on estate management when I noticed a man shading his eyes as he stared at me over the display of houses for sale in the window.

He finally entered the office, dropped his shoulder bag, and fixed his blue eyes on me with such intensity a flush raced over my neck. He was wearing jeans and a denim shirt with too many buttons undone, something not done in Canterbury. He stroked his hand through his hair.

'There's a house for sale, Black Spires, is it still available?' he asked, his voice clipped and edgy.

'Yes, I do believe it is.'

'I'd like to take a look, straight away, before I get the train back to London.'

I had come to my feet. 'Of course. I won't be a moment,' I replied.

I tapped on Mr Drew's door. Black Spires was a large country house outside the village of Wingham. It had been on the books, I'd been told, for a considerable time, and I assumed Mr Drew would want to deal with it himself. I tapped again.

'Yes,' he called, and I poked my head around the door.

'Someone wants to see Black Spires,' I explained. 'He wants to see it now...'

'Are you capable of dealing with this yourself, dear?' he asked and I felt my jaw stiffen with anxiety.

'I'll do my best.'

'Well, we can expect no more than that, now can we?'

38

His lips rose faintly and his companion turned in her chair. The widow, all in black with dark glasses, revealed long tanned legs in a short skirt and high heels in patent leather. She looked little older than me, like a senior girl when you are a junior, and had the reddest lips I had ever seen. Her expression seemed vaguely conspiratorial and, as she smiled, her eyebrows arched above the rim of her glasses.

'Well, off you go then,' Mr Drew continued, glancing at the widow. 'We happen to be rather busy.'

'Okay...' I was about to close the door.

'Wait,' he called, and produced a set of keys from a drawer. 'You won't get far without these, now will you? You do know where to go?'

'Yes, I do.'

'Be careful, there's a good girl.'

As I was closing the door, he looked back at his companion in a way that made it clear why Mother quizzed me about Mr Drew's clients when I got home each day from the office.

I rattled the keys and the man hauled his bag back on his shoulder. He stuck out his free hand. 'Roger Devlin,' he said.

'Katie Boyd.'

He held on to my hand for longer than was necessary and the way he stared into my eyes made my underarms tingle with a sudden rush of nerves.

'Right, off we go then. I don't have a lot of time,' he said, and let go of my hand.

He followed me across the road to the car park. We danced between the traffic, and he placed his bag on the back seat of the company's sky blue Mini, the reason why Mr Drew had cautioned me to 'be careful.' As I hooked into the seatbelt, I was conscious that the strap crossing my chest emphasised my breasts and my pink skirt, hemmed with flowers, revealed an awful lot of bare leg.

Not that Roger Devlin appeared to notice. He just stared out the side window as the road to Wingham curled between apple and pear orchards, the immense sky with its scattering of clouds and the fields stretching into the distance like a painting by Constable. Insects tapped against the windscreen. The traffic was light. I drove with care, but touched the kerb turning a tight corner.

'My God, what the hell do you think you're doing?'

'I'm sorry...'

'Sorry. You have passed your test, I assume? The insurance isn't valid if you haven't.'

'Yes, at Christmas, actually, six months ago.'

'It shows. How old are you?'

'I beg your pardon?'

'You heard what I said.'

I took a breath. I was tempted not answer. I don't like being asked personal questions.

'Eighteen,' I said finally.

'That's all right, then.'

With his voice raised, I had caught the burr of an Irish accent softened by years in London, and his dark eyes below a mop of curly dark hair were as shiny as the black pearls on the necklace my grandmother wore. I was hot, my neck burning, and my back was wet against the car seat. I had forgotten my sunglasses and my eyes hurt straining against the strong light.

We passed a Saxon church with a flag hanging indolently on a pole, the flint of the walls gleaming like stars. I dropped a gear to climb Pedding Hill, and slowed behind two cyclists, a boy in front, a girl in a white dress behind him. She stood to get better traction and her dress blew up, showing her white knickers.

I became aware that my own skirt had risen over my thighs when he glanced at my legs levering the pedals. I kept my hands on the steering wheel, not daring to ease my skirt down, and he looked away with a faint shake of his head. The exchange of looks was momentary, but I missed the turn to Black Spires and had to double back. He tutted.

'You do know where you are going?'

'Yes, I just missed the turn, that's all.'

'I've got a train to catch.'

'We'll be there in a few minutes,' I said, and I could hear the desperation in my voice.

'That's alright, you're doing okay,' he replied, and tapped my leg just above the knee, the familiarity of his open palm on my bare flesh both shocking and, at the same time, a relief that his anger had subsided.

He opened the window and my hair tossed about my face. I slowed as the road narrowed and the humid smell of old trees and bushes entered the car. The lane was shaded between high hedgerows and I felt as if we had entered a tunnel that would take me, as the rabbit hole took Alice, somewhere completely unexpected. I had set out on the journey with the intention of charming my way into making that first sale. I had been ready to give up at the first hurdle, the first tap on the kerb, and now told myself that the way to deal with a bully and get what you want is to respond positively to their demands.

Every adversity has the seed of an equivalent or greater benefit.

It was one of Sister Theresa's pet phrases and I said those words to myself as Black Spires came into view. I turned with a smile.

'It's beautiful,' I said, and he nodded thoughtfully as he replied.

'Damn right,' he agreed, and we stepped out of the car.

He reached into the back for his bag, took out a camcorder and slowly panned the surroundings. He filmed the façade, leaning back to capture the slate spires; they were black, shiny as the widow's patent leather shoes. The house was a folly. It looked Gothic with its block stonework and arched windows, but had been built in Victorian times by a wealthy botanist who had walked across Borneo and amassed the world's largest collection of butterflies. I was rattling off the history as the eye of the camera paused on my face.

'I make up my mind whether or not I want something by taking pictures,' he said. 'Just pretend the camera's not there. Can you do that?'

'Yes, of course.'

'Photographs without people are usually dead. A figure puts the dimensions into perspective,' he added, and I nodded in agreement.

The house was circled by tall trees. There was a half-moon of lawn with a sundial at the centre and, at each corner, facing away from the house, two crumbling statues that looked Greek, but were probably replicas. There was silence except for the hum of insects and the lilting song of a nightingale calling from the bushes that arched over the porch. It stopped abruptly, fluffed up its feathers and stared directly into my eyes. As the camera turned back to the house, the bird lifted from its perch and vanished into the glare of the sun.

We followed the York stone path to the entrance. I had a problem opening the door, and Mr Devlin stepped in to save the day.

'There, you have to be strict with door locks, show them who's boss,' he said.

We entered an open hall with black and white tiles, marble busts and a sweeping staircase. He took from his bag a stills camera, a Nikon, hung it around his neck, and continued filming as we made our way into a wide living room decorated with portraits staring down from carved gilt frames. As I passed the mirror above the fireplace, the image I glimpsed didn't look like me at first, my lips red from where I'd been unconsciously biting them, my hair wild after being blown about in the wind. I paused for a moment. I was in a sort of trance and came back to my senses when I saw Mr Devlin behind me in the reflection. He wasn't smiling as he pointed to the corner.

'Stand over there, Katie, I want to show the piano in front of the bookshelves,' he said. 'Is the piano included in the price?'

'As far as I know, everything is included,' I answered.

'Everything?' he repeated, and I nodded. 'That's good. I hate quibbling over small things, don't you?'

'Yes, I suppose so.'

I posed beside the piano, a Steinway with gold lettering, and recalled watching Bella in the music room practising. Bella always knew what she wanted and went about getting it with a blend of audacity and submission, the resources I needed at that moment. He clicked his fingers to draw my attention.

'Will you do something?' he said. 'Try and relax. Look as if you're thinking to yourself: if I play my cards right, I might just sell this house.'

He must have been reading my mind because that's exactly what I was thinking. The camera whirred, Roger Devlin moved closer, so close the lens almost touched my nose, then backed away again.

'The camera likes you,' he added.

I felt a little shock like static electricity and, when I smiled, he clapped his hands three times.

'And there's me thinking your lips were always stuck in the same position,' he remarked. 'You're not nervous, are you, Katie?'

'No...yes. No. I'm not sure.'

He laughed and I laughed.

'Come on, let's go outside.'

The living room opened on to a long garden containing the hoops required for playing croquet. We exited through the French windows. He was behind me, filming again as I walked across the lawn. He took a number of stills, then went back to the camcorder.

'Take your shoes off, I want to get one of those, you know, barefoot on the grass shots.'

I did so. His voice had grown mellow. I was getting somewhere. The grass was like velvet, warm between my toes. The garden was an island surrounded by a sea of fields. The whir of the camera was rhythmic, soothing. It struck me that we were miles from anywhere, and how unusual it was for me to be alone with a man I didn't know. I watched two pink butterflies dance in a spiral then disappear.

'If only England was always like this,' he said, breaking into my thoughts.

'If only,' I repeated, and felt as if a bond had forged between us.

He mopped his brow with a white handkerchief and I noticed another one of the buttons on his denim shirt had popped open to reveal a gold cross on a bed of dark wiry hair. He gazed up at me gazing at him, then turned to study the back of the house. The spires pierced the blue dome of the sky and the windows behind small balconies were like glittery eyes looking back at us.

We continued the tour, the modern kitchen with high tech appliances, the dining room beyond with a dozen chairs around a walnut table, the extensive library, big as a ballroom, where the Victorian lepidopterist had kept his collection of butterflies.

'Yes,' he remarked, and our eyes met again. 'It's the perfect location.'

I was hot and felt a shiver of pleasure. Half of one percent of the sale price was almost £10,000.

'Shall we go upstairs?' I said.

'You bet. I want to see everything.'

He followed me back into the hall, filming at the same time, then stopped to throw his camera bag over his shoulder. I was still carrying my shoes and was about to put them back on.

'No, don't, just hold them,' he said sharply. 'Climb the stairs slowly, will you. I love this space and I want to get it just right.'

I started off.

'No, no, come back. Let's start again. Look a bit dreamy. Arch your back and swing the shoes with the rhythm of your movement. Think about something wonderful, your boyfriend, something like that.'

I set off again. I was good at taking stage directions and had once played Romeo in the school's production of Shakespeare's play with Bella, naturally, as Juliet. Mr Devlin remained at the bottom of the stairs. He shot a side view of me as I ascended, my head thrown back, my shoes loose in my fingers. Suspended from the ceiling was a huge chandelier made up of hundreds of pale pink shades like glass roses and it wasn't my 'boyfriend' who slipped into my mind, but the gardener peeking at me through the trellis in the garden at home.

We toured the five bedrooms with their en suite bathrooms and came to a halt on the balcony overlooking the garden in the largest of the rooms.

'Lovely view,' I said, and he turned away.

He set up a tripod at the end of the bed with its embroidered white lace canopy, attached the video camera so that it reeled off a wide angle shot of the room, and took various stills with the Nikon, the snap, snap, snap of the shutter like a steady pulse.

I opened the doors to the walk-in closets.

'There's masses of space,' I said, but Roger Devlin wasn't interested in details.

'That's what you expect, the price they're asking,' he returned. 'Now, stand over there, to one side of the window, in the light.'

I padded barefoot back across the grey tiles. The shutter snapped over and over. I had thought when you shot into the light the image was ruined by the flashback, but when he showed me the photographs in the view screen, my features were highlighted against a pastel background.

'Nice, eh?'

'Amazing,' I said.

'I'll get some printed off for you,' he promised, and stood back with that intense expression he had. 'Now will you do something for me?'

'Yes, of course...'

44

'Undo a couple of those buttons,' he said, pointing at my blouse. 'I want to get a shot of the sun on your shoulder.'

He spoke in a way that left no room for thought or discussion. I obeyed instantly, releasing the top two buttons. The collar wouldn't stretch back far enough and my fingers, as with a will of their own, unsnapped another two. The blouse opened to reveal my shoulder and the tops of my breasts in the pretty white bra I had chosen as if fate had lent a hand in my dressing that morning.

'Good, good, that's nice, very nice. Look over your shoulder, push out your hip. Come on now, come on, give it to me, baby, give it to me...'

He kept talking, the camera kept snapping, and, it's funny, but I knew what to do. I'd seen a million models in magazines and had pretended I was a model, peering into the mirror in my bedroom. I would pucker my lips and glance over my shoulder to see if my bottom looked cute when I tensed the muscles. All girls do the same, I'm sure, and it seemed perfectly natural in front of the camera.

'Katie, take it off now, turn around. I want to shoot your back. Do it slowly, the way you walked up the stairs. Just those last couple of buttons. You can do it. Let's get some really nice shots...'

His Irish lilt was stronger, mesmeric, compelling, his words like drumbeats, steady, melodic. I could hear the pounding of my heart. My skin was sheathed in sweat and it felt cool as the camera snapped and the buttons popped and I dropped my white blouse nonchalantly to the floor.

'Good, good. Lift your hair above your head and let it fall, always slowly. You could model, you know that. Didn't I say, the camera likes you? Turn now. Turn towards me. Lean forward, that's it. That's fabulous.'

I leaned forward. I swivelled my hips. I arched my back. The more I glammed it up, the easier it was.

'Katie, we're going to do something interesting now. I love this skirt. I want you to spin around like a ballerina and let the skirt swirl around the top of your legs. Do you think you can do that?'

I didn't answer. I listened to the camera shutter snapping. I crossed my feet and began to turn, gathering speed, the skirt rising like a hula-hoop. The room was shady except for the path of crystal light sliding over the balcony with its galaxies of golden dust. I grew hot and giddy and, when I came to a stop, he wasn't smiling. He pointed at the hook on the side of my skirt.

'Unhook that,' he said sternly, waggling his finger. He leaned in close, his dark eyes like the nightingale I had seen in the garden. 'Lower the zip and then do one more pirouette. Hold the skirt together before you start and let it swirl around and fall. Let's try and do it in one take.'

He stood back and I turned again in a circle, the dancing girl, dancing to the mood music, the race of my heart, the swish and snap of the camera. I raised my hands. The skirt moved with me, spinning faster and faster until it was claimed by gravity and fell in a pale pink pool about my feet. I stepped to one side and, what went through my head was how glad I was that I was wearing white against my suntan.

'Let's keep going,' he said, tossing my skirt and blouse on a chair. 'We're really getting somewhere.'

I kept posing, turning, thrusting out my hips. I felt as if things inside me that had been balled up were untangling. My skin gleamed in the shaft of light. I wasn't sure what to do with my hands and, when I gripped them behind my back, I realized I was pushing out my breasts.

He stared into my eyes. I smiled. He looked serious.

'Katie, will you do something?'

He didn't say what. He just looked at me and I nodded.

'Take your top off for me.'

The words came from his mouth like a coil of silver smoke and seemed to hang there as if in tiny cloud.

Take your top off for me.

It was such a simple sentence. Such a simple request. My nipples were tingling. I wanted to release them, give them air. The sweat on my back turned cold and made me shiver.

'Take your top off for me.'

He said it again, his smooth voice deeper, darker, the words no longer a curl of smoke, but words whispered from far away. They reached me like a recording that had been slowed down.

Take your top off for me.

Just as I often knew what Mother was going to say before she said it, I had known Roger Devlin was going to ask me to take off my top. But the *'for me'* tagged on to the sentence made the request appear so courteous it was difficult to say no without seeming disrespectful. I felt flustered, embarrassed, confused. As we had entered the tunnel of hedgerows at the end of the journey to Black Spires I had made a pact with destiny and destiny was taking its course.

'I can't do that,' I finally mumbled.

'Katie?' He waited.

'Yes.'

'I won't tell you again.'

'But...'

I sensed rather than saw the faint shake of his head. The disappointment. I was just a silly schoolgirl with my head full of fantasies, a pathetic little virgin. That's what Simon had said, and the words rang through me like a funeral bell. I had failed. I would never sell Black Spires.

'Please,' I said, but my will had gone.

He raised his brow, the upward motion acting as a spring that resonated from his bright eyes to my arms. It was uncanny, a stage trick, a radio wave. As his brow went up and his eyes flashed, I wriggled my arms up my back and unhooked my bra. Like a stripper in a night club, I held the cups to my breasts before allowing the material to fall away. I had been holding my breath and let out a long sigh. We remained motionless in the amber light, my breasts standing out firm, my nipples hard and painful, pink and shiny with the rush of blood. I had always thought they were too small, but they were full now, throbbing.

He took several pictures, but I wasn't posing, just standing there.

He clicked his fingers and pointed.

'If you please.'

I went to speak but my mouth fell open and nothing came out. My breasts were already on show, sun bronzed and pretty, rising and falling with the beat of my heart. Breasts are everywhere. In every newspaper and magazine, on television, on the sides of buses.

His brow went up and he repeated the same instruction. 'If you please.'

'But...'

He adjusted the camera. 'Hurry now. Before the light changes,' he said, his soft tone whispering my own unknown desires.

Each time he asked for more, I gave more, my blouse, my skirt. My bra. I was on a slippery slide and there appeared to be no way and no reason to get off. It wasn't that I nursed a repressed yearning to stand naked in front of a stranger; it just felt natural to obey. I was used to obeying at my strict school. It was easier than swimming against the current, and I always thought I would rebel like Bella in my own good time.

Our eyes met and I watched as he used the corner of his handkerchief to polish the camera lens. He looked me up and down. There was nothing prurient in his look, and I had that sensation that came to me sometimes standing on the platform in the Underground, the rush of air, the train charging from the tunnel, the feeling of being sucked towards the edge. So much seemed to depend on what I now did, perhaps my entire future, and I felt in some way detached from the decision.

My mind was spinning and my mouth was dry. My panties fit snugly, the elastic stretching like a bridge from the supports of my hip-bones in such a way that, had he leaned forward, he would have caught a glimpse of the dark forest of hair nestling below. He didn't look down. He was still staring into my eyes and I stared defiantly back. I was determined to shake my head and say no, but my will had gone, absorbed by something more profound and overpowering. I lowered my eyes and slowly lowered the soft fabric over my hips, over the cheeks of my bottom, and down my legs. I stepped from my panties in a little dance and stood up straight with them in the palm of my hand.

He took them from me as if I had offered him a gift and what he did was so unexpected, the scene still returns to me on nights when sleep is distant and the mind has its own mind. He stretched out the damp material, stared at the faintly stained gusset and held my panties to his nose like a connoisseur with good wine. He breathed in my bouquet and tucked the perfumed triangle in his pocket.

I was naked in a beam of sunlight with a man I didn't know. He was standing back to take more photographs. Perspiration coated the split in my bottom. I was aware of the scent of my arousal and realized with shame that the obscure pleasure of that moment came, not from any expectation of what might take place, but simply from exposing myself. I was free. I felt terrified and I felt completely, totally alive. I danced around the room. Snap, snap, snap went the camera. The camcorder whirred and I was sure I heard in the distance the song of the nightingale.

A table stood to one side of the balcony. He pointed. 'Good girl,' he said. 'Lean over the surface, let's really show them what we can do.'

I spread my legs, the camera clicked and captured my most intimate parts, the crease of my bottom, my bobbing breasts, my glassy eyes.

'That's lovely. Nice. Very nice. Push forward. Come on now, push out that cute little arse. Nice. Nice. Give it to me. Give me more.'

I climbed up on the table. He didn't need to tell me how to arrange myself, you just know these things: on my hands and knees with my bottom out, my breasts hanging. I twisted and turned like a spiral staircase and the more the camera clicked the wetter I got. There were butterflies in my tummy and up in the core of my being a little fist was tightening.

'Lay back, Katie, legs up, that's nice. That's nice. Go for it.'

He was reading my mind. With my back arched, my palms with stretched fingers went automatically to my breasts. My nipples were on fire. I turned the little buds. I bit my lips. I heard the sound of the world humming outside and rose up like a beautiful cat. I ran my right hand down my side, across the bony curve of my hip and into my pubic hair. My pubes were drenched. My inner thighs were wet. The juices gushed from me, hot and sticky, and the camera kept clicking, keeping the beat. I threw my head back and would have fallen from the table where I was perched had he not caught me in his arms.

He carried me to the bed. I felt as if I had come to the end of a long race and was panting. I had masturbated, of course, many times. But holding a picture of Simon in my head had never hit the magic button and the special feeling the girls described at school had never happened to me. Roger Devlin had touched something waiting to be touched; to be concluded. Every day I looked for the letter that would say whether or not I had been offered a place at Cambridge. That long wait had tied my intestines into knots. Now, suddenly, the tangles untied. I felt a wave of sangfroid. I felt free, philosophical, relieved.

He turned the video lens to face the bed. I wasn't watching him, I was drawn to the eye of the camera, struck by its ability to capture this moment. There was doubt and confusion in my head; fear too. I would think about it all later. I would remember always. But now, I laid back on the white bed and watched Roger Devlin remove his shirt, his jeans, his black boxers.

There was no ceremony, no kissing, no foreplay. I opened my legs. He entered me immediately, pushing hard and jerking upwards at the same time. I heard a SNAP. There was a stinging flash like an electric shock that brought a tear to my eye, and I thought about the camera, how it would preserve that instant, that small tear, the pain as it changed to pleasure and spread over my features.

He moved steadily, rhythmically, up and down, and I moved with him, my back sliding against the bed-cover. My eyes were pressed shut. The soft slap and suck of our bodies pressing together sounded like waves drawing at a tropical beach. My skin tingled. Everything that had lain dormant came alive. Everything in hibernation was reborn. I was fully awake, fully conscious of my own repressed desires and passions.

I pushed down on my heels, arched my back like a drawn bow, and drew him up inside me. He moved like a piston, his breath warm and steady against my ear. Then he gasped for breath. His body stiffened and, that same moment, a shudder of contractions ran through me. I threw my head back and it felt as we climaxed as if a city of lights had lit up across my nervous system. I could see stars behind my closed eyes. I rose weightlessly from the bed and I was aware vaguely of the sun going down, the room where we lay beneath the white canopy turning slowly to shadow.

5
The Game

All writing is autobiography. If I were to write a story about a young black man from an estate in the north of England, my geographical, gender and ethnic opposite, I would provide him with patience and perseverance. I would make him quick on his feet, secretly ambitious, moody, easily manipulated and anxious to appear agreeable.

What happened that day with Roger Devlin I immortalised in a short story that lacked the fine detail that comes with experience; in writing as in life. I neglected to say that after he had severed my hymen and I screamed my way through my first orgasm, he was captivated by the spots of blood speckling the creamy smear on the bedcover. He reached for his camera and I listened as the shutter went snap, snap, snap, the steady beat the same rhythm as when he had made love to me. I laid back, breasts nursed in my palms, thighs wet, the waft of my own scent in a cloud below the white canopy.

It was Bella who came into my mind that moment. She always said people take sex far too seriously. It's just a bit of fun. I felt detached, tranquil, floating like a feather; not merely content, but the shadow of childhood had vanished in the beam of light piercing the room from the balcony. I had shed my virginity and it was rather perfect with a perfect stranger. There were no reproaches. No promises. No future. I instantly understood that sex was an unknown land to be explored, as the man who had once owned the house had explored Borneo for butterflies. Had I allowed Simon Wells to fumble his way inside me, it would have been clumsy, inept, and my journey along the diamond highway to erotica may never have begun.

Roger Devlin stopped taking close-ups and reached for his boxers. He blew out his cheeks.

'You're something else,' he said.

'Am I?'

'Damn right.' He paused. 'A virgin whore! I didn't think I'd ever get to meet one. He pulled on his jeans. 'I hope you're on the pill.'

'I'm not, actually.'

'Well, you ought to be.'

'I didn't plan on, you know...'

'Are you sure about that?'

He blew out his cheeks again and wore that look people have when they are dealing with a puppy that's just peed on the carpet.

'What if you get pregnant?'

'You'll just have to marry me.'

'I don't know what my wife would have to say about that.'

It made it even better somehow. I was the other woman. He buttoned his shirt, pulled on yellow socks, brown brogues that needed a polish; good quality. I watched and he watched me watching him.

'You enjoyed that, didn't you?' he asked, expecting praise, men, I would find, always do. A flush rose over my cheeks.

'Yes, actually.'

'You were dying to take your clothes off.'

'No I wasn't.'

He studied me for a few seconds, shaking his head. 'Well, now you'd better put them back on again.'

I rose reluctantly, padded across the room and stood looking out at the garden from the balcony. I liked being naked. I remained motionless, eyes closed, the sun warming my body.

'Come on, then, I've got a train to catch.'

My clothes were on the chair in front of the row of mirrors that concealed the walk in closets. With the sun behind me, my reflection revealed a version of myself that was different in ways that were subtle and understated. My cheeks were pronounced, rather than gaunt, and there was a serenity about my eyes that looked back as if the girl in the mirror was how I was destined to be and the girl who had woken in her bed that morning was someone else.

'Excuse me, when you've finished standing there admiring yourself.'

The light changed, a cloud must have passed over the sun. I watched in the mirror as he telescoped the legs of the tripod and placed it in the bag, the camcorder with its erotic narrative cased and placed on top. I dressed, then held out my hand.

'I think you have something that belongs to me.'

'I'm going to hang on to them, if you don't mind...'

I shook my head and wondered if he would hang my knickers on the wall as they hang the stuffed heads of stags in the corridor at Daddy's club. As I pulled on my shoes, I was still expecting him to say he was going to make an offer on Black Spires. But he didn't. I locked the house, with his help turning the key. I dropped him at the station, and I never saw Roger Devlin again – although that's not strictly true.

I have seen his naked back and white bottom many times. The video he shot of me barefoot in the garden, climbing the stairs, removing my clothes and spreading my legs was cut into a fifteen-minute film which he posted with a two-minute teaser on a website where, for 99 cents, my face pixelated, you can watch me losing my virginity over and over again.

Did I regret what had happened that day? No. On the contrary. I had taken off my clothes because I had wanted to. I could have told myself I was only trying to sell the house. But that's not true. After my long imprisonment behind the walls of school, I wanted to shrug off the past like a butterfly leaving its cocoon and be who I was, not who I appeared to be in my scarlet blazer, white blouse and blue skirt, the colours of the Union Jack that flew over the tower at Saint Sebastian's.

After being compelled by Mother from the garden into the role of secret agent in her bridge partner's office, I was ready to do something that at the time would have seemed out of character, although, with the benefit of experience, was in reality a facet of myself that had been concealed as if below a layer of dust and just needed a puff of breath to blow it away.

The moment I took off my top, I was on a journey and it felt completely natural to take off everything. When naked you are in a sense reborn. The exams were over. There were no rat-faced nuns spying on me through half-closed doors. No Mother staring through the bedroom window. Flecks of gold hovered in the sunlight; the dust blown from the mirror of my hidden self. There was a humming silence like that feeling you get in your ears when you hold your breath. I was drugged by my own sense of daring and outrageousness, that feeling of letting go, of breaking the taboo.

Ever since that time when I was caught in the showers with Bella, kissing, just kissing, I had wanted to rebel. Now, I knew what I was rebelling against: the holy sisters, Mother, the snares and traps of my class and education. I was born to marry some clone of Simon Wells, breed, have affairs, fight with my daughters and go for long walks with small dogs. Suddenly, I felt free, feverish, defiant. As I ran my panties down my legs, I started to dance, each step as if on a highwire taking me across the abyss from my protected past to an unknown future.

Timing is everything. The first time for a girl is critical: the difference between an A or a B in the exams; the life-changing event that will determine your attitude, perhaps forever. Roger Devlin wanted sex without strings; sex with a young girl because girls make men feel young. What I didn't know, I still didn't know myself, not then, but I had an intuition the moment he slid through the warm waters of my vagina, that this was right for me: sex with a stranger without commitments, with the intensity and detachment I was going to need when I began to chronicle my life as fiction.

The girl I wrote about in the short story was eighteen. Ten years had gone by and I could see now how Roger Devlin had bent me to his will through a combination of perplexing mood swings and words as shrewd and perceptive as any poet. On the journey from Canterbury to Wingham, my thighs on show, my breasts accentuated by the seat belt, he didn't take sly peeks at me, no, he stared out the side window and only spoke to criticise my driving. He made me feel clumsy, immature, inept. By the time we reached Black Spires, I was sweaty, nervous and, as he seemed so hard to please, I had become disposed to do everything I could in order to please him.

Black Spires was like a set on a film lot, the sky sapphire, the light soft and hazy. The gravel crunched beneath his leather shoes as he walked away from the car. The camcorder whirred.

I make up my mind whether or not I want something by taking pictures.

The eye of the lens was on me. The nuance was unclear. But the elasticity of words, the intricacy of words, the supremacy of words, is like the invisible power of the wind that bends the trees and acts as a drug, a soporific. Why else would priests develop that deep resonant voice that calls to your soul; or tries to?

He looked directly into my eyes.

Just pretend the camera's not there. Can you do that?

By posing the question and my agreeing, we were now complicit.

You have to be strict with door locks, show them who's boss.

The word *strict* reminded me of school where I found it easier to obey than rebel. He asked if the piano was included, implying that he was serious about buying the house. He then said he *hated quibbling over small things.*

Those small things were peeled off one by one, starting when we reached the garden.

Take your shoes off, I want to get one of those barefoot in the grass shots.

This was a direction, not a suggestion. He said the camera liked me, that I could be a model and, with those words, like a spell, I played the model. I thrust out my hips, stared back over my shoulder, eyes widened, lips pursed, bottom tensed, the object of desire I tried to create alone in front of the mirror performed for a man with a camera that formed a barrier and a bridge between us. Being barefoot is sensuous; tactile. I was reminded of the gardener staring at me in my bikini, toes tended by the prickling blades of grass, perspiration veneered on my back. The air was motionless. It felt new; unbreathed, and I watched two twirling butterflies on wings the same shade of pink as my skirt.

We climbed the stairs. He didn't tell me to undo my blouse, he asked: Will you do something for me? To which I readily said yes, and once you undo one button, it is only a question of time before you undo them all. He had tapped into my fantasies. He swept aside my social programming and made me conscious of what I believed I wanted or, indeed, did want.

Girls, most girls, want to please. They answer yes to those men who know how to pose the right questions. What I didn't know at the time, and was shocked to learn, is that there is a guide for men who want to seduce women called *The Game,* an allegedly true memoir of how Neil Strauss, a shy, inhibited guy, turns himself into a smooth-talking womaniser of the Roger Devlin school.

The technique is basically this: when a man meets a woman he desires, he doesn't look directly at her and speaks to her with indifference. Strauss suggests that in this way, the woman grows anxious to please; programmed little Pavlov's dogs that we are. At the appropriate time, he touches her in a casual way (Devlin's hand on my leg in the car), and turns the situation around by giving her something – it's called anchoring – a glass of wine, his phone number, some attention. He pays her a small compliment (the camera likes you) and uses 'trigger' words (will you do something for me?) to show that he is agreeable if she responds positively to his requests.

6
Svengali

There is a lot more to *The Game*, of course, but the message contained in the book swept into my mind that New Year's Day after lunch at *Pinchitos* and we returned to my flat.

Tom took my keys to open the door and, after the cold tramp through the frigid streets, I bathed in the warmth pumping from the iron radiators. I had left the heating on and the living room at three in the afternoon was as hot as that summer's day ten years ago. I tossed my coat on a chair and was about to unbutton my jacket.

'Wait,' he said. 'Will you do something for me?'

My breath caught in my throat.

'...what did you say?'

His request had sounded in my ears as if someone had shouted from the past. He was holding out his palms.

'I'm sorry?' he said, and I took a breath.

'I just read your mind, that's all.'

'I'd better be careful what I'm thinking.'

'Yes.' I took a beat. My heart was going pitter-patter, like rain on a window. 'Don't they say we are what we think?'

'Do you believe that?' he asked, and I shrugged.

'I have a friend who reads the Tarot.'

'Did she say you were going to meet a dark handsome stranger?'

'She doesn't like giving me bad news. Anyway,' I said, glancing around the room. 'Who is this handsome stranger?'

He grinned and threw his jacket on top of my own, pinning it down.

'Music,' I suggested, and scrolled down my iPhone: 'Avril Lavigne, Bach, Gypsy Kings, Hotel Costes, KD Lang, Melissa Etheridge, Mozart, Pink Floyd, Tribe 8...'

'Tribe 8?'

'You like them?'

'Never heard of them.'

'It's a dyke band. How about random?'
'Isn't that a compromise?'
'No, it's eclectic.'
'No, it's a compromise. Hotel Costes,' he then said, and I set the iPhone in its dock.

The room vibrated with drums, brass, maracas, a mélange of sound roaming the space.

'So, Tom Bridge, you were saying?' I continued, and he sat in the armchair.

'I said, will you do something for me?'
'You already know I will,' I replied.
He crossed his legs. 'Take your clothes off for me.'
I stared back at him.
'I am a doctor,' he added, and it made me smile.

The thing is, like that day long ago at Black Spires, it was hot and my jeans were sawing into my crotch like a cheese wire. I was desperate to strip off my clothes. Did he know that? Had I beamed out my subliminal desires and he was responding to them?

'You want me to take my clothes off?'
'Yes.'

I raised my shoulders, as if surprised, and tried not to show that I was rather pleased as I unhooked the first of the row of brass buttons on my jacket, one button leading to the next like I was playing an accordion. Being naked for a woman isn't the same as it is for a man; our clothes acquire different associations. We don't dress in clothes, we masquerade in the robes of contrivance: too tight, too small, the contours outlining shapes and displaying slivers of flesh like promises, like the trailers for a film. Nudity is a logical progression.

An idea for a story jumped into my mind, a continuation of my experiences with Roger Devlin. After being seduced, the female protagonist becomes obsessed with the camera watching her during sex and puts the films online – she always wears a mask, of course, and charges customers 99 cents to see the edited movies. She is in league with her web guy, a facsimile of my web guy, Bradley, a boy devoted to barter – he'll fix my laptop for free if I fix the irritation in his blue jeans.

'Bradley, you're twenty-two years old.'

'In my prime, right? You know what, Katie, I could give you a real good seeing to.'

'Bradley, if you put all that testosterone into repairing my machine it wouldn't keep going down on me...'

He did a little shimmy. 'You've got a way with words, Katie, I'll give you that.'

My face must have showed my thoughts; I'm an open book, a blank page.

'What are you thinking about?' Tom asked.

I stared back across the room. 'I'm not telling you,' I replied, and held the jacket out for him to inspect; it was rather gorgeous – a shade of blue that's not quite blue and not quite anything else, cerulean, kingfisher, lazuline.

'Do you like the colour?' I asked, and he didn't answer the question.

'You should wear more green,' he said instead, and paused, 'to match your eyes.'

'Yes, doctor. Would you like me to change my hairstyle as well?'

He smiled. I liked his smile, natural, full-lipped. The low sun edged his face in gold, making it hard to see his expression. I dragged the rollneck over my head and shook out my hair. He leaned forward to watch as if he were at the theatre following a scene on stage. I took a step towards him and pointed down at my boots.

'Can you?'

He untied the laces. I lifted my feet in turn so he could remove my boots, which he placed beside the chair. Next my socks, stretching them out and placing them on top of the boots with a neatness I approved of. The snake's head on my belt clasp had blue eyes, to match the jacket, a detail. I released the clasp and writhed like a plume of smoke as I lowered my jeans. I sat on the edge of the sofa to pull the material over my feet, and stood again, barefoot on the carpet.

'You have beautiful feet, they're your best feature,' he said.

'Oh,' I replied.

'Apart from all the other best features, obviously...'

'Too late, give me my socks...'

'Absolutely not.'

'I'm going to console myself counting all my shoes...'
'You can do that, Miss Boyd, in your own time.'
'Bully.'

I twirled in my underwear and was struck by a thought that took me skipping through to the bedroom. There were shoes everywhere, breeding like mice in every corner, in bags and boxes, under the bed, lined on racks at the bottom of the closet where I hide sometimes; ankle boots, riding boots, boots with moons and stars, boots with chains and silver heels, court shoes, ballet pumps, trainers, flip-flops, Jimmy Choo sandals with straps as intricate as a cat's cradle and Jimmy Choo black patent stilettos like objects of wonder in a museum. I must have a hundred pairs of shoes and culling them is like killing baby seals.

Now where was I?

Ah yes, the bottom drawer, which I opened, and stared down at the blank eyes of the mask waiting there as if with secret plans of its own. Just as when you glance at a pair of shoes and it feels as if destiny is at work, when I first saw the mask in a store in Soho, I knew we were meant for each other. My hands reached out as if drawn by the motions of the moon and I slipped the elastic bow over the back of my head. The mask fit to my face as if drawn from a mould, the curve below my eyes shaped to my cheekbones, the angle across my brow like two wings that meet in a coxcomb of tiny black feathers. I turned to the mirror and instantly felt as if I had become somebody else, someone I didn't altogether recognize, but who, I knew, would be able to glide across the dance floor at *Pink* without need for words or justification. Just as I had concealed the tattoo beneath my hair, in the mask I concealed myself beneath a veil of mystery and anonymity.

It was years ago, I was young then, and the very thought of going to a lesbian club had sent me into a spasm of fear and anxiety. The two friends who were taking me to *Pink* had promised that there was no pressure to do or be anything, although they had not taken into account that, in a mask, the pressure doesn't come from without, but from some untapped source within.

I took a long look at myself in the mirror, my other self, the masked self, and slinked cat-like back to the living-room. I clawed at the air.

'Sssss,' I hissed.

'It suits you.'

'It's to hide my feet.'

He made a hook with his finger.

'Come here,' he said.

I rolled my shoulders as I edged on all fours towards him, nose twitching. I arched my back. I purred as I slithered my paws up his legs and stood, resting my palms on his knees.

He nipped the sides of my knickers between his long fingers and thumbs. I sighed with pleasure and the air flew like a small bird from my chest. He gracefully, as if removing peel from an orange, slid the fabric over my bottom and down my legs. He took my thighs and nuzzled my pubes with his nose. Instantly I was wet. Instantly I caught my musky bouquet, piquant as an animal in heat. The mask makes me feel wanton. The drums beat louder. He turned me around and I dropped into his lap, legs open. He made me comfortable and a single finger stroked between the lips of my vagina in a soothing motion. I wriggled.

'This sweater's awful, it's all scratchy,' I complained.

'A present from my mother...'

'Can't live with them, can't be born without.'

'Cynic,' he said, and I laughed.

'There is something incredibly sexy about a girl in a mask laughing.'

'I shall write that down,' I told him.

'You'll forget it.'

'I don't forget anything.'

I nearly fell off the chair as he leaned forward to pull the fisherman's sweater over his head. I dragged at his shirt, he took it off, and it was cosier when we laid back in the same position, my spine angled across his chest, the pad of his finger moving between my legs, softly, like you might stroke a sleeping kitten. He investigated my breasts through my bra, the faint swell of my tummy, my sticky-out hipbones.

'Your BMI is in the first percentile.'

'Does that mean I'm too thin?'

'No, it means everyone else is too fat.'

He eased me away from his chest and removed my bra, placing it on the table beside the chair, one cup tucked in the other. I adore being naked, and I adore being naked in the mask even more. I laid back and he continued stroking me, his right hand between my legs, his left inspecting my breasts. I wondered if he were feeling for lumps. I didn't ask. I wouldn't have wanted to know.

'I love your breasts,' he said.

'More than my feet?'

I felt his chest vibrate and knew he was smiling. I liked being explored in this way, anonymous in the mask, submissive to his touch. His palm shuffled over my waist.

'I love your hips.' He mused for a moment. 'They're like sails.'

His tongue swept over my ear and his free hand brushed my scalp.

'I love your hair, it's...autumnal.'

'When all the leaves are falling and it starts to get cold?'

'Noo,' he replied, stretching the word. 'It's like a rainbow, no, a kaleidoscope. It's not brown or russet.' He sounded like a doctor listing symptoms. 'There are flecks of bronze and gold, red and copper.'

'It can't make up its mind,' I said.

His right hand left the place where it belonged; he twisted me to one side like a wrestler and used both hands to pull the hair away from the back of my neck. He had discovered my tattoo and paused like he was looking at a Rothko in a gallery.

'Do you like it?' I asked.

'It's unique.'

'Hardly.'

'Why's it hidden?'

'Why not?'

He brushed my hair back, straightened my mask, and looked into my eyes.

'Green,' he said.

'Unlike my jacket.'

He laughed as we got comfortable again. I knew he would be puzzling over the tattoo, the whys and why there, those questions people ask, and he already knew me well enough to know there was no point in asking. His right hand slipped over the contours of my body, his finger coming to rest back in the moist delta of curly pubes. His other hand stroked my hair, my chin, my shoulder, the length of my arm, a poem on his lips:

cranium, mandible, clavicle
scapula, sternum, ribs
humerus, radius, carpals
metacarpals and phalanges

He lifted my hand and kissed my little finger.
'Is it going to be better now?'
'It'll take another two or three months.'
I sighed. 'How boring,' I said, and he changed the subject.
'How long have you been here, Katie, in this flat?'
'Two or three months,' I answered; an echo.
'It's really super,' he said, and I thought: what an old-fashioned word; I would have said marvellous or wonderful. 'Where were you before?' he then asked.
'I thought you knew?'
'I can guess, Kensington, I'd say, maybe Notting Hill?'
'Down by the river, actually, in Chelsea. I had a little garret, you know, the poet thing.'
'Why did you move?'
'Interesting question...'
'And?'
'Hold on, I'm thinking.' I glanced down at his hand. 'This isn't the best time for thinking.'
He had cupped my breast and, like a plumber, his right hand was fiddling with the leak between my legs. He kissed my cheek below the mask and I continued.
'I needed a different landscape, you know, like Emily Brontë, she had the moors; or Daphne du Maurier with Cornwall. Did you know, it was her grandfather, George, who wrote *Trilby*.'
'I haven't read it.'
'I have, twice, actually. He invented Svengali. You remind me of him.'
'Me?'
'Yes.'
'In what way?'
'You must read the book.'
'I've got a lot to catch up on.'
'Me, too, there's never enough time.'
'Time for what?'

'For anything...writing, Twitter, working as a waitress at stupid events. I'm trying to write a blog, so the whole world knows how interesting I am, which I'm not. I've got, like, a million half-written stories; the emails keep coming, more every day. I worked it out. I'm going to have to live for 200 years and I'll still never catch up.'

'Poor baby,' he said.

I had turned to look into his eyes. I didn't want to talk about what I did, where I lived, why I had moved. I lowered my head and our lips met. He was a good kisser, a give-and-take kisser; relaxed, leisurely, kissing like someone eating melon at a picnic. I sucked his finger when he put it in my mouth and he wriggled the digit back between my legs. Life has few perfect moments. This moment was perfect, naked in a mask, his mouth roaming the nerve endings of my mouth, the pad of his finger nursing that mysterious place, so precious and vital it makes me believe that it isn't all random, all chaos, that there is some universal purpose to our lives; to everything.

Perspiration ran off me as if I had become a bubbling stream. The monkeys in my mind were still. I threw back my head and wedged my legs across the arms of the chair, his finger a hovering presence over my clitoris. I moved languidly like a dancer at two in the morning, like a leaf caught in the breeze. That small fist was opening and closing inside my belly. My breath raced. Contractions ran through me; it felt as if my insides were a length of wet cloth growing tighter as it was wrung out. The drummer in Hotel Costes filled the room with pulsing heartbeats.

I had a fleeting vision of myself in the black mask spread naked with the flame of my clitoris glowing and erupted like a burst balloon filled with water, the arc of silky discharge squirting in a shower of raindrops down my leg. I was proud and ashamed, I always had those twin feelings, and happy, too, happy in a way outside the normal register, like the first daffodil of spring can make you happy, or a snatch of Bach or Bizet.

My breath came in gasps. A snake slithered up my spine. Aftershocks raced down my legs, the ripples a flowing tide. My heart was bursting. Liquids flooded from me. I felt the same and different, my body retuned, recalibrated, replete. At the moment of orgasm you are living fully and totally in the present. An orgasm is anticipated, like the sunrise on a new day, and unexpected, like winning a prize in a competition you can't recall having entered. Time freezes and there isn't a feeling of loss, a void, a little death, but a reminder that of all human activity, none is more perfect. The orgasm is my driving force, the random consequence of meeting a stranger in a bar or at a ball and taking him home to warm the bed sheets.

The music switched to the next track. I turned in the chair so that I could kiss him again. I squeezed one of his nipples hard enough for him to recoil in pain and our teeth clashed. He bit my neck and I squirmed down across his chest until my knees touched the carpet. He went to pull me back, but I wriggled free. I loosened his belt, his jeans, his boxers. I pulled off his shoes, desert boots suitable for wandering in far away places. He was hard and I sensed his body relax as I licked the length of his cock. It was pretty, playful, the head pink, the column creamy white with thin blue veins like spider thread. I ran my tongue along the groove; the taste was feta and olives, Mediterranean, and I wanted to feel his sperm on my face.

I often ask myself why I like being down on my knees in this way and assume the appeal was grafted on to my DNA by the repetition seven days a week during the school year in chapel. With my bottom resting on my heels and my elbows on the ledge of the pew in front of me, I stared at the life-sized carving of Saint Sebastian, the young Centurion martyred for his love of Christ by a flight of arrows. As I reached puberty and the first unexpected tingles began to prick my nipples, the statue began to appear to me less as an example of sacrifice than a symbol of masculine virility, a counterweight to the convent's toxic cocktail of oestrogen and exploding hormones. With his strong thighs half hidden by a toga, muscular chest, heavy lips, sharp cheekbones and dreamy eyes, Saint Sebastian looked more like a lead guitarist from a progressive band than a Christian martyr; more contemporary than historic. In my bed at lights out, alone for a moment with my own thoughts, the whittled saint with the woodworm holes drilled into his toes and sandals became an object of desire and also absurdity when I recalled the allegory of the sculptor, who makes religious images by day and kneels before them to pray at night. It's hardly surprising that I always preferred Camus to Sartre.

Tom had slid forwards in the chair, bettering the angle for my assault. I sucked his cock in the same steady way that he had nursed my clitoris, my lips moving slowly, gently, back and forth. His fingers locked at the sides of my head. I paused to nibble the sleek helmet before swallowing it down once more, sucking and licking, pausing to give my jaws a rest, and drawing the soft outer skin between my palms. I sucked his balls, one, then the other and plunged his cock back down my throat. I gagged momentarily, taking the entire length beyond my tonsils, then out again, up and down, the music far away, the light changing as the sun slipped from the wintry sky.

His grip grew tighter. I thought he was going to come and anticipated the stream of his semen pouring down my throat. But he stopped suddenly, grabbed the scruff of my neck and pulled me to my feet. He kept hold of me in this way, like a caveman grasping me by the hair. We crossed the room to my bedroom where he tossed me across the saffron sheets christened the night before.

I laid back, head on the pillow. He straddled me backwards, dipped between my legs, slid his palms beneath the cheeks of my bottom and his tongue oozed back into the soggy pool of my vagina. His cock swayed above like a battering ram at the gates of the castle keep and I opened my mouth to allow him entry. The pleasure of having his tongue tending my clit and his cock in my throat was almost too much to bear and I felt a spasm like a hot needle pass through me. I was like a thirsty creature at a salt lick lapping away, my dribble keeping his cock oiled, my throat expanding and contracting as I gulped it down. His tongue parted the cowling about my clitoris like the prow of a ship furrowing the sea. The little bulb was throbbing, and I had that rare feeling of transcendence, that my whole body had become one erogenous zone, a feeling bathed in the miraculous and sublime.

My heart beat faster. I licked and stippled, a painter with a fine brush. I sucked the bulbous head like you suck an ice cube. I bit down, his body grew tense and he withdrew, the motion jerky, unexpected, and I would have cried bitter tears but he slid round and eased up inside me, lips on my lips, his chest pinning me down. The spasms, paused like a video, started again. I arched my back, pushed down with my heels and gasped as his cock reached places never reached before, the membranes vibrating with unfamiliar sensations, my muscles firming and softening like a sea anemone swallowing a giant fish.

He had been silent all the time I was sucking him off, but now he started to pant like a runner at the end of a race. I could feel the tension across his shoulders, in his loins. I could feel myself coming and held back. The feeling started in my chest, ran down through my tummy into my womb and I roared as a climax like a tidal wave gushed through my body.

Tom was overcome by my spasm. He tensed, slipped from me as he was about to climax and, just as I had wanted, as I had telegraphed into his mind, the creamy stuff like milk from an urn poured over my belly, my breasts, my face, a long stream of semen, sticky as glue, body hot and tasting of bitter chocolate. He held on to his cock like it was the short handle on a whip, pumping out every last drop and I licked it up like the greedy girl I am.

He dropped to one side, snuggled under my arm and lay there panting, fondling my breasts; two gladiators given their freedom. He was puffing for breath.

'You're amazing, Katie.'

He turned my nipples in his fingers, then rubbed them with the flat of his palm. We were quiet for a long time, dozing. He stroked my hip bone. I loved the feeling, that sense that time was suspended. The shadows had folded into darkness and the mirror on the closet looked like a grey door that would lead to another dimension.

After making love, there's nothing like making love again, slowly, idly, like walking without a destination, or swimming in a warm sea. I had some bread and eggs, some Comté from Borough Market. I'd make a cheese omelette and open the bottle of red wine I'd brought back from Spain and had been saving for a special occasion. I would have just one glass, I decided, and keep refilling his glass. I wanted to know more about Tom Bridge. I wanted to know everything, and I wanted to wake up with him next to me in the morning.

When the telephone rang in the next room, it sounded like a car bomb and the vision shattered like shrapnel through glass. I could just make out Lizzie leaving a message, and I suddenly had a cramp in my foot. He slid his arm from under my neck.

'Do you need to get it?' he asked.

I shook my head as if trying to shake away the sound. He turned on the lamp.

'I have to go,' he said, a sigh in his voice. 'I have a dinner tonight with some colleagues. It was arranged ages ago.'

I didn't say anything. He stroked my cheek. The phone message came to an end.

'Can we have breakfast together?' he then asked and I shrugged.

'I don't eat breakfast.'

'Can we not eat breakfast together?' he insisted; his eyes above me were bright, even with the light from the lamp behind him. 'And can I take you to lunch?'

'I'll have to check my diary.'

'With my sister?'

'Your sister.' I thought for a moment. 'Is she going to inspect me?'

'Probably.'

'I don't know if it's a good idea. Sisters don't like me.'

'I can't believe that.' He bent down and kissed the tip of my nose. 'I'm sorry I have to go.'

He swung around and stepped away. As he left the room, I was struck by the ivory white of his round bottom between the tan on his broad back and strong legs that could have been carved by the same sculptor who had shaped Saint Sebastian. He returned dressed, the tail of his scarf over one shoulder. He sat on the edge of the bed. The smell of sex in the room was overpowering, an aphrodisiac; the devil's perfume. I felt bereft and tried not to show it.

'I'm sorry,' he said again, and I sealed his lips with my finger, something men never like.

'Don't apologise. I'd promised to see a friend anyway.'

He knew I was lying and I knew he knew, and he knew I knew he knew.

It was a pact.

7
Stucchevole

From school with strict cheerless nuns to university, where I came under the severe hand of my tutor, I identified with the eponymous Trilby the moment I opened the pages of George du Maurier's novel of domination and submission, a book with an undercurrent of eroticism that can only have slipped by the censors by its sly subtlety and incisive examination of the human condition.

Set in the Paris Bohemia of the 1850s, it is in Trilby where we meet Svengali, a name from fiction that has found its way into the language, like quixotic, Scrooge and Catch 22. Svengali is a music teacher and would be impresario with a perfect ear and an eye for the main chance. Trilby O'Ferrall works as a laundress and artists' model. She is young, pretty and vulnerable. All the men she meets fall in love with her, which forms the body of the book. When she enters the orbit of Svengali, he becomes obsessed with making her his protégée and a singing star; a Diva.

Although Trilby is tone deaf, she is susceptible to hypnosis, another of Svengali's dark arts. Under his power, she performs in a trance. They travel across Europe, making their fortune, until Svengali has a heart attack during a concert in London and Trilby, as she sings on, is shown to be talentless without the maestro's influence. Having been acclaimed in high society and lived among the élite, Trilby O'Ferrall returns to her former role in the laundry, aware that her only gift is her fading prettiness, the fate of most women.

The moment he left the warm sheets and the door clicked shut, I had that feeling you get when you are lost in a strange town and night begins to fall. I curled into the chair where he had watched me undress with my book of cuttings, tears seeping into my eyes. My hands trembled and I squeezed my fists together, hurting my finger as I did so. I could see the tremor of my heart through my skin and was tempted to crawl into the darkness of the closet.

Car lights flickered across the wall. The man on the art-deco lamp puffed on his cigarette. A helicopter rattled the windows; they are always there, watching, filming, reading our wretched emails. I had suffered panic attacks before, but not for a long time, and I couldn't work out why it was happening now. He wanted to return for breakfast, have lunch, take me to be inspected by his sister. What was I panicking about?

I stood beneath the hot needles of the shower and the creature in my chest slowly grew still. I dried myself in front of the mirror, my reflection veiled in steam. I dream sometimes of flying solo in the fastest jet ever seen, or riding in a rodeo, bareback on a stallion, or grilling small fish for friends on a shady terrace in Spain. We live the life we live and I often wonder what it would be like to live another life far away beyond the window, somewhere warm with long sunsets.

It was raining again, continuous streaks slanting down in razor slashes, as if the banks and City buildings were an aberration to be razed like Sodom and Gomorrah. The sky split with lightning. I counted the rolls of thunder, one, two, three, four miles west along the river, where my parents were making their plans for the evening; when love goes, kindness stays.

After dressing in old things, I made an omelette, opened the bottle of wine and the phone buzzed with a text as I filled the glass.

- Missing you already xx

A smile lifted my lips and I hated myself for being so pathetic. I keyed in my reply.

- Only two kisses?
- For now. And here's two more xx
- x

The exchange made me instantly happy, ridiculously so, and I remembered Lizzie had left a message. I called back.

'Hi sweetie, it's me,' I said.

'I thought you must have died. How's lover boy?'

'Not sure yet. What are you doing?'

'I'm meeting Ray at ten.'

'Fancy a drink at *Jacques* first?'

'I could manage that,' she said after a pause, and I caught a hint of reluctance; a benevolence. 'About nine?'

I poured the wine down the sink, took two bites from the omelette and went to look at my shoes.

*

Jacques is a champagne bar in Dean Street close to *Groucho's,* haunt of TV people and screenwriters, intense men with wild eyes and thumbed scripts in shoulder bags. *Pink,* scene of my capricious youth, is nearby. So is the French House, where George Orwell wrote items for the BBC during the war and Francis Bacon, in the years following, entertained friends and hangers-on. He said the job of the artist is *always* to deepen the mystery.

The job of the writer, then, is to pose questions, not answer them. You enter a novel as you enter a house of strangers, not knowing who you may meet or what might happen. Like a mirror maze, you must follow the reflections and distortions to the secrets veiled by the words. Bacon also said, Champagne for my real friends, real pain for my sham friends.

It was in *Jacques* where I often sat on a high stool at the bar plotting my stories. A skinny girl in tight clothes writing in a notebook has a magnetic pull on those in the shadows. I was conscious of this, conscious that the man or woman who drew up the stool beside me would inevitably ask the same question: what are you writing? Writing is like a religion to those who don't practise, an act of faith for those who do.

On the occasions when I did accept company, it was only with those who had gone beyond the predictable, restless souls with an air of abstraction, of ambiguity.

You're not searching for a publisher, are you?

I'm not searching for anything.

Aren't we all searching for something?

Perhaps I've already found it?

You wouldn't carry a notebook if you had.

I would, on hearing the right code, accept the gift of a glass of champagne with the understanding that I would be travelling somewhere that night in the back of a black cab.

Was a glass of champagne my price; does every woman have her price? It's not as simple as that. It is the promise of novelty more than danger that makes my pulse race and I have suffered the consequences. There are men who can't resist kicking the heads off flowers. The white wall calls out for graffiti. Our ancestors sacrificed virgins to appease angry gods and the angry men who invent them. Abusing a casually met girl is the natural response to those primordial genes, a pleasure seldom but sometimes shared.

The bar in *Jacques* forms a long arc, allowing those perched on stools to see who is present at the zinc counter and who, with the benefit of the mirrors behind the bar, sits at the tables or dances on the polished wood circle of the dance floor that holds in paler wood the silhouette of a seahorse. It is where, on somnambulist nights, I have resisted the flutes of champagne offered by men with primitive desires and danced alone to my private thoughts.

Valmont places a glass before me and slowly pours. He is that rare thing, a quiet Australian; he is originally from Lyon and is making the customary pilgrimage back to Europe. He has never asked what it is that I write in my notebook.

'Bonne année.'

'Bonne année.'

He fills a shell-shaped dish with almonds, another with green olives. The music is soft, guitar and piano, a fusion, unidentifiable. I adjust my hair, flicking a loose curl back into the nest, a mannerism men at first find amusing and quickly tiresome.

I set my phone on mute, swivel in my seat, glass in hand. I adore these moments, the champagne bubbles fizzing; time suspended.

The lights are amber and grow like strange fruits with tulip-shaped blooms from the high ceiling. The walls are decorated with old black and white images of Paris blown up and vaguely distorted, the Eiffel Tower, the Seine with barges laden with coal, the bridges and street lights.

A girl sits alone in the corner, the amber light making a halo above her head. She wears a sleeveless white dress with thin straps quite like my own. The dress sparkles with sequins and her wide lips open like a fish as she tilts back her glass. She places the empty glass down on the table as a tall man with dark hair and a moustache paces across the dance floor towards her. He looks determined, uncompromising. I can't hear what he says, they are too far away, but the girl nods her head as he speaks and I can imagine his words as he lowers himself into a chair.

He turns to face the bar; he has the eyes of a cobra, black as obsidian, and clicks his fingers in the way of confident men from faraway places. Valmont, without hurry, carries a bottle and a bucket of ice to the table. He opens the champagne, the deep-throated pop of the cork like a canon from the *1812* finale. He pours two glasses. The girl smiles. She has blue eyes, a pretty retroussé nose. Her skin is luminous, the firmness revealing her age, eighteen, perhaps, her arms like streamers of white ribbon flashing in the semi-darkness. Her blonde hair is gripped in a chignon, and a ring with an ice-blue stone sparkles on her finger. She is Russian, most probably. They have appeared like a new species of orchids, tall sullen girls hard to read, sleek as new cars.

A smile lifted my lips as I recalled suddenly the way Tom had removed the bandage from my fractured finger and checked the movement. Like a watchmaker. I admired the look in his eyes, lively, concentrated, without guile. He made love aware of my every motion, the steady articulation of my legs, a rower in a skiff, the roll of my back, the way I opened myself fully to take him inside me.

After making love, making love with the same man rarely recaptures that sense of vertigo and wonder, the magic of it. With Tom, this man of whom I knew nothing, a stranger with tousled hair and soft hands, each touch of his flesh intoxicated me in a way only satisfied by more of the same. I could smell his smell about me even now. His tone, when he spoke, was deep, melodious, like the plucked strings of a cello, a voice used to being listened to and obeyed. There is a word in Italian: *stucchevole,* so delicious, so exquisite, just a little can be too much. I was besieged by a yearning, a craving, a burning desire. My heart had opened like one of those mysterious flowers that only bloom at night.

Love and sex have never been confusing to me. I have Roger Devlin to thank for that. That summer's day at Black Spires had not left me with a sense of loss. On the contrary, I had driven back to the office with a sense of well-being. My dream of selling the house had been a delusion. Once you undo one button, the light comes on. You leap from the diving board. Mr Devlin had spied the misty island of my deepest instincts. There were no strings, no promises. Our lips never touched. It was just sex. I had turned virginity into a fetish, a phobia, and cast it aside with a sense of relief and liberation.

I've done it, I thought, I've finally done it.

As we passed through the tunnel of overhanging bushes into the sunshine, he ran his palm over my bare leg.

'You're something else,' he said

And I thought: I'm not, but I will be.

'Thank you,' I replied, and he took a photograph of me in profile.

'I'll send you a copy,' he added, but never did.

I dropped him at the station and the rest – the rest is fantasy.

They say after your first time you feel different and it's true. It's like getting over a long bout of illness. That night, I kept running upstairs to look at myself in the mirror. My lips seemed to be fuller and my cheekbones rose over the hollow of my cheeks; I ran my fingertips along the ridges of bone, the shape anticipating the mask waiting in the future. I was about to begin a journey and the butterflies in my tummy were like tiny fluttering hands packing a suitcase. Yesterday I was a girl, I thought, a child. Now I am not. Five years of anxiety and exams had washed away on the tide of Mr Devlin's raucous climax. My eyes sparkled like the lawn after being watered by the sprinkler and contained an expression impossible to interpret. I had rather enjoyed parading half naked in front of the gardener without knowing why. Now, I knew why.

I adjusted the mirrors, pulled off my clothes and studied myself from every angle. My spine had bowed, pushing out my bottom, and I had grown an inch taller. The last pubescent traces of baby fat had slipped from my cheeks and chin and seemed to have gathered around my breasts. I couldn't resist turning and squeezing my nipples, they were pert, delicate, the colour of coral, and tingled as if with the minute stabs of a thousand needles. Was I pregnant? I didn't even care. The lips of my sex were moist and, when I touched myself, my fingertip had the fragrance of the sea on a sunny day. It was the long hot summer of 2003. I was deeply tanned, quite beautiful, I thought, a small vanity, and felt in touch with my true nature.

The weekend came and there was just one person in the world with whom I wanted to share my secret. I called her. I packed two dresses, two pairs of knickers and a toothbrush in a shoulder bag. I kissed Mother on both cheeks and caught the 6.20 train from Canterbury to London. I stayed with Bella in a flat she shared in Notting Hill with Tara Scott-Wallace, one of the twins from school.

Bella knew the moment she looked into my eyes that I had finally left the cloying confines of Saint Sebastian behind me. She threw her arms around me.

'Esto Quod Es,' she said, and kissed my lips.

It was the school motto - Be what you are.

'I am.'

'A little tart?'

'Absolutely.'

'I am so happy, Katie. Was it that, what's his name, Simon?'

'Noo...'

'Was he a poet? A svelte handsome Lord Byron?' she asked and I laughed; we'd studied him in literature.

'No, actually, he was old with a bit of a belly and a gold chain around his neck.'

'How marvellous, my dream,' said Tara, and we all hugged like we were back again in the dorm.

Bella brushed a curl from my eye, an oddly male gesture that came naturally to her. She had been born with feminine charm and masculine determination in equal measure. She had once written an essay on all the things Romeo and Juliet had done wrong and what she would have done to bring the Montagues and Capulets together. I have a photograph of her in costume in the school play and study it when I have to make a difficult decision. I try to work out what she would do, then do the same. She had from the age of fourteen always been conscious of her innumerable talents. She had waltzed into school after living in Italy and proceeded to seduce everyone, each to their needs. She knew what she wanted and exactly how to go about achieving it, the opposite of me, the opposite of Tara, languid, gamine, with big brown eyes and perfect features, identical to Saskia, her twin, two dolls straight from the factory. They were my rivals, my mentors, my oldest friends.

Tara and I watched Bella perform at a gig that night, her career was just starting, and after the show they took me to *Pink* in Wardour Street, where I would come to learn that where sex with a man carried an air of menace, sex with a girl was like slipping into a bath of bubbling water.

I had been cloaked in the shadows of my family, class, education, my own secret ambitions. A little membrane had snapped and my eyes had opened. I understood why Mr Drew was offhand with me, men will either fawn over a young girl or feign disinterest. I knew why Mother was constantly on the verge of a nervous breakdown. She was a beautiful woman who must have missed afternoon sex with strangers and was forced to find her pleasure among the bridge players and golfers of rural Kent knowing, no doubt, that Daddy, an Orientalist, was with a girl half his age practising his language skills. People adore sex but take it far too seriously, an error I had no intention of making.

8
Black Dwarf

My one concern after driving away that day from Black Spires was waiting for the letter I knew was coming to finally slide through the brass flap on the door and fall to the doormat. Like a death row prisoner, it was like waiting for a reprieve or a death sentence, that something not merely personal, but universal, was suspended within the contents of that letter.

When I arrived home each day from Drew Butler, I searched the places where Golo hid the mail and took my disappointment with me out into the garden to catch the last of the sun. The trees on the horizon at this time of day were bronze like statues and a pink and pale blue glow illuminated the sky. It was, we would learn, the hottest summer on record. I was as brown as teak. Old people were dying from dehydration, the environmentalists warned us that global warming was destroying the planet, and there was a ban on garden hoses, which Mother told the gardener to ignore.

Now, ten years later, when everyone talks and texts nonstop on their smart phone, the very notion of waiting for a letter seems like a literary device. I started to imagine the communication was lost in the post, or had never been sent in the first place. In an unkind moment, I did wonder if the missive had come and Mother had hidden it for reasons that would never be fully explained and would be put down to the onset of menopause.

Then it arrived, a pale dun envelope with a smudged stamp, and I had that feeling I imagine parachutists have the second they pull the rip cord, a tug, a lurch, fear and relief. It was Saturday morning, hot already. The French doors were open. Golo had left the letter on the breakfast table and I heard as I reached for it what I'm sure was a nightingale. I rushed back upstairs, the envelope in trembling fingers. I peeled back the gummed flap, a war bride opening a telegram. Destiny doesn't run in straight lines. I had reached a crossroad, and the contents of that letter would send me in one irreconcilable direction or the other.

Mother poked her head around the door. She was in her dressing gown, velvet slippers with embroidered initials, no make-up.

'It's come?' she asked and I nodded.

'And?'

'I haven't looked yet.'

'Best get it over with.'

I pulled out a sheet of paper with a crest on top, glanced at the words in the first paragraph and tears welled into my eyes. I ran into her arms.

'You got what you wanted,' she said.

I sniffed back my tears. 'I worked for it, Mummy.'

'We all know that,' she said, and shook herself free. 'You must call your father, and Matthew.'

'I will.'

She always wore heels. In her slippers, I was taller, I realized.

'Well done,' she said.

'Thank you.'

She left the room, closing the door. She was pleased for me, I knew that, even if she was unable to show it. I glanced back at the letter, the words fizzing like a struck match. The touch-paper had been lit that day. My life was starting; Mother's was in stasis. She had achieved and acquired the things she had wanted and was aware that there were other landscapes she may have crossed. We set out on a certain course. It is hard to change direction, harder still to turn back down a path littered with regrets. We get one life and I wanted to do everything, be everything I could be. Be myself. At school, there had been moments of boredom and melancholy. Now, I was free. I stood at the open window. The sky was a shade of blue that doesn't visit England often and the lawn was as green as an emerald.

It was mid-afternoon for Father. I could hear the pleasure in his voice when I called him. Fresh tears filled my eyes and it occurred to me that I always cried when I was happy and was stoical when sad; the English way.

My brother was more down to earth. He was fifteen, sailing his passion, and was in Cornwall taking part in a regatta.

'That's not going to make life easy,' Matthew said. 'First Father, then you. They're going to expect me to do the same.'

'You'll be starting uni when I'm leaving.'
'Dead men's shoes, that's all I need,' he said, and I laughed.
'Are you winning any races?'
'No, not really. We don't want too many winners in one family, it wouldn't be fair.'
'Nothing's fair.'
'Yes, I know, it's all, what do you call it, random chaos.'
'That's what Mother calls your room, Matt.'
'Anyway, bloody well done.'

I dressed in a white bikini and grabbed a book; *Harry Potter and the Order of the Phoenix*, the latest from JK Rowling. The wet grass was cold underfoot. My mind was empty like a suitcase in a cupboard. I read without hearing the words, closed my eyes and saw myself dancing naked through the dusty light at Black Spires. Now I had been offered a place at the college of my choice, it felt as if these two disparate turning points were connected, that the first had, by some absurd act of wizardry, intervened in the second.

Golo lugged a table into the garden and placed it in the shade of the rose arbour. She spread out a cloth from Provence; it was green with yellow parrots on swings and loaves of country bread. She placed at the centre a vase with lily-of-the-valley, the white blooms mysterious as pearls.

Mother wore a white cotton dress with a lace top and a large straw hat with polka dots in pink on the white hatband. She looked pretty, immobile, a china doll. I could always tell her moods by the faint twitch in her right eye, the vacant look, like she's just missed a train. She had made marriage her career and her husband was on the other side of the world.

'How's your father?'
'He sends his love?'
'Does he now? I'm sure he's pleased.'
'Over the moon, he said.'
'What a peculiar thing to say. You're so alike.'

We sat down with a bottle of sauvignon blanc in a bucket of ice, my glass topped up with fizzy water.

'This weather,' she said, and sipped her wine.

The air was baked. The roses were fully open, the petals heavy with perfume. There was no breeze. I could hear the soft murmur of a bee and remember how the bottle of Perrier gleamed in the sunlight, the beads of condensation like diamonds, a dark circle spreading over the cloth. Golo had made Caesar salad, far too much. She was from Bolivia, Golondrina, 'swallow' in English, the bird, not the action, plump as a peach, her mission to fatten us up utterly hopeless.

We sat quietly. Mother kept refilling her glass. It was too hot to talk, and it was a relief when Golo came waddling out like a conspirator.

'Misses Boiled...'

'Boyd.'

'Misses Boyed, is Simon.'

'Simon?' I gasped.

'Do tell him to come through,' Mother replied.

'Really, I wish you hadn't said that.'

'Why? I thought you were, whatever.'

'Well, we're not.'

He appeared and she smiled. She lifted back the brim of her hat and her eyes lit up.

'Simon, what a pleasure.' She called Golo. 'Bring another glass, will you, dear, and a chair.'

He stood beside the table as if at ship's rail sailing away from port. He was wearing a tee-shirt with the words *Black Eyed Peas* on the front and a stain on the shoulder. He was as white as clay and I had an urge to tell him about Mr Devlin.

'Hi.'

'Hi.'

'The clever girl has made it into Cambridge. Her father's old college,' Mother said, and he looked away from me as if surprised by a distant sound.

The wine bottle was empty. Mother left and he remained standing there at the table in his stained tee-shirt.

'That's great,' he said.

'Thank you.'

'You didn't mean what you said, you know, those emails, like, like just like that.'

'I did.'

'But why? Why, Katie? You promised.'

'I changed my mind.'

He was breathing heavily, panting, clenching his fists, revving himself up.

'Is there someone else?'

I thought for a second. 'Yes,' I replied. 'Me.'

He wasn't sure what I meant. 'What...'

I pointed at myself. 'Me. It was always about you, what you wanted, what you want...'

'You did, too.'

'Not any more.'

'Well, let's see what happens. We can go out tonight. I'm back now, go into town or something?'

I shook my head. He was pleading, throwing out his hands, jaw tight. The urge to mention Mr Devlin had gone. Like enemies, it is best to keep old lovers, even if they were never lovers, as friends.

'No, best not,' I said.

'Moving up, then, are you, Katie?' He shook his head and looked at me properly, really for the first time. 'You look fucking...fucking amazing. Maybe I'll see you on the way down.'

He turned, marched off, paused and glanced back.

'Bitch,' he spat.

He passed Mother without speaking. She had returned with a second bottle of wine and sat with a look of pleasure crossing her features.

'A thwarted lover, dear?' she said.

'No, not really.'

'Always be nice when you give them the sack. It pays.'

'I was just thinking the same.'

'So we do have something in common after all.'

The bee had sunk its head into the nectar on the rose hanging above me. It flew off, buzzing, as we clinked the rims of our glasses.

'Here's to you, Katie,' she said.

'Thanks, Mummy.'

She sat back. 'It never crossed my mind to go to university,' she said. 'I thought it would be a complete waste of time.'

'It's different now.'

Again, she lifted the brim of her hat. She studied me for a long time, my face, my shoulders, my breasts in the white bikini top.

'Not really,' she replied. 'You could just find an older man, there's lots of them about, someone who likes fishing and shooting, and golf. Those things they do. While he's in the country, you could swan around Kensington with different lovers.'

'Like in a Luis Buñuel film?' I said and she shrugged.

'I've never been interested in all that psychological claptrap. I'm not even sure what bourgeoisie means.'

'Middle class,' I said.

'Really? I thought it was an attitude more than a designation.'

'Well, yes....'

Mother had never spoken like this before, of love and lovers. She didn't know about Roger Devlin, I was sure of that, but was aware that something in me had changed and the way Simon Wells had stalked off had revealed what it was. She stared at me through the vase of lily-of-the-valley.

'You have become quite a beauty, but then, you know that, don't you, Kate?'

I shrugged. 'I'm alright,' I said.

'No, dear. You have become...' she paused, 'that obscure object of desire.' She refilled her glass, leaned back in her chair. 'It is a burden as well as a gift.'

Once, in a restaurant, as a man was leaving, he leaned over my table and whispered, 'Don't think you're special, because you're not. You're nothing.'

What had I done to offend him? Was my voice too loud? Too plummy? Was my skirt too short? He had seen something in me he didn't like. Had Tom seen something he did like? Or was I just a stray girl with whom to see in the New Year?

It felt more than just that to me. But did he feel the same?

I grow anxious when happiness comes near. I grill myself with the same dreary questions. Who am I? Where am I going? What makes me me? What do I want? What do I really want?

There is a game we used to play. You ask a friend, if they had to stop being human and become an animal, what would they be? Immediately they answer, you say, there are no vacancies for that particular animal. What is your second choice. The first choice (often a lion, a wolf, a leopard) is what we think we are; the second is what we really are (a poodle, a fox, a snake). I can't remember my first choice, but my second was a giraffe – aloof, an observer, partial to the sweetest leaves.

I look into the mirror and it seems sometimes as if the person in the reflection is wearing a mask, that there is someone quite different looking out through my eyes, the hunched, haunted figure I call Black Dwarf, my avatar, the portrait of Dorian Gray that hides in the cupboard. I have always surrendered to Oscar Wilde's counsel: The only way to get rid of temptation is to yield to it.

The mirror reveals each day someone different. Time never sleeps. It moves, bends, spirals. Our cells die and new cells come to life. We grow tired repeating ourselves. Something had been shifting inside me, slow and delicate, like a lizard stalking a fly. An ennui had slipped like a sour smell into my daily routines; perhaps that's why I had moved along the river from west to east?

Was Tom another symptom of this feeling, or the catalyst for something new; something definitive? It was as if I had wished him into being and he had appeared in the dying seconds of the old year; the first day of the new.

Why had doubt so overwhelmed me the moment he left my bed? When he said he had a dinner, my first instinct was that he didn't. There was someone else, his girl, his wife. Trust is a dying species; the tigers, the orang-utans. There is a shop nearby with a sign in whitewash across the window saying SALE – Final Day. It has been there for three months. We have lost confidence in politicians, bankers, advisers, doctors. We don't trust ourselves. So how can we trust anyone else?

When he left I sat curled in the chair listening to the whine of the helicopter, Black Dwarf rearranging like a spiteful juggler the spirals of my DNA. The feeling, so quick to arise, passed with those two iPhone kisses, so little and yet so much.

Jacques.

An amber glow.

The sound of the piano keys like footsteps.

I sipped my champagne. The bubbles burst in my nose and I had a sudden urge to giggle, to be silly, to be that girl at the corner table with her pale arms and breasts pushing over the dip of her sequinned dress. Happiness is the suspension of disbelief; a brief ignorance.

I looked away, adjusted my hair, recrossed my legs and hooked my heel behind the metal ring of the stool. I reached for my phone, as if anticipating a text, and the machine vibrated; a creepy preconception, the opposite of déjà vu. I often get a sense that my phone is watching me and have the odd desire to throw it in the river.

Lizzie is in Old Compton Street, two mins from J.

Valmont is watching me and pours the Cristal before I ask.

She makes an entrance in red, her colour, her waist cinched by a tight belt, stressing her breasts and hips like ripe fruit, her legs long in high pointed shoes. She threw her coat over a chair.

'Am I late?'

'No.'

'Then you must be early. That's a first.'

'I spend more money on cabs than I save in rent.'

'And how is life among the poor and downtrodden? Ghastly, I'm sure.'

'I like it.'

She sipped her champagne and smiled. 'Mmm, that's better,' she said; she looked at me closely, like the doctor with my finger. 'You have that glow.'

'You'll have it later.'

'Yes, my dear, but in different places.'

Ray is a soldier, a sergeant in special forces. He does things in shadowy places, Iraq, Afghanistan, Libya, Lebanon. He has special needs.

She threw up her shoulders and viewed her surroundings with that self-assurance that imposed itself on the amber-lit space. Her gaze took in the men who had arrived too early; the couple in the corner, the girl reminding me of Fay Wray from the original *King Kong*. The beast was leaning forward and drummed a finger on the table as he spoke. Lizzie's dark lashes fell over her eyes like camera shutters, recording everything. There was a deliberation to her movements, as if each gesture was considered before being put into action. Her eyes opened fully as they turned back to me.

'Now, why are we here?'

'I don't know. I just wanted to see you.'

'I know you better than that. Why aren't you seeing him?'

'He had a dinner with old friends.'

'And he's lying?'

I shook my head. 'No, I don't think so. He's not like that.'

'They are all like that.'

She took another sip of champagne; her lips were the same colour as her dress and she left a ruby red print on the glass.

'You like this one, don't you?'

'We made love for, like, four hours, and when he left, I felt...bereft.'

'That's one of your words.'

'Bereft, desolate, forlorn, fretful. It's totally weird.'

'Sounds totally wonderful.'

'We're going to have lunch tomorrow with his sister.' I took a second. 'Sisters don't like me.'

'Of course not, they dream of incest,' she said, and fixed me with an intense expression. 'What's he like in bed?'

'You are so personal.'

'I'll put it another way: what's he like in bed?'

'Firm, but patient, kind and thoughtful...'

'Just like my grandmother.'

'He asked me to undress for him; well, told me, really. I wore the mask, you know the one, and it *really* turned him on. When he told me he had to leave, I felt totally...'

'Bereft?'

I nodded.

'Sounds promising. Good looking, good in bed...curious that he should be alone on New Year's Eve.'

'I was alone.'

'Two curiosities make a plot. There has to be someone else, it stands to reason.'

'Then I shall just have to kill her.'

'That's what I like to hear.' She paused. 'If you like this one, you mustn't give away too much of yourself. Keep him in suspense.'

'I'm not writing a book.'

'Of course you are. It will be your best.'

I cheered up. 'You think so?'

She didn't answer. She didn't like being prodded for compliments. She stroked the back of my hand. I loved her. I love Daddy, Matt, even Mother...sometimes. But Lizzie was the only person who knew me, the me inside me, the me who got lost in the mirror and hid sometimes in the closet. Bella had moved to America, taking the twins with her. She was big now; she had a fan club, her own hairdresser. I write books, heaven knows why, and Lizzie made me feel as if I were her student, which wasn't surprising as she gave classes in creative writing to prisoners at Wandsworth Jail. She reads the drafts of friends' books, writes honest reviews that always have a word of kindness, even if the review is harsh. She designs book jackets, takes marvellous photographs and looks forward to Ray Fowles arriving and leaving in equal measure.

'How long is Ray here for?'

'Two weeks. That's about as much as I can stand. Especially now.'

'Ah, do tell?'

'It's not as if I'm being unfaithful....'

'An excursion to *Pink?*'

'I'm especially partial to girls,' she said, her words rolling from her tongue as if she were swallowing melting chocolate. She paused again, shrugging her fine shoulders. 'Anyway, Ray doesn't need to know; he wouldn't even care.'

A man appeared in a navy blue suit; his tie too tight, face flushed.

'Hi, gals, I'm Bob, what are you drinking?'

Lizzie looked over her shoulder. 'In a champagne bar?' she asked.

'Hey, that's right. Two more glasses?'

She glanced at Valmont, raising her eyes a fraction; he knew the drill. Bob leaned on the bar beside her, foot resting on the rail. He was looking at me, forcing Lizzie to turn towards him.

'Where are you from, Bob? she asked.

'Kansas City, USA.'

'What do you do in Kansas, Bob?'

'I'm a banker, you know...'

'A banker. How fortunate.' She turned wide-eyed in her seat. 'So, you're the one who bankrupted the economy and went off with squillions of dollars?'

'I wish,' he replied.

'You didn't?'

He held up his two palms like a cowboy surrendering in a Western. 'I'm a wheat analyst. I work in futures...'

'You mean, you're not filthy rich?'

'No, lady, I am not...'

She leaned forward with an unnerving smile and lowered her voice to a hiss. 'Then save your money and spend it on your wife, Bob. That's the future.'

'What? Hey, listen, I was only being friendly.'

'Then go and be friendly somewhere else.'

His face grew redder. 'I wasn't interested in you, anyway.'

She glanced at me, then back at the man. 'You know something, Bob, I don't think the feeling's mutual.'

I gave him a shrug and he stared back at Lizzie.

'I've met some bitches in my time, lady, but you take some beating.'

'Never a truer word been said, my dear,' she replied. She threw up her hand to look at her watch, a small silver Cartier. 'I'm going to have to go.'

She slipped to her feet as the young blonde left the bar with King Kong's hand resting on the small of her back. The girl was wearing a fox fur coat that swayed around her long legs. The door opened and I caught a glimpse of the drizzle in the street lights.

'I'm going, too,' I said, and Lizzie's brow rippled.

'Is this love?' she asked, and I shook my head.

'Lust, I imagine.'

We stood outside, waiting for a taxi, the neon signs along the street making the night seem darker. I looked up at the sign, *Jacques,* a signature in pale green letters, and it occurred to me that I would probably never go back there again.

9
Someone Else

He kissed the inked scroll on my neck, my shoulders, the hills of my spine, those little dents at the pit of my back that I look at sometimes in the mirror, so mysterious, as if two fingers have been pushed into a balloon. He fondled my bottom as if it were pastry dough, kneading the soft flesh and making it rise. The grotto behind my left knee, my right knee; my feet.

'My best feature,' I said, and rolled over to face him.

He was smiling. I adored his smile, his good teeth. 'Yes, quite the best. But I am growing rather fond of your Achilles' tendons, they're in pretty good shape.'

'That's a relief.'

He planted watery kisses on the sinewy flesh above my heels, one after the other. 'Now you are protected,' he said, and propped himself up on one elbow. 'You know something, you remind me of Helen of Troy. She had green eyes...'

'Didn't she sink a thousand ships? Quite apart from starting a war.'

'At least it was a noble cause.'

'About as noble as two blind men fighting over a photograph.'

He laughed. 'You *do* have a way with words.'

'That's what Bradley says.'

'Bradley?'

'My web guy. Twenty-two and as randy as a sack of rabbits.'

'Two blind men and a sack of rabbits. You're all over the place, Ms Boyd,' he said. He brushed my hair back and his expression changed. He had slipped into his thinking face. 'I don't know Greece at all. I'd like to visit Troy.'

I adored his voice; its depth, its timbre. I had written in my notes that it sounded like a cello. The words on the page had seemed overblown as they hurried out on to the screen. But it was true, his voice was cavernous. It resonated as if my intestines had arranged themselves into highly-tuned strings.

'I love your knees,' he said, and kissed them.

He continued, my belly-button, my breasts that flamed, the concave of my throat, his progress across my body soft as the horsehair on a bow, the down-strokes firm, the up-strokes tender. I had sat at my computer when I arrived home from *Jacques* with that feeling you get after a long flight, tense and edgy. While the world sleeps, words in the night become mosquitoes that I chase around the room, squashing them in bloody pools that I press on the page, the screen. Nothing came. No buzz. No torque. No whisper. I was in another time zone. My heart thumped. My hands felt bloated and clumsy.

A branch from the tree outside tapped on the window like the finger of someone who has forgotten their key and wants to come in. Beneath the flowing strokes of his fingers I had become a musical instrument gently weeping, tears like glass crystals streaking my cheeks. He swept them up on his tongue as if they were too sacred to squander and I recalled reading that Hindu women save tears in a phial to spill at their husband's funeral.

'You're crying,' he whispered.

'It's what I do when I'm happy.'

'Why are you happy, little Katie?

'I am not so little...'

'It's a term of endearment.'

'Endearment,' I repeated, tasting the word, filing it away like a nice pebble found on the beach. He had shaved that morning, washed his hair. It was the colour of walnuts with highlights bleached by the sun. His eyes, flecked with gold, had a look of intensity, of curiosity. His cock nestled against my tummy.

'What are you thinking about?' he asked, and I wondered what he had seen in my eyes, and whether we see what we want to see, reflections of our own musings.

'I'm thinking about who I am going to be when I meet your sister.'

'She'll be crazy about you.'

'You don't know sisters,' I said, and he licked my nose.

His weight pressed down on me. Our lips met, the sound like the closing of a hotel door. We kissed and we kissed, snatching for breath. Making love requires no thought. You move as the fronds of a palm tree move in the breeze. It is all instinct. All wonder. I adored kissing. Kissing him. A really good kiss is like a secret you want to share. There are no words to describe it. A really good kiss reminds you why it's hard to decide on the right lipstick. Time expands with a really good kiss and you add another few seconds to the end of your life. His finger traced an arc over my cheekbones, and I felt that second day of a new year as if I were on a bridge burning to ashes behind me.

The kiss extended like quicksilver over my chin and down in a line between my breasts, my tummy, gurgling still from the almond croissants and cappuccino he had brought with him in a yellow bag. An arrow of light darted across the room. I heard the drum of the traffic; people returning to work.

He eased my legs apart. I pressed down on my toes and arched my back. I was always happy being naked, like this, with him, the light moving like a tide over the ceiling. The tip of his tongue rang the divine bell, that sublime stupa, the sweet spot, and I floated off on the liquids that wet my thighs. We imagine that there is a special man who will make us feel special in special ways, not with words or gifts, not with glances, even eyes, but in the way that he makes a perfect fit inside us.

When he entered me, I held him as a drowning person would cling to driftwood. He came quickly, gushing, his breath in my ear, the speck of dribble on my neck like a raindrop, a tear. I gripped my hands behind his back. There was a zing of pain across my finger. I held him tightly. I wanted his essence inside me where it would stay warm and I would feel it all day.

We kissed slowly, breathlessly, the after love kiss, and I despaired at that part of myself who conjured up at that moment a picture of Lizzie in *Jacques* when she said, 'Two curiosities make a plot.' There has to be someone else, it stands to reason.

Does it? Is there? The kiss faded and there were words on his lips.

'I'm sorry I had to leave yesterday, it was a boring evening, I can't tell you.'

'I had a marvellous time,' I said. 'I met my best friend at my favourite bar and drank oodles of champagne.'

'Is that what you usually do?'

I thought for a moment. 'I don't usually do anything.'

'I'm reading *Dancing Girl*,' he said. 'You really do know how to write.'

'Knowing how to write and knowing how to write is not the same thing.'

90

'I can't wait to find out how it ends. Do they stay together?'
'I can't actually remember.'
He laughed. 'Don't worry, Katie, I'm going to finish it.'
I liked hearing the sound of my name on his cello tongue; it sounded as if he were talking to someone else.
'I'm not worried,' I told him. 'I mean it. While I'm writing a book, I'm obsessed with my baby. I love them. I wipe their tears and nurse their scars. When I start something new, I forget about them.'
'That's quite amazing.'
'I learned it from my mother.'
'When am I going to meet her?'
My head lay nestled against his side and I replied with a vampire kiss, sucking hard and biting the soft flesh of his neck. He squirmed and pressed back.
'More, more. I love it.'
I bit the same spot. I kissed his lips. His eyes. I blew in his ear. His cock stiffened and slid back inside me. We made love again, leisurely, deep in the moment, my movements unhurried, gradual, continuous, like Duchamp's *Nude Descending A Staircase*, each figure the same but different, motion captured and released.

Pink underwear. It's always right. The Zara tweed jacket with red lapels, skinny wine-red trousers, lace-up brown boots. I left the door open so he could watch me dress. Men are intrigued by our clothes, by the hooks and buttons, the straps and elastic that bind us together. When I entered the living room, he had his hands behind his back and a crooked smile I couldn't interpret.
'I nearly forgot, I have a present for you,' he said and produced a yellow ball with a smiley face.
'Thank you.'
He placed it in my right hand and stretched my figures about the soft surface.
'Squeeze,' he said. 'It's an exercise ball. It's for your finger.'
'I thought it was for me.'
'You can share it. Good girls know how to share things.'
'Yes, daddy.'
We kissed and we kissed. He grew hard and it wasn't easy tearing ourselves away from the warm sheets calling from the

bedroom. I dragged on a quilted coat, a grey wool hat, and my cheeks burned with cold as we clattered down the stairs and out into the street.

Tom bought *The Times* in the corner shop where Mr Patel glowered from behind a counter stacked with chocolate, aspirin and chewing gum. With the red spot on his forehead and a yellowing moustache, Mr Patel wore that look people have when they reach a certain age and realize their dreams were just dreams. He was snappy with his customers, his daughter, who limps and never smiles, his wife, whose drawn face as she fills the magazine racks makes me think of the Danaides, those spiteful wives from mythology who murdered their husbands on their wedding night, and were condemned to spend eternity filling a bowl from jugs perforated with holes, a futile undertaking I thought I might explore in a blog.

'Happy New Year.'

Mr Patel's head jiggled from side to side. 'Yes, another one.'

I pulled my hat over my ears: 'It's freezing out.'

'What do you expect, in England?'

He glanced at Mrs Patel as he spoke and she looked away. Was it her fault they were in London, not Mumbai?

'Happy New Year,' I said, but she didn't answer.

Tom tucked the newspaper under his arm and an old-fashioned bell rang as he held the door for me.

We crossed the road, skipping between the traffic. On the corner, a woman in a green sari studied a mannequin in a shop window dressed the same as herself, a scene that reminded me of a story by Ian McEwan. Next door, at Khan's, two boys, thin as reeds in crocheted hats, unlocked smart phones in a cat's cradle of wires and pulsing lights. A steel necklace of vehicles jangled by, filling the air with silver smoke, blaring horns, threats in so many tongues it made me feel as if we were on our way to Babel. It was noisy, chaotic, vibrant, and it occurred to me that where I lived now was more inspiring than where I had moved from, that I had been living like a genie in a bottle and now I was free. I grabbed Tom's arm and squeezed in beside him.

'Tell me, what is your deepest desire?' I intoned. 'Your wish is my command.'

He was reading the headlines as we walked along and stopped. He took my shoulders.

'That you're for real, Katie. That I'm not going to wake up all of a sudden and, poof!' he said. 'You're someone different.'

I had been light. Playful. He was deadly serious.

'I can try. But it's not easy.'

'Why?'

'To know who you are and just be that person.'

'I don't have that problem.'

A frown formed on his smooth brow and a lump grew in my chest.

'Then you're lucky,' I said. 'Sometimes, I'm moody and want to hide away from the world. Sometimes, I feel angry. Or empty. Sometimes, I'm writing and the words won't come. Sometimes I tell Mother I'm never going to speak to her again, then I call her next day.'

'And sometimes, you're happy, I assume?'

I pulled on his scarf and stared into his eyes. 'Yes. That's my default. But I get the blues, like everyone, viruses, crossed wires. It's normal.'

'Some girls think being moody is attractive. I don't.'

'Neither do I,' I said. 'And it's not attractive when men are moody, either.'

'You're right. I'm being a complete pain. It's hard to explain...'

'You can try.'

'No, it's nothing, really.' He trailed off and shrugged. 'I just think you're too good to be true.'

'Of course I am,' I said and the frown had gone.

We kissed. I had never liked kissing in the street, it seemed so crass, so cliché. It's what they do in advertising.

Two women in veils pushed by, seeing nothing, ignoring us. Tom tucked the paper in his coat pocket and put his arm around my shoulders. We continued around the corner where stacks of red suitcases stood in pyramids behind the 'SALE - Final Day' sign, and it struck me that it wasn't so much a ploy, a deception, as a philosophical statement, that any day is potentially the final day and you shouldn't put off doing what you want to do for some far away time. Buy those blood red cases, travel to Troy.

As we made our way down the steps into the car park, he started singing, his voice magnified over the low roof. The fact that he was singing, and quite loudly, seemed out of character, although,

93

in truth, I had no way of knowing. We were in the time of mystery, the time when love is thin ice that you skate over half believing it is going to break at any second.

'You have a nice voice,' I said.

'Oh, no, I wasn't singing was I? It's a nervous habit.'

'Do I make you nervous?'

'Absolutely not,' he replied, and turned. 'Well, a little.'

'Good, I'm glad to hear it.'

I followed him into the shadows asking myself why I had said that; why, when you clearly like someone, there is an absurd inclination to show otherwise. We reveal false versions of ourselves, a protective veil we weave with words, then wonder why there are misunderstandings. He opened the door to an old Land Rover streaked in mud. I kissed his cheek and he kissed me on the mouth until I pulled away, breathless.

'I just love kissing in car parks,' I gasped.

'You do it often?'

'All the time. Car parks, the street, bus stations...'

'I don't believe you've ever been in a bus station.'

'In Paris once.'

'I knew it.'

We kissed again and he slapped my backside as I hauled myself up into the cab.

'You are so predictable, Tom Bridge,' I said and he laughed.

With the doors closed, I caught the familiar smell of stables and moist earth. My seat had split seams and bounced up and down as the engine fired. The gear box grated. He reversed, swept up the curving incline and lurched into the traffic as if casting off into an empty sea. He spotted an opening, accelerated and switched lanes. The car behind blasted its horn.

'You have driven before,' I remarked.

'It's a jungle out there,' he replied, foot hard on the gas. 'In Sri Lanka the roads turn to mud in the monsoon. It's like driving in blancmange.'

'Did you bring the car back with you?' I asked, and he laughed.

'No, no. Course not. It belongs on the farm. Tamsin and Joe drove up in two cars and left it so we had wheels.'

'That's kind.'

'They always think of those things. They're quite amazing.'

'Isn't everyone amazing, in their own way?'

'Not at all. But they are. They've just got it together, you know. Joe's American, an economist turned financial consultant...'

'One of those.'

'Can't live with them, can't put them all behind bars. He's got an office in the City and manages to spend most of his time working from home,' he said. 'Tamsin's a busy bee, baking and sewing, growing things. She started making ceramics, vases, coffee sets, all that sort of stuff, and it just took off.'

'I hate her already.'

He laughed again. 'They've got horses and dogs – and the children, of course.'

'Three children?'

'You are a spy. How did you know?'

'It's the fashion.'

'I don't think that's the reason...'

'It's quite an achievement.'

He glanced sideways for a moment. 'What, having children? It's not difficult.'

'Not having them. All the other things that go with having them.'

'Do you want children?'

I cleared mist from the side window and glanced out. 'Some time,' I said, but he can't have heard me.

'Sorry?'

The vehicle shuddered, the cogs grinding like an olive press. 'Yes, some time,' I repeated in a louder voice.

He shot by a line of buses. The road was clear for a moment. We followed the river; it was slate grey, the colour of an old pipe, the surface serrated by the wind. Flickers of light slid across my knees as we crossed Blackfriars Bridge. The Tate Modern came into view, the Oxo Tower and, in the distance, Shakespeare's Globe with its mock Tudor façade and the sudden recollection of Julian Rhodes in a red duffel coat and white fur hat like a pantomime woodcutter.

Julian had been anxious to meet the director of *Much Ado About Nothing*, a rising star straight out of Cambridge, not that we got to see him that autumn night when Julian had tickets. What I did remember was sitting on my hands with freezing feet uncertain whether I should identify with the witty, alluring

Beatrice or the intense, yielding Hero, the two female leads. It was Shakespeare's genius that I found in myself a fusion of both these women. I could be shrewish and sharp-tongued as well as compliant. I took offence easily and was quick to lie back and submit. The play ends with two marriages, Beatrice with Benedick, Hero with her beloved Claudio, an uncommonly positive resolution for Shakespeare and for me, too, as it turned out.

'Have you been to the Globe? I asked.

'No, we must go,' he replied. 'That's what I miss most about London, the theatre, the galleries. I'm becoming a philistine.'

'Yes, that's what I thought,' I said and he laughed, a deep, rich laugh from the diaphragm. He crunched into second, accelerated, and eased back through the gear box.

The A3 took us through Kennington Park and Clapham Common. The sky was pale and watery, devoid of birds, the sun like a mourner at a funeral. I watched a jogger move through the cold trees, vanishing and emerging again. I thought about the Danaides. Mr Patel. Jo and Tamsin – baker, potter, mother. Tom was doing something he believed in. Something that mattered. Father the same. I was more like Mother, filling my days with the intangible, an occasional job waitressing, an odd sort of masochism.

'What's it like in Sri Lanka?'

'Incredible,' he said. 'I love it. The people are unspoiled. They're not like us. They're not grasping to have more than they've got.'

'You mean they're happier because they have less?'

'No. Not that...'

'People looking for work, single mums, teenagers on sink estates, they're not celebrating their poverty.'

'Now you sound like *The Guardian.*'

'No,' I said. 'I sound like me.'

'You're right, that was below the belt.' He paused. 'The thing is, we have higher expectations. Maybe too high. The banks, the corporations, the internet; we're one world when the developing world is still developing. We had a Parliament in England for three hundred years before women got the vote. They have these insane wars and expect the Afghans to create the same kind of democracy in five minutes. People I meet, every day, every single day, have integrity. An honesty. The Tamils aren't trying to be something, succeed, all the stuff that's important to us.'

'Are they really more honest? I doubt it. People are people. Good and bad...'

'It's different. It's hard to explain,' he broke off, glanced at me, then back at the road. 'If you book a sleeper on the train, you are expected to give the ticket clerk an extra couple of rupees. It's his job to sell the sleeper and the baksheesh is a sort of thank you. In the developing world where wages are low, you bribe people to do what they are actually paid to do. In our world, we bribe people to do what they are not supposed to do, what's illegal. It's a different mindset.'

'Just sounds like different types of corruption to me.'

He laughed. 'I'm, sorry, I'm being too serious.'

'I don't mind that.'

'I know, I just bang on too much sometimes. The world's turning to shit and it doesn't have to. It's such a pity, it would take so little to make it work.'

'Your voice changes when you're talking about Sri Lanka.'

'Really?'

'You love your work.'

'I suppose.'

'That's when it stops being work.'

'Writing must be the same.'

'On good days. And there aren't many of those.'

He ran his hand over my thigh then squeezed the tendons at the side of my knee, just softly, but enough to make my leg shoot out.

'Ouch.'

'That didn't hurt.'

'Yes it did. And it was a surprise.'

'Don't you like surprises?'

'I love surprises.' I squeezed his knee, really hard, but he didn't react. 'And I love my present.'

I took the yellow ball from my pocket and threw it from hand to hand.

'You should exercise that finger at least ten times a day. It will heal more quickly.'

'Yes, doctor.'

He gathered speed to beat the traffic lights and turned right. The Land Rover was like a fairground ride throwing me about in the seat.

'Sorry, I get impatient. Driving is such a waste of time.'

'I thought it was the journey that mattered more than the destination?'

'That would depend where you're going and how you're travelling. A walk around Troy would be about the journey. A drive down the A3 is a necessary inconvenience.'

I squeezed the yellow ball. The necessary inconvenience for me was being inspected by his baker mother potter sister. The road was clear. We gathered speed. Trees and hedgerows flashed by. The seat rocked on ancient springs. I had lost my sense of balance, of equilibrium. I understood how strangers met and fell into bed, not how they met and fell in love. I wasn't sure what falling in love meant. The very notion seemed so corny, so arbitrary, so fragile. And after falling in love, it rarely lasts. Love is a noun as well as a verb, a treacherous construct. If you fall in love you exchange one life for another life. Was I getting ahead of myself? Was that look in his eyes and the touch of his hands something he had cultivated, a professional quality, that what seemed imperative to me was merely a passing romance for him?

'Is there someone else, Tom?'

He eased his foot off the accelerator pedal.

'No, Katie, there isn't.'

'I just wondered.'

'There was. It's over.' He paused. Our eyes met for a fraction of a second. 'I could ask you the same question.'

'Yes, over. Dead as old tombstones. An actor whose neck had a permanent crick because he couldn't stop turning to look at himself in every shop window.'

'That's why you were alone on New Year's Eve.'

It was a statement, not a question. He had obviously thought about it. Same as me.

'Bad timing.'

'Or good timing?'

'Yes, good timing.'

He squeezed the tender spots below my knee again.

'Ouch, you really are a sadist.'

'I can't help it. I just love to hear you squeal.'

98

'That's what dominants say to submissives.'

'Oh my God, I forgot I was with an expert.' He paused. 'You must have done loads of research?'

'Is that a question?'

'I'm not sure really.'

'I have a vivid imagination.'

'That I do know.'

He changed gear. The Land Rover rattled more at low speed. The going was slow through Guildford. We stopped. Tom bought two dozen winter roses. They were pale yellow, like dying suns unaware they were already dead. He pulled back into the line of cars. There was a sign and he pointed.

'Albury. Nearly there.'

We curved through bends that rose and fell through the Surrey Hills. He listed the places we drove through, Foxholes Wood, Newlands Corner, Silent Pool, Farley Green, names from storybooks, and I thought, love finds you when you aren't looking for it. It is a surprise like unexpected happiness. A dead flower that suddenly comes to life, so fragile you are instantly terrified.

10
The Way To Live

He turned through an open five-bar gate and we bounced over a track that turned in such a way that the entire house came into view like a painting of a lost England.

'Bramley,' he said.

The house sat in the fold of two hills. It was long and low, two-storeys below two peaked roofs, the dormer window between them bringing light into what must have been a huge attic made for storing memories. Some blue had seeped into the sky and the light of midday lent a powdery flush to the white façade.

The door was open and two Airedales charged out barking as we came to a halt. Tamsin followed, waving the dogs away. She had good legs in flat shoes, solid but shapely, a fast walk, back straight; she looked like a round-the-world yachtswoman with dark blonde hair piled on her head, a broad, heart-shaped face, sea blue eyes that missed nothing.

'You managed to get here in one piece, then?' She kissed her brother, then gave me a hug, squashing the roses. 'So, you're the fabulous Katie Boyd. Lovely name. Good name for a writer,' she glanced at Tom. 'He's going to lend me your book when he's finished. Not very good for royalties, I suppose.'

She took the flowers.

'They're gorgeous. I bet this was your idea. He's totally useless.'

The dogs ran in circles. Tamsin held on to my hand and I bathed in the perfume of her life, the laundry, pottery, freshly-baked cakes. Tom stood to one side jangling the car keys.

'Thank you, I'll take those,' Tamsin said, releasing me to take the keys, which she slipped into a pocket. She paused a moment to study her brother. 'You look like the cat that swallowed the canary,' she added, and I was conscious of the bond between them, the love, and suddenly missed Matt.

Tom looked at me. 'You should wear more yellow,' he said.

As I was about to respond, we were interrupted by three children who swam into view, all talking at the same time.

'Have you seen Dr Watson?'

'Are you Katie?'

'Who do you think she is, silly?'

The children were Gretchen, Hugh and Clemency; eleven, eight and six; candidates for a Christmas card.

Gretchen, in jodhpurs and a red riding hat, had the same quick movements as her mother, a games captain in waiting, a girl who would dry the tears of other girls and take on the bullies. She was holding Clemency's hand and the child stood in muddy green boots, studying me as if I were a piece of bric-a-brac at a fair she wasn't sure whether or not she had a place for in her life. She was darker than the other two, like her father, I assumed, with grey eyes and chestnut hair in a ponytail. Hugh was an angel from a painting with full pink lips, dreamy blue eyes and white-blonde hair. He wore a silver calliper from the knee to the ankle on his left leg and moved with astonishing speed on aluminium crutches gripped about his forearms. His voice was slurred, but so slightly he sounded like an old tape recording that had slowed down.

'One at a time, one at a time,' Tamsin said over the sound of the barking dogs, and the girls deferred to Hugh, the male.

'You have to come and see Topsy, she's just done an enormous poo,' he said.

'Perhaps Katie's not interested in Topsy's poo, Hugh.'

'It's enormous,' he insisted. 'Are you Tom's new girlfriend?'

'Hugh's got a girlfriend,' Clemency said; it saved me the trouble of answering, and made me wonder how many old girlfriends Tom had brought to Bramley.

Hugh shook one of his crutches at his sister. 'No I haven't.'

'Oh yes you have,' said Gretchen. 'Daisy Oakthorpe. I saw you kissing.'

He shuddered. 'It was awful. I hate her...'

'Don't say hate, darling,' Tamsin told him. 'Now leave Katie alone.'

Hugh looked back at me. 'Do you want to come and meet Topsy?'

'Yes, I'd love to.'

'Hold your nose, Katie, he's not kidding,' Tamsin warned me.

She shooed the dogs inside. They gave her a surprised look, then waddled off like a pair of Teddy bears behind her. Gretchen took my hand and we followed Hugh as he wind-milled around the house towards the stable, a long, brick building with open doors and the tang of Topsy's poo.

'Come and see mummy's pottery first,' Gretchen suggested and Hugh just missed as he leaned out to give her a swipe with one of his crutches.

'You always do that,' he said.

'No I don't. Anyway, just for a minute.'

We made our way to the barn opposite the stable and I was struck as I entered by the sense of calm creativity. The smoothness of it all. It was like a surgery with two potter's wheels, an electric kiln, deep steel sinks, the vague smell of ammonia. There wasn't a trace of clay or slip on the floor, and the walls were lined to the ceiling with shelves mounted with finished work. When Tom told me his sister was a potter, what ran through my mind was the cute china tea sets with flower designs that Americans take home from Canterbury and Windsor. I had misjudged. I often do. Tamsin's work was original, contemporary, her plates and vases embellished with pixelated lines of wine red, bottle green and gold, the contours drawing the light, and I remembered the way Tom that morning had worked me through his hands as if I were a soft wet substance he was shaping into someone else.

I reached for one of the plates and ran my fingers over the surface. 'They're so good,' I said, and turned to find Gretchen cuddling a black cat with big jet eyes as shiny as the porcelain.

'Mr Holmes,' she told me. 'He's terribly sad. He needs cheering up.'

'What a wonderful name.'

'We call him that because if we hide something he always finds it,' she answered, and her blue eyes darkened. 'Dr Watson's missing. He's been gone for two days. We've searched everywhere.'

'I'm sure Mr Holmes has looked.'

'That's what mummy said.' Her gaze shifted to the display on the shelves. 'Mummy makes it all, well, not everything. Pammie and Janice help, and I help sometimes.'

'Come on, we're wasting time,' Hugh shouted from the doorway.

We turned to leave, and at that moment, Tom came in.

'We were just going,' Hugh said.

'One minute,' Tom replied, holding up his finger like a minute hand. 'Did you know, when I was your age I wanted to run away with the circus?'

'Honestly?'

'Cross my heart,' said Tom.

He took three coffee cups from the shelf and started juggling, the cups passing from hand to hand, as fast and as nimble as a surgeon. Each cup he tossed into the air went higher and higher and I half-expected and half-wanted him to drop one. I had been holding my breath, and we all clapped when the performance came to an end.

'Another skill,' I remarked.

'You mean I have others?'

'Oh, yes, and you know what they are.'

'They? Plural,' he noted.

I was saved again by Hugh. 'Come on,' he said, and we followed him out. 'Will you teach me how to do that, Uncle Tom?'

'Absolutely. But not with the coffee cups.'

Hugh's eyes lit up. He really did have the face of an angel.

The barn, the stable and the house edged three sides of the courtyard like a stage set, a private world looking over the undulating landscape. In the paddock, off to my left, the horse jumping bars stood forlornly under a coating of frost. The apple trees lined up in the orchard had the appearance of a surrendering army with extended arms, and the pines on the hillside were motionless like frozen plumes of smoke. The clouds had cleared. There was that moment of brightness that comes sometimes into the sky on cold January days, and I could see for miles in every direction. There were no other buildings, and I felt instantly that sense of reprieve you get when you leave the city and arrive in the heart of the English countryside.

We entered the stable. The poo was impressive and overwhelmed all other smells. Topsy clattered her heels in a skittering dance. She was a friendly, black fell pony with the tragic face of the endangered species to which she belonged, as Gretchen informed us. Razor, the grey, Anglo-Arab, as proud as a

Saudi sheik, stood 16 hands; daddy took her out at daybreak every day before locking himself away in his office. Tamsin's Cleveland Bay was named Henry V; mummy had won 'millions' of prizes at jumping events and an assortment of rainbow-coloured rosettes were pinned on a board.

'Do you ride, Katie?'

I was stroking Topsy and turned to Tom. 'Yes. I used to.'

'It's so peaceful here,' he added, as if making a point, which I didn't grasp.

Tamsin interrupted my thoughts, her voice, deep as Tom's, singing out across the courtyard.

'Lunch, everyone. Boots off. Hands washed. It's on the table.'

We left the horses and shuffled out. The Airedales chased around the courtyard and ran in behind Tamsin. The children went ahead. Tom pulled off my grey woolly hat. He threw it into the air and caught it again.

'I love your hat,' he said.

'You can have it if you want,' I replied.

I shook out my flattened hair like one of the horses. He put the hat on and pulled it over his ears.

'Do you like it here?'

'Yes, it's...it's like a dream. The children are amazing. They're so...unaffected.'

Tom marched off towards the side of the house, paused mid-stride and threw the hat back to me. 'Here,' he said. 'I left something in the car,' and disappeared.

There was a tap low on the wall outside the back door. The girls had gone in and I watched Hugh wash his shoes and the bottoms of his crutches.

'Do you need any help?'

'I'm okay, thank you. I do everything for myself,' he answered. 'At school they call me the Iron Man.'

'Better that than the Tin Man,' I said and his hair danced about his face as he laughed.

We entered the mud room with its assortment of tack and riding hats. I hung my coat. Hugh dried his shoes on an old towel and I followed him down a corridor lined with bird prints. The calliper and crutches stalked along like the legs of a tripod. He leaned to the left before turning into a dining room with logs spitting in the fireplace and Christmas cards looped above the stone chimney on strings of red ribbon.

That same moment, Joe appeared with a dish of potatoes flecked with parsley.

'Katie, hi, I'm Joe. Good to meet you. Love the roses,' he said, glancing at the alcove behind me. 'Hope you brought an appetite?'

'I certainly did. I'm starving.'

'That's what we like to hear.' He turned away, then turned back to speak to Hugh. 'Guess what mom's made?'

'Don't tell me, it's asparagus, right, dad?' he said, the slowness adding a touch of irony to his reply. He glanced at me. 'I hate asparagus. It tastes like string?'

'I'll tell you what, I'll eat yours when no one's looking,' I said and his eyes lit up. I had made a friend for life.

The flowers were arranged in a vase with Tamsin's stylized rings of colour and stood on a side table below a wall lamp with a vellum shade. The dogs had taken up positions either side of the fire like a pair of sphinxes with extended legs and paws. The kitchen was half-concealed by an arch, the walls either side shelved with books; hardbacks, paperbacks, the non-book books you see on shop counters filling the narrow, wedge-shaped spaces where the arch joined. The ceiling was supported by beams and the lattice windows looked out over the hills.

Tom entered holding a case of wine as Joe reappeared with a dish of vegetables.

'For the cellar,' Tom said. 'Louis Bernard, Côtes du Rhône, 2007.'

'Sounds interesting. Should be ready next year.' Joe called out. 'Table, please,' and the children came hurrying in from different directions.

With his head almost touching the ceiling, Joe Hirsch had the stooped posture of the excessively tall, cropped hair, thin lips like a pink scar and round glasses. He had the distant, aesthetic look of a don, or a poet, and the silvery grey eyes bequeathed to Clemency. He was wearing a black tee-shirt, faded jeans, trainers with orange laces like it was dress-down Friday. He projected an air of being laid back, but I sensed an aloofness, a shrewdness, that behind the wire-rimmed spectacles, that could have been on loan from Gandhi, his brain was conducting millions of calculations per second.

Tamsin appeared bearing a golden pie with a domed crust, the swirl of steam like an escaping ghost. She had changed, how she had found the time I couldn't imagine, and was artlessly chic in a velvet dress the same shade of red baked in her porcelain, the bodice cut to reveal high firm breasts over a flat tummy. She had brushed her hair, it was thick, dark, a shade like old bronze, and I found myself doing that thing I do, judging others, comparing myself.

'Steak and kidney. I did check you're not a vegetarian.'

I glanced at Tom.

'The...what do you call them? The meatballs.'

'Ah, yes, albóndigas,' I replied.

'What's that?' Clemency asked, and I could see the likeness to her father, her little brow rippling as she took in information.

'Meat balls, silly,' Gretchen told her.

'I'm not silly...'

'Smells wonderful,' I said, and Tamsin fixed me with one of those looks Mother gave me when she was irritated by something.

'I admire vegetarians. But it's so tedious when they bang on about it.'

'No, no. I eat everything,' I said quickly, and Tom waved his hand in protest.

'She eats almost nothing,' he corrected.

Joe had returned to the kitchen and came back with a gravy boat and a dish of roasted asparagus with shavings of parmesan.

Tamsin sat at the head of the table, closest to the kitchen, with Tom on her right, Hugh on her left. I was directed next to Hugh with Joe beside me, the girls opposite. Tamsin cut the pie, serving me first, the savoury smells as they exploded into the air adding to the ambience, the mood, or perhaps my own mood, the odd feeling that I wasn't taking part in a family lunch, but being inducted into a secret club like the Bullingdon at Oxford, and that being a member would carry unforeseen obligations as well as privileges.

We helped ourselves to vegetables, the gravy that poured thick as honey with its hints of red wine, fennel and mustard. The Airedales remained well-behaved beside the fire. A violin concerto played in the background and the winter light added an ethereal glow, a patina of well-being. I looked about to see if there were a camera crew recording what was, with a surface glance, just a family sitting down to lunch, but had in the soft light a feeling of being rehearsed, being performed, that we were taking part in a documentary that would be titled *The Way To Live.*

Like a puck in ice hockey, the conversation skated back and forth across the table. Everyone talked and everyone listened. There were no quiet moments. We heard the kissing incident again and Hugh said he didn't really like girls, except his sisters. Joe spoke about the 'uptick' in the markets. It was good for everyone. Unemployment was a social sickness; a disease. It destroyed lives. He was a dove with the eyes of a hawk juggling contradictory positions.

He poured red wine from a decanter.

Tom talked about the Holi festival in Sri Lanka when everyone throws paint and perfume at each other in the street, and the children at the orphanage thought he had turned into a devil when he appeared with a red face.

'It's fun, but sort of tragic,' he said. 'The paint used to be made from herbs, neem, turmeric, stuff I don't even know the names of, but actually helped offset colds and viruses when the weather changed. Now, they use synthetic dyes that are toxic and have the opposite effect. The tradition's the same, but instead of being healthy it's dangerous.'

'Traditions that have lost their origins are the hardest to break,' Tamsin quoted. 'Who said that?'

'Oscar Wilde or Samuel Johnson, it's always one or the other,' Tom replied.

'I think it's JK Rowling,' Clemency proposed, and her dad laughed.

'I wouldn't be surprised.'

Hugh took advantage of this moment to slide his plate closer and I transferred his asparagus to my own. He then told a convoluted story about a boy with a chocolate passport that melted while flying from America to England. He mashed his food so that it looked smaller and didn't eat a thing. Tamsin, who had, of course, noticed the asparagus ploy, forked up a small chunk of kidney from Hugh's plate.

'For the blue team,' she said.

He took the piece of meat, rolled it around his mouth and chewed it down, the ritual fulfilled. Gretchen explained.

'Daddy and Clemency have grey eyes and are so greedy they eat everything.'

'We're not greedy, are we, daddy?'

'Except when it comes to marzipan dipped in chocolate,' he said.

'Yes, yes, I want some. I want it now.'

'So do I,' said Hugh.

'That's not going to happen,' said Tamsin, and glanced at me with neat white teeth in her pink smile. 'The blue team are epicureans and the grey team are bon vivants.'

Everyone laughed. Everyone seemed satisfied and Clemency changed the subject. With that odd fascination with death that often visits small children, she was sure Dr Watson was dead, like Harold, the hamster, and Mr Holmes would need counselling. Joe thought Dr Watson might have gone to visit Marmalade, the ginger cat that lived over the hill at Hawley House, and promised to go out and look for him again after lunch. Tom said he would go, too. There was nothing he liked more than a good walk in the country.

'That's a plan,' said Tamsin, glancing at me.

We drank the red wine, Muga, a Rioja, 2003, the year of the heat wave; of Roger Devlin. Joe thought life too short to drink bad wine. The steak and kidney pie had been cooked with mead instead of water, and the grey team had second helpings.

'Katie?' Tamsin asked, a wedge of pie balanced on a serving spoon.

'I'm in the green team. We don't believe in coalitions,' I said, and won a laugh from Tom.

Gretchen followed her mother into the kitchen with the dirty plates and helped ferry out individual dishes in the shape of apples cut in half, the set made by Tamsin, the crumble with apples from the orchard.

'That's where the house got its name, Bramley,' Gretchen told me. 'We have trees that are, like, five-hundred years old.'

'Two hundred,' Clemency corrected.

Gretchen turned to her father. 'It's five hundred, isn't it?'

'Sorry, honey, she's right this time.'

There was cream in a glass bowl. I assumed it was home-made. Joe stood, his head skimming the beams, and threw an extra couple of logs on the fire. Red sparks danced up the chimney and the Airedales swivelled their heads to watch. I accepted more wine. I wasn't keen on desserts, but the crumble was delicious, and I ate it all.

'When are you off again?' Joe asked Tom.

'Another two weeks,' he replied; the first I'd heard of it.

'You know they've started oil exploration in the Cauvery and Mannar basins?' Joe continued. He sat. 'At least that'll end the country's dependency on imports.'

'Is it a good time to invest?'

I thought Tom was probably joking, but Joe removed his glasses and thoughtfully polished them on his linen napkin before answering. 'I don't really like to give advice, the markets are driven more by emotion than common sense. But, yeah, I'd say so. Future wars are going to be about resources.'

'Haven't they always?' said Tom, and Gretchen continued.

'Why do they have to have wars all the time?'

'It's man's nature,' Tamsin answered, and gave her daughter a conspiratorial look. 'And we girls have to pick up the pieces.'

'It doesn't matter how much people have got, they always want more,' said Joe, and everyone laughed as Clemency waved her napkin in the air like a flag.

'Yes, more, I want more.'

Gretchen had finished her apple crumble and Tamsin sent her out into the kitchen to help herself.

I finished the Rioja in my glass. Smooth, deep, the taste of Spain; warm days below blue summer skies. Yes, life is too short. The children asked permission to leave the table and went off to do those things children do on winter afternoons. Joe brought a tray with coffees to the library, an unpretentious room with books higgledy-piggledy on the shelves, a television and another log fire. The dogs wandered in and stood gazing at Joe with dull expectant faces. He drank his coffee, placed the cup back on the tray, added a log to the fire and spoke to Tom.

'Shall we?'

Tom had opened a book, which he tucked back in its slot on the shelf. He turned to me with a smile I was growing used to, curious, enigmatic. 'Don't let her bully you,' he said, and glanced at Tamsin. 'Lovely lunch, as always.'

'Yes, thank you. Bye, Thomas.'

Joe whistled, the Airedales bolted out and Tom closed the door behind him as he left the room. Tamsin pushed off her shoes, tucked her legs beneath her, and yawned as she stretched out on the sofa.

'Oh, I'm so sorry, Katie, it's been a long day.'

'I imagine all your days are long.'

'I can't begin to tell you,' she said, and then she did.

Tamsin sang in the church choir with Gretchen. Hugh didn't enjoy all the starting and stopping at rehearsals; he was one of those people who, once they started something, want to see it through to the end. Clemency was a 'committed agnostic.' Her youngest daughter considered it scientifically impossible that Jesus had walked on water or raised Lazarus from the dead. She was, at six, sceptical, inquisitive and had one of those memories like a filing cabinet with everything neatly tucked away. Gretchen was more like her, organized, industrious, 'a busy bee,' she said, the words Tom had used to describe Tamsin.

She removed a clip and shook out her hair; it glimmered like gold in the thin light. Just as Tom's tone changed when he talked about Sri Lanka, Tamsin's voice took on an intense quality when she came to Hugh. He had the eyes of the blue team, but the intellectual potential of the grey. He suffered from non-progressive cerebral palsy, a condition that normally begins during pregnancy or at child-birth. Tamsin didn't say, but I got the feeling she blamed herself for Hugh's disability and her mission was to put it right, put the world back in balance. Her life was a canvas on which she had painted a portrait of herself against the landscape at Bramley, the scene illustrated by the horses, obedient dogs, inventive pottery, her clever husband and super-kids. Hugh was undertaking oxygen therapy to reactivate malfunctioning brain cells and was taking elocution lessons with 'an old Shakespearean hand.' He was a work in progress, the unfinished detail at the heart of the canvas.

There was silence, less reflective than theatrical, a re-crossing of those good legs, an obligation to take part in this game of show and tell. When the red wine reaches the bloodstream there is a yearning to tell the truth; it bubbles out of you like sweat, like tears, like a confession that leaves a sour taste in the mouth. Better a well told lie than a tedious truth. Truth is flexible, malleable, a yellow exercise ball, a chunk of wet clay that can be shaped into a spiralling futuristic vase suitable for pale winter roses or a little black devil with whiskers and a grinning face.

Time to tell, but tell what? She wants to know who I am but I don't know who I am. It's just an insane question that strikes you – that strikes me, in moments of doubt – and even in those moments there is another part of me, a reflection, a shadow in the corner asking why I am suffering this feeling. There are those, Mother for one, who say I have everything. If only life were that simple. We see the façade, the exterior. We can't see the rooms and compartments inside other people's heads. There are many ways to live, to love, to aspire. The mountain only has one peak but there are limitless paths that you can take to reach it. The secret, they say, is to find your own path and stick to it. What they don't tell you is that the path is invisible. If you find it, or imagine you've found it, you follow the path in the dark with nothing to guide you but self-belief. Knowing who you are and what you want is only one part of the puzzle. Conquering doubt and growing wings of self-confidence is the inner core of self, and there's always the Black Dwarf to pull you back down when you feel the air beneath your wings and start flying.

Life is too short for cheap wine and good wine pours itself from the bottle. My head was full of grey matter turning darker. It was hot, the fire blazing. I took off my jacket.

'More coffee?'

'No. Thank you.'

Her smile was patient; relentless.

I write. All writing is tenuous, abstract, self-indulgent. The ultimate fear is that nothing means anything and it is that fear that haunts you every time you stroke the keyboard and watch the words slip from your head to the screen, pinning them there like an accusation. Apart from writing, how do I caricature myself in a few lines? Cambridge, that box that's always ticked. Whispering spires and damp cobbles. The first story published in an erotic magazine. Trips to Singapore to visit Daddy – a spy, bureaucrat, I'm never sure of the difference. The abandoned attempt to learn Chinese. Marketing. Waitressing.

Boyfriends?

What do I say? What did I say?

A film clip of forgotten faces flashed behind my eyes, a journalist, a photographer or two, a sculptor, the gay set designer sampling alien fruit; actors, they are such fun, such narcissists. It all seemed so shallow when I compared myself to Tamsin and her busy-bee ring of activities and achievements. She knew who she was, where she fit into the universe, her life in some strange way given greater significance by her beautiful son and their biblical quest to cast off his crutches and speed up the tape of his gently blurred voice.

'You are so lucky to be a writer. It's so creative.'

Was this a question? Am I lucky?

'Yes, except for the migraine, the insomnia, the long hours with the words like mosquitoes...' I paused.

Was I plagiarising myself?

'Like moving ants you try hopelessly to arrange in some sort of order. The feeling that nothing's ever perfect.'

'Is that so important with erotica? I thought it was all, you know, rumpy-pumpy.'

'A lot of it is.' I sighed. I had been out-manoeuvred. The steak and kidney felt like lead in my gut.

'Why did you choose erotica?'

'You sound like my mother.'

'Really? I suppose people say the same things. We're all a bit of a cliché.' Her expression changed. 'Are you close?'

'No.'

'Tom says you're rather brilliant. He's a good judge,' she said. 'It's such a relief he's his old self again after Marie-France. I knew she was trouble the moment I laid eyes on her.'

'Marie-France?'

'Oh, you don't know her. She was awful. Awful. She broke Tom's heart.'

'Oh.'

'I'm sorry, Katie, I didn't mean that. It's over. I assure you, and thank heavens for that.'

'Marie-France,' I said. 'It's a beautiful name.'

11
Kamarovsky's Girl

Who among us has not dreamt, in moments of ambition, of the miracle of a poetic prose, musical without rhythm and rhyme, supple and staccato enough to adapt to the lyrical stirrings of the soul, the undulations of dreams, and sudden leaps of consciousness. This obsessive idea is above all a child of giant cities, of the intersecting of their myriad relations. – Baudelaire, from *Le Spleen de Paris*

In the last days of Soviet Russia, two groups of people disappeared through the vanishing iron curtain: the former apparatchiks turned oligarchs, who had obtained the deeds to the nation's natural resources, and the party insiders at the defunct ministries, who were going to help them spend it.

Leon Kamarovsky was one of the latter. An adviser on French art at the Ministry of Culture until its dissolution in 1991, he was a guest at the marriage of a former KGB general who revealed after hurling his glass in the fireplace that his young bride, tall, blonde and with an interest in fashion, had refused to submit to his fondness for restraints until he found them a home in France. The two men wept, the Russian way, and, in the beat of those sobs, the young art attaché heard the sound of opportunity knocking.

Kamarovsky had travelled to Paris on official delegations. He had always enjoyed the city, the language, the river turning gold at sunset, the girls with their swaying nonchalant walk. Like a fly buzzing against a window, thoughts of seeking asylum had moved often through his mind. But to do what exactly? And with what? Even now, with the frontiers open, unlike those who had got their hands on the oil and gas, the Chigalls and Kandinskys in The Russian Museum were an unmoveable feast.

By the time the general dried his eyes and filled another glass, he was committed to Kamarovsky's proposal that he, Kamarovsky, a French speaker, journey to France to find a suitable property. With a small retainer, he left immediately, such was the general's misery, and every day through the coming weeks faxed back photographs and details of the houses he had visited. They spoke regularly on the telephone and, sight unseen, the general finally agreed to buy a 17th century chateau in Sancerre, a hilltop town noted for its gourmet restaurants and fast road links to the couturier shows in Paris. With its wistful towers and high arched windows, the chateau satisfied two preconditions: it was flooded with light and had wide vistas in every direction, the opposite of the general's office in the Lubyanka Building with its windowless cells and abiding demons.

It was the start of the global boom in house prices that ended with the banking crisis and the worst depression since the 1929 Wall Street Crash. But that was to come and, in the heady years of the nineties, Kamarovsky found, as few men do, his *raison d'être*. With their innate fear of inflationary spirals and fluctuating exchange rates, Russians with bulging suitcases were eager property buyers and the French nobility, who had inherited their chateaux without the funds to maintain them, were willing sellers.

Kamarovsky travelled from the austere agricultural towns of the north to the sun-washed Côte d'Azur, from the Alpine slopes of Saint-Jean Montclar to Biarritz with its faded hotels and neglected boulevards. The small city was like an ageing beautiful woman in a dress from another season, an echo to Kamarovsky of the Russia he had left behind. He stood on the long wind-blown beach in this forgotten corner of south-western France with the waves filling his vision. His eyes welled-up in tears, real tears, as he realized for the first time that he was free. Free of morose Mother Russia. Free of the party, the past. Free to be whoever and whatever he wanted to be. As he walked back to his hotel, it was as if he had left behind on the empty beach an empty shell, the husk of the past. He pulled back the wide doors at the Hotel du Palais and it was a different person who stepped across the threshold.

Leon Kamarovsky was tall, dark with wide cheekbones, a hooked nose, like some Caesar on a Roman coin, full, sensitive lips, dark hair and deep-set almond-coloured eyes, a reminder of the forebears who had migrated west from Kazakhstan a century before his own journey westward to Paris and Biarritz. He was immensely strong but light, supple, like a dancer with a dancer's sense of rhythm and timing. Free from the cropped brush cut customary at the Ministry of Culture, he wore his dark hair swept back in a shiny wave and grew a moustache that added maturity to his firm features. In 1992 he celebrated his thirty-first birthday, a milestone in the age of a man, thirty being connected to the twenties, of youthful vanity and excess. At thirty-one, he reasoned, it was time to lay the foundations for the future. With his Emile Lafaurie suits in pale colours, long walks following street plans through the bejewelled fabric of French towns and cities, and a love of sea swimming, be it the Mediterranean or the Atlantic, he grew lean, bronzed, and was one of those men who turned the heads of women when he passed.

Arranging the purchase of the chateau for the KGB general provided Kamarovsky with a reputation as a fixer, a man who got things done; great success often begins with a minor triumph. He sought out properties for the new Russian entrepreneurs, yachts and berths to keep them in, rundown hotels needing a cash injection, there were a great number in Biarritz; empty castles, abandoned vineyards, towns hungry for a shopping mall. He took commissions from the sellers, not the buyers. Those men who had slipped through the crumbling walls may have shaken the dust and debris from their collars, but remained what they were. They knew Kamarovsky would never cross them and he knew, if he did, he would be cast off, most probably from the deck of a yacht at night with his throat slit and his feet weighed down with a rusting bust of Joseph Stalin.

He travelled the country by road and rail, adding properties to his portfolio. Like a convert to Buddhism, he had become a Francophile, a believer. He read the French poets, Paul Verlaine, Arthur Rimbaud, Charles Pierre Baudelaire. Just rolling out those names and hearing their prose on his tongue made Kamarovsky feel in touch with something hidden and abstracted deep in the core of his being. He listened to the radio, watched movies in half-empty cinemas and read aloud in hotel rooms in an incessant battle to wear down the burr of his Muscovite accent.

In 1995, he found himself in Beaune, in the Côte d'Or. He stayed at the *Hotel de la Poste,* an old coach house, and strolled the mediaeval streets of the walled town. He sat in the main square with a glass of burgundy. He liked the way the French enjoyed their wine, drinking for pleasure, not regret. *Un verre de vin pour le bonheur.* From beneath the shade of an umbrella, he watched the promenade, men with good shoes and brisk walks; women with bare arms and straw hats, the fine gaps in the weave letting in flashes of light like silver fish that swam over their faces. Those women at whom he smiled responded with a faint lift of the shoulders and smiled back. It was another custom he appreciated, that French women accepted a man's admiration of their beauty, as a man may admire a painting in a gallery, for what it was, not for what it might imply.

After lunch, he followed the ring road around Beaune and took the scenic route to Nuits Saint-Georges, 'the world's most illustrious wine village,' he'd read in the guide. Flies tapped against the windscreen and birds lifted indolently from the road as the vehicle approached. The country lanes curved between vineyards and fields of ripening crops, a landscape unchanged for centuries, and he felt when he saw the sign for Saint-Nicolas Grand-Moulin that vague sense of accomplishment that comes at the end of a long journey.

Saint-Nicolas Grand-Moulin was a large country house with a defunct oil mill that began life in the Middle Ages and had been extended in a palette of styles ever since. The windows were shaded by red shutters, dark as rubies against the necklace of large-leafed ivy coating the walls. The building, on three floors with a cellar, stood in a wide stretch of parkland in the still of a summer's day, the earthy, subtle tang of rural France, like a woman's scent, overwhelming his senses.

He stepped from the car as the owner of the house made her way towards him across the courtyard.

'Bonjour.'

'Bonjour.'

'Monsieur Kamarovsky,' she said without smiling, and offered her small white hand. 'Sibylle Durfort. *Bienvenue dans ma maison.*'

She studied him as if she were looking into a mirror to check her own reflection, or through binoculars at an empty landscape. The study was brief, just a second, but mildly intimidating, like the fleeting gaze of a senior figure in the politburo.

'You would like to see everything?'

'Yes, yes I would,' he replied.

'Do come.'

They entered Saint-Nicolas Grand-Moulin, it was surprisingly cool after the rising heat of the stone courtyard, his gaze drawn constantly to Madame Durfort's erect slender figure as he followed her through rooms with marble fireplaces, frescoed ceilings and carved Provincial furniture, the walls adorned with paintings in gilt frames. A piano and cello stood in the shadows of the music room, the objet d'art precisely placed as to appear arbitrary. He paused before leaving the library.

'Is that a Cézanne?'

'It was once,' she replied. 'Now it's just a copy. Like everything.'

'Not your house.'

'No, my house is my house.'

He followed her up creaking staircases and along corridors lit by sunlight that ran in strips through the half-opened shutters. He liked the way she moved, so light it was as if her feet barely touched the floor, the way the light filled her hair, it was pale, like honey, and lifted from her neck with stray strands falling from a tortoiseshell clip. In a sleeveless, ivory-coloured shift and rope-soled espadrilles that tied about her slender ankles, Sibylle Durfort was ethereal, a fleur-de-lis, delicate, elusive. She was ten years older than him, he thought, and he was reminded suddenly of that day on the windy beach in Biarritz when his soul migrated from Russia and fixed itself in France.

They entered a large room on the top floor.

'My studio,' she told him, and shrugged as if to dismiss the implication.

He studied the unfinished painting on the easel. It was a pastel landscape with a lemon sky, pink fields and blue trees vanishing into mist, the result alluring and mischievous, even transcendental. More paintings were hung and stacked against the walls, scores of them.

'They are wonderful,' he said. 'You have so many.'

'When I finish one, I start another.'

'Do you have shows?' he asked, and the way she looked back over her shoulder gave him once more that feeling of being clumsy; uncivilized.

'No. Nothing like that,' she answered.

He followed her out to the balcony. What he could see was rolling green fields divided by trees that turned hazy along the horizon, the view when it transferred to the unfinished canvas softened, impenetrable.

'It's so peaceful,' he said.

'Like the eye of the storm,' she continued. 'Wherever you go in France it is the same distance. We are in the middle of everything and the middle of nothing.'

'That would have advantages.'

'I suppose it would.'

Their eyes met for a moment, and he gave away a secret, something you should never do in a negotiation.

'I like the house, I like it very much,' he said.

'Yes, so do I.'

'Then why sell?'

She nodded her head and swept a stray strand of hair from her eyes. 'That is easy to answer, Monsieur Kamarovsky, I have run out of money. But then, of course, you must know that.'

He wasn't sure what to say and was saved by the sound of an approaching vehicle. They looked out from the balcony and he could see the roof of a white car through the hedgerows.

'Ah, the children,' she added.

He followed her back downstairs and they left the house as the car came to a halt. The nanny was driving, an English girl; even the French had grown aware that English was indispensable. A boy ran up and hid behind his mother, peeping out timidly with the same expression as the miniature white poodle that chased after him. Nicolas was six, pale and blonde, like his mother. The girl was ten, tall for her age, with her mother's knowing eyes. She strode towards him, nodded in that typically French way, and shook his hand.

'Bonjour, Monsieur.'

'Marie-France,' her mother said.

'Bonjour.'

Her eyes fixed on his and Kamarovsky experienced the same feeling of inadequacy that had pinpricked his shell the moment he had met her mother, that sense of being assessed and found wanting. The girl entered the house while Madame Durfort, with Nicolas and the dog for company, continued the tour, the outbuildings with relics of ancient farm tools, the old mill, the chapel, the stone altar pitted by the woodworm of time. They arrived finally back at his car and he could hear above the courtyard the sound of a cello being played capably if inexpertly in the music room.

A cello. Of course.

It all sounded so...so romantic, so otherworldly, so...so foreign. I felt...parochial, cosseted, inadequate, English.

We had stopped at a station.

'Do you have a photograph?' I said.

He reached for his iPhone. 'I thought you'd looked already?'

'I may have said I did, but I didn't.'

He glanced back at me, shook his head, then scrolled through the files. 'Just one.' He gave me the phone. 'You can delete it.'

I studied the image. Marie-France was precisely how I had imagined her to be. She was my age, but had about her a wisdom, a knowledge; experiences I could barely envisage. No smile lifted her lips and she had that look in her grey eyes of someone who was being photographed against her will. Her hair was the colour of ripening corn, one side tucked behind a small ear with a drop earring, a pixie chin, arched eyebrows, a look of vulnerability and strength, the face of a woman men want to protect and ravage.

I returned the phone.

'You haven't deleted it.'

'It's not mine to delete.'

He did so, so that I could see, as if it made a difference. Marie-France had been important in his life and she remained, a scar, a wound, distinct and layered, as clear as a crystal ball that collects the light and leaves stains of shade as it turns. The sun was going down and Tom's face, too, through the carriage window, was divided like a costume mask in light and shadow. I wondered if he had ever intended to tell me about Marie-France? Or whether Tamsin had advised him to? Or whether there was some collusion, that he had asked her to break the ice before he told me? It was the sort of thing I would do for Matt.

We had left Bramley after the men returned with the missing cat. It was exactly where Joe had assumed it would be. He dropped us at the station. We would be home as night was falling.

Doors slammed. The train gathered speed, constantly moving, up and down like an algorithm. I pass exams by studying my notes the day before. My memory is specific, short-term, the opposite of Clemency Hirsch. I listened as Tom continued and, next day, I wrote everything down as if Marie-France and the Russian were characters in the book Lizzie Elmwood had said I was going to write.

Kamarovsky drove slowly through the heat haze that still afternoon in early summer and his dry heart burst to life like a flower in the desert. His mouth was parched, his eyes watery behind dark glasses. He had been struck by a lightning flash, a *coup de foudre,* an unexpected sense of urgency and passion so powerful a pain crossed his chest and he thought for a moment he was having a heart attack.

He pulled into the shade of a tree and stepped out of the car. He loosened his tie and took deep breaths like a runner at the end of a race. He was beside a vineyard, the grapes growing plump, each row of vines hemmed by a rose bush with pale pink blooms. He had seen roses marking the vines all over France and wondered what purpose they served beyond the beauty of being. A bird with blue-tipped wings landed on the branch of the tree and he couldn't recall what type of bird it was, the word mislaid in Russian as well as French. He was tired of living in hotel rooms, his sense of being on the outside of life looking in exaggerated more than assuaged by the one night affairs that marked his journey. Kamarovsky shaded his brow and gazed across the landscape. He doubted that there was a more beautiful place on earth.

He clapped his hands. The bird flew away, taking with it his self-doubt, his sudden anxiety. He straightened his tie and climbed into the car. He swept his hand through his dark hair and smiled as he studied himself in the rear view mirror. Intelligence is knowing what you want and making the right decisions to reach your goal. A smile touched his lips as he fired the engine. The driver on a tractor waited as he turned the car in the narrow road. He waved and the man touched his fingers to his beret and waved back. You never knew where you stood with the French. They were rarely open. They didn't weep like the Russians or welcome you noisily like the Italians and Spanish. They could be amiable, charming in subtle ways, and he took the friendly gesture from the farm hand as an omen.

Without mentioning his intention to acquire Saint-Nicolas Grand-Moulin, he invited Madame Durfort to join him for dinner. That night, they became lovers.

What Kamarovsky admired in Sibylle was her self-assurance, the serenity easily mistaken for arrogance, or perhaps it was arrogance; her remoteness, her poise, the pastel paintings she had never shown. She was from that class of old families all across Europe – I know them, I am them, the haves who have grown used to having less, conventional, prudish, innately xenophobic, clinging on with good accents in draughty houses they can't afford and who work for a living, media jobs, columnists, designers, artists.

The deeds to Grand-Moulin moved into Kamarovsky's name, but little else changed. Not on the surface. He continued to work tirelessly those coming years. He bought hotels and apartment blocks off plan and sold them when they were built. He still negotiated for the oligarchs, they are not men to whom one says no, but from the old mill in the middle of everything and the middle of nothing he avoided all things Russian and exercised his artistic gene writing poetry in French. He grew his investments as you grow Pinot noir black grapes with patience and love and, when the crash came, he was sheltered, as only the rich are, behind the walls of banks with initials not names in Switzerland, Dubai and the Cayman Islands.

Madame Fournier, in fact a mademoiselle, the plump housekeeper with peasant wisdom and pastry skills that validated her family name, organized life at Grand-Moulin. Nannies came and went. The children learned English. Sibylle painted. She was thin by nature and grew thinner, sharp-angled, a woman transforming from an object of desire to pity. The qualities Kamarovsky had admired in Sibylle, her aloofness, her superiority, traits she had passed on to her son, became the wall that went up brick by brick between them.

When he wasn't at school, Nicolas spent his time in his room with his collections, butterflies under glass, crusaders acting out battles with Saladin, obsolete coins and books of stamps that had belonged to his father, whom he worshipped like a fetish and had barely known. Kamarovsky was an intruder, an invader from the Kazakh steppes, and Nicolas, in an oedipal sense, believed he had stolen his mother.

Marie-France, by contrast, had an instant affinity with Kamarovsky. He was a man, and men do things. They make you feel in touch with something and you're not quite sure what it is. She laughed when he pronounced words wrongly or borrowed phrases from Baudelaire, and when she laughed, he laughed at himself. He built a tennis court and swimming pool behind the mill – 'how gauche!' whispered mother, but used it nonetheless. He bought a white Vespa. He taught Marie-France to drive, there were paths all over the estate, and when he was away, she raced the scooter through the country lanes without a licence. Kamarovsky appealed to her wayward side and she, in turn, gave him a feeling of belonging, something he had never felt in Moscow or between the sheets of Sibylle Durfort's four-poster bed.

At fourteen, Marie-France was as tall as her mother, a child-woman. She reminded me of me at that age with small breasts that itched and tingled, long legs, hips and bottom smoothing, shaping, reforming. It is a cliché, but the cliché is always true. Girls are butterflies and at fourteen they feel the air below their wings and fly through the glass walls that imprison them. She would have been like me, giddy and confused, happy one moment, melancholic the next, me studying at Saint Sebastian, she at the music academy in Beaune, mythic twins separated at birth.

Kamarovsky drove an old black Citroën he had bought because Marie-France had fallen in love with the svelte lines that may have reminded her of herself, all is vanity; it was long, poetic, sleek as a spaceship. He would collect her from the academy and they would visit art galleries and bookshops in time lost country towns where they sat in the shadows of churches and forts and ordered tea and pastries that he ate hungrily and she never touched.

She took his arm as they strolled back to the car and heads turned as if the dark Russian and tall slender girl with her face hidden by a hat were figures from a fairy tale. Did they stop in the forest on summer days? Did she take her cello from the car and sit on a tree stump in a glade playing Bach's Prelude to the 1st Suite? Did they climb into the big back seat with the soft grey leather in the long sleek car, read poetry, discuss art and literature. Kamarovsky would surely have read *Lolita*. Was he Humbert Humbert? Or Svengali? Or Rasputin?

He called her *mon petit poisson,* my little fish, and that summer when she turned fifteen she sunbathed naked beside the pool and grew as dark as he. Sibylle didn't notice or didn't care. She thought of her daughter, if she thought about her at all, as Kamarovsky's Girl, a foreign flag hoisted over a lost French colony. Sibylle's solitary ardour was her painting. She painted dark cityscapes with angular shadows crossing blank walls and bleak empty plazas. She signed her canvases in red with the name Kamarovsky and, at his prompting, showed her work to favourable reviews all over France.

Nicolas withdrew as if into the shadows of those unknown cities. His passion was his crusader figures marching eternally into battle and at night when Kamarovsky was away, Marie-France listened for the sound of her brother's footsteps as he scurried along the corridor into the big bed in his mother's room.

Tom fell silent for a moment. We had stopped at another station. A girl got on and sat further down the carriage singing softly to the music playing on the headphones she wore like earmuffs. It had begun to snow. It would be dark soon, the days short, the summer far behind and far away.

After receiving warm reviews in local papers and magazines, Sibylle Durfort left the serene eye of the storm to do an interview with the infamous poison pen of the art critic for *Le Figaro.* The critique, illustrated with photographs of her work and Sibylle in her studio, was unusually generous and her cityscapes in silver frames began to fly, like migrating geese, from the gallery walls. Astutely priced at 10,000 euros, Sibylle's art hit that golden mean figure that touched the nerve endings of both the old rich and *nouveau riches,* who believed in 1999 that the paintings would go up in value and the champagne bubble would never burst.

In the autumn of that year, she had a show in Dijon featuring for the first time her pastel landscapes, Kamarovsky, her familiar imprimatur, now scrawled like streaks of blood in the bottom right corners of the canvases. Dealers were calling from New York, Frankfurt, Barcelona. Sibylle Durfort was acclaimed, sought after: at forty-six she had reached artists' heaven, the airy space between the twin-peaked mountaintops: recognition and financial independence.

Those winter months she worked night and day on a fresh theme, merging her landscapes and cityscapes in what became known as 'autoscapes' – the curving graphs of the autoroutes with their bridges and service stations, the drivers and passengers faceless automatons isolated in steel cases, snappy cars like small dogs beside 16-wheel behemoths, like Trojan horses, smears of red lights and white lights in night parallels skirting nameless towns and dividing forests and field, day and night, the rational and the insane.

All life is random. All life is absurd. A snap of the fingers and it's gone. A shooting star is already dead by the time we see its light. There is no reason, no purpose; except reproduction. The animals know that. Our cells know that. Sibylle Durfort's last exposition was in Villebleven, sixty kilometres from Beaune. She had hung the show with her new work. The catalogue had gone out. It was January 2000. A new year. A new millennium. Snow coating the hills. Ice on the road. She skidded at speed, the car struck a tree and she broke her neck.

C'est la vie.

Such is life. Such is death. These things happen and when they happen it seems in some strange way as if they were meant to happen, that synchronicity has an eerie will of its own. The conjunction of the car, the ice and the tree rely on the human element – an excess of speed, alcohol, fatigue, the gift of self-determination that makes us the masters of our own fleeting pause upon the planet.

Forty years before, almost to the day, Albert Camus, at the age of forty-six, was the passenger in a car that likewise hit a tree outside Villebleven. Like Sibylle Durfort, he died instantly from a broken neck. The coincidence – celebrated author, celebrated artist – turned the mills of the national press, and they kept on turning. A book was published a year later. A production company acquired film rights. Was it an accident or suicide? Had someone tampered with the car brakes? Who was Kamarovsky, that *éminence grise* whose name appeared in blood on the Durfort canvases? There was no note, just an abiding mystery, an unquenchable suspicion.

No doubt because her mother was showing in Villebleven, Marie-France had received at Christmas a copy of Camus's *L'Étranger*. Was it coincidence, to use that fateful term again, that

I, at the same time, was reading *The Outsider,* the English translation? Or is this particular novel a life experience that girls of a certain age and class inevitably meet, a reminder, like menstruation, of the absurdity of life and the irrationality of death?

The Outsider explores the premise that man's search for the meaning of life makes no sense in a world devoid of eternal truths or values. Meursault, the book's antihero, is a lowly French clerk who kills an Arab on the beach without apparent motive and is condemned more for absurd than rational reasons. The novel is a wake-up call, the moment for putting childish pleasures behind you, and, once awake, you never go fully back to sleep again.

I felt sick. The red wine had turned sour in my stomach. While Tom told the story it was hard to focus on the lives of Sibylle Durfort, Camus, of Villebleven, a minute dot on the map. I could only think about Marie-France. While she was fifteen, I was fifteen. She had a brother four years younger than her, as do I. Tom was four years younger than his sister. We were boxes within boxes. Russian dolls. We were joined by geometry, a cat's cradle of curving looping lines of invisible thread. We were finger puppets with someone else's finger in our rectums. Marionettes with palms and soles connected to strings and we danced to tunes we could almost but not quite hear. All that I was and all that I did was charted and tainted by the inevitable, an inescapable connection to providence. We are free to choose, but choice is hidden within the cage of luck and happenstance.

Kamarovsky became the children's guardian. The housekeeper and English nanny maintained continuity and the earth circled the sun, or was it the sun that circled the earth to mark the movement of time? Marie-France joined Le Conservatoire de Lyon. She grew a long fringe to conceal her eyes and hid herself in her music. The death of her mother had given her focus and sealed her destiny as a concert cellist. Nicolas moved to Paris to live with an aunt and attended boarding school where he wet the bed and wrote long letters to his sister that she never read. They saw each other during the holidays at Grand-Moulin and, late at night, with the moon's glow seeping through the shutters the pitter-patter of footsteps echoed once more along the upstairs passage.

They met at a concert in Paris. Tom had just joined Médecins Sans Frontières. Marie-France was quarter part of an all-girl quartet playing to raise funds for the charity. They had both entered new phases of their lives and were drawn together as stars are drawn by the pull of the moon. They met again two weeks later when she performed in London and while the two violins and viola travelled back to Paris, the cello stayed. They found a flat in Putney with curving windows overlooking gardens and trees, and I pictured his cello tongue licking her cello body with mist sliding over the Thames and Bach's Air on a G String in the background.

That was two years ago, a little more, time enough to see those parts of a partner that at first remain hidden. Marie-France was distant, reserved; she kept a tight grip on her emotions, and what Tom said he admired was her ability to make decisions with scant reflection, to leap without looking back at her reputation as a musician in Paris and start again in London. His long weeks away with Médecins Sans Frontières suited her new life as a jobbing cellist, the work never hard to find when you have the good fortune to be a beautiful woman.

That summer when they visited Grand-Moulin, Tom came to understand why Marie-France had readily abandoned her career to move to London. Yes, there was a spark, a fire, a passion – he avoided the word love with its disturbing connotations, a word the English don't like to use except when they talk about their horses and dogs.

He had noticed during those months together that the pale blue moons below her eyes and the furrows tracing her brow had faded and gone. At Grand-Moulin, they came back again, the indistinct bruising that follows restless nights, the lines on her brow fine as cracks on old photographs. Marie-France turned into another person; she spoke differently, dressed differently, she looked different. She became the girl-woman bound to the past by Nicolas and Kamarovsky, by the knotted chain of their shared history, by the memory of standing beside a brass regaled oak coffin in the graveyard at Saint Symphorien, the church in Nuits Saint-Georges, among strangers and ghouls with autograph books drawn by the charisma of celebrity and death.

Neither Marie-France nor her brother or guardian had ever been interviewed and had read the book about Sibylle's death as if it were a palimpsest scavenged from the waste basket of Albert Camus, an early draft of something that should have been burnt. They had watched like passengers peering down through clouds from an aeroplane the film version that had gathered up the fragments of that icy night of the new millennium and cast on screen a noir mystery in the monochrome images of a retro nouvelle vague, the art director drawing upon Sibylle's autoscapes that, against market trend, and confirming the investors' sense of self-congratulation, had risen ten-fold in value and become icons.

They partnered for tennis. Kamarovsky played each point as if life and death hung in the balance. He doubled with Tom so that Nicolas could play with his sister and I imagined her in a short white skirt with long legs and agile movements spinning the ball in ways that were complex and unreadable. They swam in the pool. I dressed her in a white bikini, and imagined the eyes of the three men following her every move, every shrug, her expression hidden by a straw hat, her feet bare, lively as fish.

They sat below the trees at a table set with salad, saucisson and local cheeses. The sunsets were long and golden. They watched the swallows turn hoops in the sky, the birds joined as if by a single consciousness. Kamarovsky added ice to the wine, a sacrilege, and they clinked their glasses in tribute to health, wealth and the time to spend it, a Spanish toast, he said, his eyes orange in the twilight, his bare arms thick with coarse black hair like fur.

Kamarovsky was charming, loquacious, in a good mood. Since the death of Sibylle, he had begun to write, he said, to the sound of old recordings of Marie-France playing the cello and had devised what he considered was a unique way to reach a private utopia. He wrote poetry in French, translated his words into Russian, then translated the Russian back into French. He had published a compilation of his work under the title *L'âge de Conséquences*. He gave Tom a copy, the book bound like a bible in black with gold-leaf titling, his broad signature in red a one word psalm to the past.

'Read. It will help,' he said, and Tom didn't know what he meant.

'Help what?'

'Why, everything. It will help you understand.'

The heat of the day had warmed the vines and their scent wafted in the air. It was early July, the light lingered and stars burst into the pale green sky. They drank a great deal, old burgundies from another century, and Tom's head was spinning like the universe domed above his head.

'It's like a painting,' he observed.

'Magritte,' said Marie-France and Kamarovsky smiled.

'You remembered.'

'I remember everything. '

'You remember that time at the Louvre, when Sibylle had her show?'

'No.'

Kamarovsky glanced at Tom and threw up his shoulders as he came to his feet. He left the table and returned with the cello from the music room.

Marie-France was balanced on the back legs of her chair, her heels on the table. Nicolas was stroking her feet.

'Play, *petit poisson,* play some Tchaikovsky,' Kamarovsky said. He straightened her chair. 'Careful, you will fall and break your pretty head.'

Nicolas refilled his glass. 'Always Tchaikovsky. I hate Tchaikovsky.'

'The man who hates Tchaikovsky, hates life.'

'Who said that? Not you.'

Nicolas's face was ghostly in the pallid light and Tom was struck by the paleness of his blue eyes, the fineness of his skin, the little twist of his narrow mouth as if he were sucking on a sour olive.

Marie-France tuned the cello, musicians seldom say no when asked to perform. She turned the pegs, the tone of each string variations on a heartbeat. She hoisted up the skirt of her sleeveless white dress and clutched the instrument between her bare legs. Tom had observed this same motion many times, but that night in the feudal air of Grand-Moulin it felt carnal, primitive, something normally hidden rashly and unexpectedly exposed. She played the Nocturne in D minor, the notes like stars slipping into the night sky. Her eyes pressed shut, her playing face a mask as she entered the esoteric world of the music.

'Look, she doesn't play the cello, she has sex with it. She fucks it.' Kamarovsky's words rasped like a wind from the north. 'Art is either political or sexual. I am right, no?'

Nicolas smashed his glass on the table and waved his bloodied fingers at Kamarovsky.

'You're repulsive. You're an animal. You disgust me.'

'Not so much that you don't take my charity.'

'You, you, you piece of shit.'

Nicolas rushed off. Marie-France played. Kamarovsky refilled Tom's glass.

'Ignore him. He is in love with her,' he said.

'And you're not?'

Kamarovsky thought about that. 'I am a man. The whole world wants to fuck her and she only wants to fuck the cello.' He paused, a smile touched his features. 'And you, you have her. *Vous êtes un homme intelligent,* Doctor Thomas. A clever man. You didn't answer my question. Art, it is political or sexual? Or what's the point?'

'Maybe there is no point.'

'Then you are an existentialist.'

'I should check he's alright. He cut his hand.'

'Leave him. He is a mummy's boy with no mummy's breast to suck on. A man has to be a man. This boy has never become a man.'

Marie-France opened her eyes and her piercing gaze across the table sent a shock like a pulse of electricity through Tom's bones. It was like she was another person, a stranger. That look could have been great love or great hatred; he would never know which.

'Take no notice. He likes to be insulting.'

'Nicolas cut himself.'

She shrugged. 'Do what you want,' she said.

She spoke in French, which she never did. Kamarovsky switched from French to English with an ease Tom envied. It seemed the British were born to hoist their flag over every nation where the sun rose and never learn their language. He struggled with Tamil and often missed nuances in French.

Kamarovsky drummed his fingers on the table. He glanced at Marie-France. Then he turned with a concentrated, slightly irritated expression, back to Tom.

'All art has to move you, whether it is on canvas, in the cello, in the words of the poet. If it doesn't move you, what is the point? And if it does move you, what is the point? Ah, you see, perhaps I, too, am an existentialist. But maybe not. Maybe there is a point. The point is to touch your senses, your soul,' he picked up a knife. 'To carve as a knife in the right hands carves beauty from a block of wood. To do this, to move you, art must be sexual or political. I am right, no?'

Marie-France stopped playing, the Nocturne in D minor complete. 'You are always right. Even when you are wrong you are right.'

'Is that why you love me?'

'That's why I hate you.'

Kamarovsky laughed. He cut a piece of cheese, pared off the rind and dropped it in his mouth. Marie-France closed her eyes. Her hair fell over her face and she started to play a piece she had been developing. Tom had followed its evolution when she practised in the bay-windowed room overlooking the river and perceived in the notes the sound of moving water and night planes gliding over the city.

Kamarovsky spoke softly. 'It's new, no?' he asked.

Tom nodded. Kamarovsky leaned closer and listened like a bird watcher listening for the song of a rare bird.

'Art is a gift. You have to keep asking,' he pointed at the sky, 'before the gift is given. She doesn't compose music, she channels it. It comes from up there,' he said and switched back to his former thesis. 'Political movements are driven by the sweat and spit and semen of words. We have Lenin and Trotsky to thank for a century of war and chaos. Trotsky, he was a fine writer, you know that?' he asked. 'It is rubbish now, just history. You can't change the past or the inevitable. Marxism was doomed to fail.'

'Didn't Marx say the same about capitalism?'

'Of course, and he was right. They are both doomed to fail as we are all doomed to die. Just as politics is dying,' he continued, raising his finger. 'We live now in *L'âge de Conséquences.* Politicians serve the corporations, the banks, the vested interests that keep them in power. The world has lost its way. There will be more disasters, more terrorism – one day, the banks will collapse and our money will be as Voltaire said, worthless scraps of paper. Artists do not know this. They do not think, they feel it in their souls. They can't express themselves through the issues of the day, there are no issues, and they are left with just one life-line to hang on to: the sexual.'

He glanced at Marie-France. The bow was going back and forth across the strings of the cello. Sweat darkened in rings on the dress below her armpits and ran in slippery beads between her breasts. Her skirt had risen up. You could see the feathery pink wisp of her pants, her thighs tightening, the muscles glossy with damp.

'Look, look now. Look at her play and you will see yourself.'

Tom glanced quickly at Kamarovsky and back again at Marie-France. The Russian continued, his voice a chant, a prayer, a poem.

'You are moved and that which is moved is between your legs. I am not mistaken. You suffer an insatiable hunger. You want to be the cello gripped by her thighs. You want to feel the bow crossing your flesh as it crosses the strings like a whip across your back. You want to pay penance to your desire. Why did God in his infinite folly give her such beauty? Such ability? What was he thinking? What did he want to do to us, we mortals?' He paused. 'He wants to kill us with her beauty. That is what she does when she leads the orchestra, our *petite* Jeanne d'Arc, our virgin leading the hordes into battle. Every man wants her. Every woman wants to be her. It is a burden only a very special woman could carry. Marie-France is that woman. You are a lucky man, Doctor Thomas.'

Their eyes met for a moment and Kamarovsky was silent. A bird landed on the table, snatched a crust of bread and flew off again. Marie-France bowed frenetically, as if drugged, as if sawing through metal bars, her music unknown, haunting, the chords pounding, seductive. Her dress was soaked, her breasts visible through the fabric, her legs drawing the cello deeper inside her. Kamarovsky was right. She was making love and Tom watched, mesmerized by this display of auto-eroticism. The choreography of her fingers fretting the arm of the instrument was a ballet, the bow was the tongue of a whip flashing in the hot sirocco night, and Tom that moment didn't feel as if they were in the middle of everything, but on the edge of everything. He was holding his breath, as you do before orgasm, and when her composition came to an end, his brow burned in fever.

He heard the soft clap of hands behind him and turned. Nicolas was standing like a ghost among the trees. Marie-France propped the cello against her chair. Her hair was wet, her face silvery in the moonlight. He watched her cross the grey flagstones and throw herself into the pool, a fallen angel in her white dress. Nicolas pulled off his shirt and slid into the cool green water.

'Come in, it's beautiful,' she called. She was smiling, girlish, fourteen years old.

Kamarovsky was watching him.

'Now you see,' he said. 'To understand something is to be liberated from it.'

Tom was drunk. It was like a dream he couldn't fathom. Marie-France slipped out of her dress and left it on the side of the pool.

'Come, come. Take your clothes off.'

He stripped naked and dived into the water. She kissed him on the mouth and kissed her brother on the mouth. It was strange but not so strange. It was the age of consequence. He understood. The stars folded and when they made love in her childhood bedroom, the moon peered through the shutters and white tears ran down her cheeks. She cried for her mother, she cried for the past and she cried because, for a moment, she was happy.

Next day, the sun high, the sky lazuline, they drove to Lyon, left the hire car and flew back to London. They never spoke of that night. The present is quickly the past and Marie-France had to prepare for her first major performance playing the solo in Bach's Concerto in C Minor, the purported Casadesus forgery. Kamarovsky sat at his side and I was reminded once more of Svengali as Tom described the packed house at the Royal Albert Hall coming to its feet like the flock following the call of Jeanne d'Arc. She shared her mother's genes and, like her, Marie-France Durfort was born to have her name picked out in lights.

Tom was away more often. It suited them. When they were together they were content and when they were apart they were busy. They did intend to make another visit to Grand-Moulin the following summer, but after her recital at the Royal Albert Hall, Marie-France was in demand and was whisked off to Prague, Glyndebourne, Salzburg, Edinburgh. She was booked for the opening night of the Proms in July. Tom had arranged his diary so that he could return from Sri Lanka and planned to meet Kamarovsky so that they could attend the concert together.

Tom paused and took a long breath. His eyes were cloudy. 'You know, I wonder sometimes if we ever get to know another person, I mean really know them.'

He glanced out from the carriage window. It was snowing, large flakes, the sort that settle, and I remembered that morning when we were walking to the garage and I'd asked him his deepest desire. He had grown serious: that you're for real, Katie, he'd said. That I'm not going to wake up all of a sudden and, poof, you're someone different.

The train was slowing into Waterloo. The girl down the carriage had removed her headphones and I watched her rub the steam from inside the window to look out. I turned back to Tom. He buttoned his coat, as if to delay the end of his story, to think about what he was going to say.

'My work was unpredictable. I was more involved back then in raising funds than caring for the kids,' he continued. 'I had to fly back to London unexpectedly. I called and sent a text, but Marie-France isn't a telephone person. She turns them off when she's practising and forgets to turn them back on again. I thought I'd surprise her.'

He bought flowers at the stall outside Putney Station. He strolled along the river, the light golden in the trees. There are moments in July, on sunny days, when London becomes the most beautiful city in the world. The house was silent. The downstairs neighbours were away. He heard the sound of laughter as he opened the door and it stopped as he walked along the passage to the bedroom.

He paused. The lights of Waterloo were grey like mist.

'They were in bed together,' he said, and I knew he was going to say that. I had been holding my breath.

'Kamarovsky,' I gasped, and he shook his head.

'No, no. She was with Nicolas. She was in bed with her brother.'

'That's...' That's what? I had run out of words.

'I shut the door. I wasn't sure what to do, what to say. I mean, what do you say?' He was shaking his head. 'She came out

133

in a dressing gown a few moments later but in those few moments, something had gone, broken. It was over.'

'They were...' again my words ran out but he knew what I wanted to ask.

'She said no, it wasn't what I thought. When I was away, Nicolas got the train from Paris. He lived in a room Kamarovsky paid for and told everyone he was writing a book. Her brother needed her. They were linked by the past, by death, by the life at Grand-Moulin, by something...existential.'

'What does that mean?'

'I don't even know. Nicolas had always climbed into his mother's bed. Marie-France allowed him to continue. It was what he needed, to feel her next to him. She had been born with the gifts, the beauty, the thing you need to get through it all. It was fucked up...'

'I'm sorry.'

It's what English people say when we don't know what to say. When someone bumps into you, you turn and say sorry. If you don't understand something you say sorry. I didn't understand, not really, and I was sorry.

'When I said I didn't have anywhere to go on New Year's Eve, it was true. I moved my stuff into my folks' place next day. I never saw her again.'

'When was it?'

'July, last summer.'

'You kept the photograph.'

'It's gone now. In every way.'

I wasn't sure what he meant. The train jerked to a halt. Doors slammed. The cold moved like an ice drift along the platform.

The girl with the headphones was just ahead of us. She tripped and fell, landing on her knees. Tom rushed forward to help her and she looked disappointed when she realized he was with me.

We took a taxi. The snow fell and kept falling, coating the pavements, the roofs, the parked cars. It sat in white bonnets on the trees and blew like white butterflies against the windscreen. The sky was black and a single star glowed on the horizon.

12
Thirteen Days

I felt trapped inside my clothes. I shed my coat and jacket, long scarf, woolly hat. Night had come. Snow coated the windows making it feel as if we were in a tent on an ice drift cut off from the rest of the world, from the tolling bells of the past. The Victorian lamp created a warm glow and the smoking man still waited, the same ironic look on his thin face.

'Are you rushing off?' I asked him, and he shook his head.

'No, Katie, I'm not rushing anywhere.' He took a step closer. 'It's the past. Dead and buried. You wanted to know. I wanted to tell you.'

'Yes, thank you.' I wasn't sure what to say. 'Thank you,' I said again.

'For what?'

'I don't know. For taking me to see your sister.'

'I probably shouldn't have. She can be so over the top.'

'No, not at all. It was nice. The children are lovely.'

'They're great.'

'I wanted to eat Hugh, he's like chocolate.'

'He's quite something.'

We were saying those things people say when they don't know what to say. There was a cloud in the air, a small cloud, almost invisible. He hung his coat on the back of a chair. I sat and removed my boots. My toes were cold.

'Did you ask Tamsin to mention Marie-France?'

'No,' he replied. 'But it's just the sort of thing she would do.'

'She's very...protective.'

'That's one way of putting it.'

I stood. It was still snowing. 'I'm going to take a shower.'

I left him in the living room studying my corkboard and wondered if I had pinned up anything too personal or frivolous or stupid? And what did it matter? We dream of letting go, of being, not thinking, but remain attached to our chains. I dumped my clothes on the wicker basket and stood below the jets of water, turning the hot tap higher. My head throbbed. My finger hurt. My stomach burned. Red wine at lunch. It always does that. My thoughts whirled like cars at a funfair ride, a glimpse of the future. Time's flow was out of sync. I saw film clips from a long July night, a cello pulsing on the soundtrack, slender legs around the instrument's thorax, a haze of yellow hair, nude bathing in the moonlight.

Phantoms of steam escaped as the shower door opened and he stepped inside like the genie from the lamp. I was glad he'd come, like this. He looked into my eyes and we kissed. We kissed and we kissed. His hands curled around my body, gathering me in, and I thought not only this moment is present, the past is always present. The way he kissed my neck and shoulders is an echo of the way he kissed her shoulders. Life is a continuum, a landscape we cross with the future ahead and the past a breath away behind. The water beat down, scalding like needles, and I clung to his neck like a dancer in a night club. His cock slid across my tummy and I imagined a bow crossing cello strings. We are prisoners of our thoughts. He clutched my shoulder blades.

'They are like wings,' he said.

'You didn't know I was an angel?'

'I had my suspicions.'

'We have strict orders to keep it secret.'

He zipped his lips with his index finger and I turned off the tap.

We dried.

'Give me a few minutes,' I said.

I went through to the bedroom, glanced at myself in the long mirror and saw a girl with green eyes and an expression I had never seen before, neither happy nor sad, not blank, not expressive. It was the expression you might have staring at an equation, a stray date that means something, but you can't work out what, and it probably doesn't matter. I crossed the room. I opened the drawer containing the mask and a memory dropped like a leaf into my head, wearing it at *Pink,* feeling more confident now that I knew I was going up to Cambridge, now that Mr Devlin had removed the unnecessary; the clutter. You always remember your first, it's true, but I no longer thought of him as the tempter, the seducer, but a messenger summoned from my own psyche, the key to a cache of infinite possibilities.

I held the mask out and the vacant eyes stared back. Naked I felt as if my soul was exposed, my thoughts could be read. In the mask I felt protected. I eased the elastic strap over my head, adjusted the fascia to my cheekbones and glanced again at the mirror. The acid in my tummy had gone. Masked I am me. Masked, I can do anything. Be anything. I had worn the mask for him before, but it was different now. Something had changed, as a dress changes with a different pair of shoes. I coiled my left hand into the Louis Vuitton velvet handcuffs then, behind my back, slid my wrist into the velvet casing and closed the snap. My shoulders straightened, my spine bowed in an inward curve, and the dead cells in my head drifted from my parted lips like funeral ash.

That New Year's morning when he left my bed, I fell into a restless sleep and saw in a dream an imaginary future with Tom and pale blonde children and a white horse that may have been a unicorn, his sister's life, or someone else's life. The dream came back into my mind and it seemed now, as I stood masked and cuffed before the mirror, that it wasn't only someone else's life, it was someone else's dream. The story I was writing was no longer my story. It was her story.

The door opened. I watched the mirror's reflection and remained with my back turned as he approached through the thin light. He ran his palms down my arms, describing the narrow v to my bound wrists. He kissed the nodule at the top of my spine below the tattoo and stroked my rib cage that concealed a red bird that fluffed up its wings. My heart beat faster.

'You are beautiful, Katie,' he said, and turned me towards him, turning away the past like a thief at the door.

Time had been in stasis.

It races now. Like clouds before the wind.

Our lips touch. He holds my hair away from my face, above my head. He cups my cheeks. His hands are potter's hands that move me, warm me, shape me, turn me towards the bed and down on my tummy. I wriggle to my knees and bury my head in the pillows, my legs open in an arch ready to receive his tongue that glides into the wet delta of my sex as a bird homes to a nest. He reached the dome of my clitoris, his touch lighting a million stars. My stomach muscles tense and a spasm of unimaginable pleasure

137

passes through my body to my eyes that loosen tears beneath the mask and run unseen down my cheeks.

He takes a grip on my thighs, his palms with fingers spread pulling me back, his cheeks buffering against the cheeks of my bottom. The motion is rhythmic, musical, each pulse sweeping me higher like a kite free in the sky. I give everything, all I can find in my shallow being bred from a shallow life conjuring words. I understand the psychology and doubts and shortcomings of my characters. I know why they do things, what they are striving for. I create their problems as I create my own. I have on the edge of my perceptions that Black Dwarf feeling that nothing means anything, that I am trapped in an eternal search for something that doesn't exist.

It is January, the time for new beginnings. I feel on the verge of a resolution, a turning of the page, a time to metamorphose, and be someone else. I am swimming under water. Contractions ripple through me in delectable tremors tinted by an odd sort of irony, a contradiction. My half-hidden face is pressed into the bed, my hands locked in velvet cuffs. I am for a moment floating, suspended, all feeling, all sensation, and my orgasm comes in a seismic roar that makes me weep.

I roll over. He pulls the mask back from my eyes and licks the tears from my cheeks.

'You're crying.'

'You know I always cry when I'm happy.'

'Then I am happy you are crying.'

He drops the mask on the floor, rolls me on my side and releases the catches on the handcuffs.

'You don't need these now.'

He stares into my eyes and I wonder who it is that he sees. He draws closer. His cock slides up inside my cleft and it seems at that moment as if I am her and she is me and we are one, my twin, my avatar, my nightmare. He comes quickly, warmly. We lay there panting and I feel as if I am waking from that dream with the white horse that may be a unicorn, that the future containing the creature, whatever insight or symbol it represents, contains him, too, Tom and me, and perhaps I am the white horse with spreading wings.

*

We went out, stamping through the cold night like two figures in a snow dome. Our boots crunched. Our breath froze. A bus grated by, ghostly faces hidden behind misted windows, and I wondered who those people were, where they were going. So many people, so many lives. I remembered after grandpa's funeral going to his study filled with books and bibelots that had meant so much to him and now meant nothing at all. I took his old hardback *Roget's Thesaurus* to remember him by but never use it. It's quicker on the net and words like people go out of date and die.

We chose the Turkish restaurant. I picked at some cheese, black olives, sipped a glass of white wine I didn't want. The light was yellow. Four men in the window seat sucked on a shisha that bubbled like indigestion, smoke curling over the low ceiling. Tom ate hungrily and drank beer, his knee bobbing below the table, a bundle of revved up energy. Jangly music. Candles in red glass holders. A vinyl tablecloth. He tells me about a boy of twelve who had lost his entire family in the war, mother, father, siblings, cousins. The boy, his name was Ghanan, never uttered a word for two years and the first time he did speak he spoke in English. 'Thank you, Doctor Tom,' he said. 'I will become a doctor. Like you.'

He called for another beer.

'All the time he wasn't talking, he was listening. We can learn so much if we just remain quiet.'

I looked back into his restless eyes and remained quiet. On the wall next to him was a poster with a picture of the Blue Mosque. He drank his beer, holding the neck of the bottle. We had known each other a few days and it seemed as if we knew everything about each other and nothing about each other, that no one ever really knows anyone else. He reached for my hand.

'You okay?'

'Perfectly.'

'You seem different,' he said.

'Different from what, from when?'

'More...thoughtful.'

'You said this morning, God, it seems like a hundred years ago, you said you didn't want to turn around suddenly and find I was someone else. You said you didn't like moody girls.'

'I don't.'

'I'm a moody girl...'

'No you're not...'

'Yes I am. I was sad on the train. Now I'm happy. My moods change. They change in a second. When I see someone begging in the street it makes me feel instantly upset and confused...it makes me depressed for the rest of the day.'

'That's a lot of reactions?'

'I am upset because people are forced to beg in the streets and we are such a rich country. This isn't Sri Lanka. I am angry with myself because I always have the same set of thoughts: I should give this person money, £5 one way or another makes no difference to me. And, at the same time, I'm thinking: he's probably a heroin addict and he'll just get another fix, or buy a can of beer. I should give my £5 to the Salvation Army. The whole cycle is repetitive. It's boring. It's confusing. We want to do the right thing, but what is the right thing?'

'Katie, most decent people think like that, it's normal.'

'That's good. The last thing I want to think is that I'm special.'

'You are special.'

'I am not Marie-France.'

He sat back in his seat. 'She's not special, Katie.' He paused. 'No one is.'

We were quiet for a moment. He reached for the basket of pita. I thought about Marie-France playing the cello at the Royal Albert Hall, her brother creeping to her mother's room, to her room, the mystery of incest, the ultimate transgression, if that's what it was. I watched him scoop up the last of the humus. He looked back across the table.

'Why the mask?' he asked.

'I like it.'

'Me, too.'

'Why?'

'I'm not sure...you seem more relaxed, freer, I suppose,' he said.

'You don't wear a mask to disguise yourself but to show who you really are. In the mask I am me, Tom, without it I am moody and don't always know who I am.'

'Well, whoever you are, I think you're amazing.'

'I'm in my amazing mood. It could change at any second.'

'I wish I'd never said that, about, you know, moody girls,' he said and there was a touch of laughter in his voice. 'It's not easy meeting someone new and trying to find out who they are.'

'Tell me about it.'

He swigged his beer. 'You're the writer.'

'You're the doctor.'

'I fix broken bodies. Heads are your department.'

I glanced up at the Blue Mosque and he followed my gaze. 'When we leave Troy, we should go to Istanbul,' I said. 'I have a friend there who paints murals.'

'I can't wait.'

'Let's go home,' I said and he waved his hand for the bill.

There is nothing like making love after you have made love. I have said this before. It is the nature of our minds to keep coming back to those truths that guide us. We carry in our heads readymade sentences and phrases like snatches of music, jingles that repeat themselves. When you make love after you have made love there is no urgency. It's like the last swim before sunset when the water is warmest and your skin prickles with salt and sun.

I woke with the morning light and listened to his breathing. It was slow, regular, untroubled. His eyelashes were long and thick. I could see the rapid eye movement behind his closed lids and judged by the faint smile on his lips that he was dreaming about something without myths and monsters. He was leaving in thirteen days and I was greedy to have him with me and inside me every one of those days.

He stirred. His eyelashes flapped and I kissed him.

'You're awake,' he said and we touched lips.

'Maybe you're seeing me in a dream.'

His expression changed. He was fully awake now. 'I did see you in a dream, at least I think it was you.'

'Maybe it was someone you used to know...'

'Katie.'

I rolled over and scooped the mask from the floor where it had been dropped. I held it over my face.

'Is that better?'

'Yes,' he said. 'Definitely. It was you. You were dressed in that blue jacket with lots of buttons and you had your back turned.

Then you turned around. You were holding something, a spider, I think, or a crab. You went to say something, then I woke up.'

'A spider!'

'A tarantula or something, it was huge.'

I squirmed. 'I wonder what it means?' I said.

He shrugged. 'It doesn't mean anything. Freud's a joke.'

I laughed.

His cock nudged my hipbone.

'Hello,' I said. 'Someone's awake.'

I disappeared below the sheet. His cock lay bathed in the perfume of our sex, sperm with its vanilla zing and girlie discharge, a fruit shake of chemicals I'd read made you feel high and happy. His knees stretched the covers in a ridge over my head and I felt as if I were in a cave. As he grew harder in my mouth, I wondered why I liked this so much, why it felt so right and natural to be in the warmth below the blankets, eyes pressed shut, my teeth fixed with that twin impulse to be tender and to bite down hard on his throbbing manhood. I sucked his balls and a sigh shimmied through his legs. He was constantly edgy, always anxious to be doing something, going somewhere: obscure meetings with mysterious colleagues, across the fields in search of the missing cat, out into the fresh snow to eat black olives and see London dressed as a Christmas card. For a moment he was in the moment.

His hands reached under the covers and his palms came to rest on the sides of my head. I became a robot girl, my mouth a perfect rictus, my lips furled back, the trunk of his penis slipping in and out of my throat with piston-like ease and rhythm. There is nothing more feminine than sucking cock. It is oral sex that separates us from the animals. My breasts were on fire. My pussy was wet. The whiff of my own arousal filled the cave. I wanted him so much, it hurt.

There is a word I have always avoided in my writing, my life, my thoughts. That word is love. What does it mean? How do you deal with it? If you find it and lose it, how do you get over it? Love is something you feel and when you feel it you can't trust it or define it. How can you sustain love for a long time? A short time? You may love your family, your friends. But you don't invite them inside your body.

I slithered up his chest and he slithered up inside me. He lay back like a figure carved in the landscape, and I adored being the pilot taking our little craft up over the updrafts and turbulence. By rolling rather than rocking, a rhythm men find hard to maintain, like being led while dancing, I felt the oscillations over my G-spot and a rippling effect against my clitoris, the simultaneous vibrations driving a charge as if between two terminals and lighting my body like a city at night. I arched my back, he stiffened, I shuddered and cried out loud enough to wake the Romanian girl from her slumbers in the flat downstairs.

13
Someone I Don't Know

We made love every night and every morning. The days grew warm and wet, as if spring were coming, and the buds on the trees were fooled into opening. I carried sunglasses as well as an umbrella as we set out to find little pop-up bakeries and coffee shops for breakfast. My inclination was to stick with somewhere I liked and return knowing what to expect. Tom preferred the unexplored and unexpected.

He collected the paper from the corner shop where Mr Patel was running a duster over a display case containing cigars.

'Good morning,' I said.

'And who should we thank for this fine day?' he replied with a question.

Tom pointed at the ceiling. 'Perhaps someone upstairs?'

'Ah, you mean Mrs Patel?' said Mr Patel, and it was the first time I had ever seen him smile.

'Have you made a New Year's Resolution?' I asked, and he shook his head from side to side.

'Yes. Yes. Yes. Every year the same. I decide to live for one more year.'

'Just one?'

'One at a time is more than enough.'

He smiled again, twice in one day. The bell over the door chimed as we stepped into the street's noisy chain of grinding traffic and turned at the first corner into the warren of architects' offices, new galleries and shops selling vintage tee-shirts, candles and cupcakes. There was a smell of fresh paint, croissants and coffee. East London was humming. You could hear the song of change in the air, the light that had once beamed down on Chelsea, Notting Hill, Camden, shining now on Wapping, Dalston, Haggerston. The sun lifted over the rooftops as we turned into a narrow passageway lined with horse posts and cobbles like dark winking eyes.

'London's magical when it's like this,' he said.

'The upside of global warming,' I replied, and he shrugged and seemed sad all of a sudden.

'A few degrees in Europe means blue skies. A few degrees south of the Sahara and there's a famine,' he said and I bit my tongue. 'Look back over the last hundred years, where's there's oil there's war.'

'Then we have to end our dependency on oil.'

'Absolutely.' He laughed. 'Then they'll find something else to fight about – water, most probably.'

He read *The Times* one day, *The Guardian* the next, seeking balance, staying informed, putting a frame around situations, giving them focus, perspective. He didn't believe everything was hopeless, selfish, existential, but a work in progress in which he and we and everyone played a part. He was plugged in and it made me feel as if I were observing the world like a graceful tree in an ink drawing above a rolling river.

One afternoon when he was called away to a meeting, I took the plastic bags filled with discarded clothes from under the bed and felt lighter leaving them at the charity shop. I studied my shoes and left them unculled for another day. I squeezed the yellow ball and my finger felt stronger. I went to the gym and could smell him on my sweat when I sprinted on the running machine. I bubbled in the hot pool and, clean and creamed, was ten minutes late for my appointment with the manager at the Nat West.

Angela Pelling worked at a glass desk in a glass office, her name on a metallic strip inserted in slots on the door in such a way that it could be removed as easily as it had been dropped into place, a suggestion of corporate impermanence. She was my age, squat and stocky with the beginnings of a moustache, rings on her thumbs and pens of different colours in her blazer pocket. She stared for several seconds at a computer screen, then turned and stared at me over red-framed glasses.

'You are aware that you're late? I have other appointments, not only you.'

'Yes, I am so sorry, Mrs Pelling.'

'Miss Pelling,' she corrected.

She glanced briefly back at the monitor, folded her glasses in front of her, then spoke as if the financial crisis were my fault, the fault of people like me who expect credit and neglect to honour their obligations. Banks support international trade, small businesses, large companies. Banks keep our money safe. Banks are a pillar of the community. Banks can't run on debt. The system only works when those with broad shoulders carry their part of the load, she said, and I wobbled my head like Mr Patel in the corner shop.

I was sitting at a sideways angle to the desk, legs crossed in dark brown skinnies from Anthropologie, a tan leather jacket with a fake leopard collar and knee-boots ornamented with brass fittings. My cheeks glowed from the workout, my pinned-up hair was half-unpinned, the wiles of the wind, and my lips were a shade of Lizzie Elmwood Christmas present *Chanel* pink. If I were a character in one of my books it would not have been hard to understand why Miss Pelling was going on so, and about things that were inaccurate and vaguely irrelevant.

The overdraft was the result of Simon Singh suddenly demanding three months rather than one month advance rent on my new flat and it had been paid off by the time my appointment with her had been made. I wondered, with the plethora of pens and the shadow over her lip, if Miss Pelling had a satisfactory love life, and I would love to have known if she knew that Miss Pelling spelled misspelling. I caught a glimpse of myself in the glass wall separating us from the machines where lines of broad-shouldered people did their banking and the reflection showed someone all shiny and relaxed. What misspelling needed was a lover, and if she had one, well, she needed another, that it was love, or sex, or both, that oiled the wheels of the human soul. Angela Pelling seemed to have exchanged her soul for the name plate tentatively slipped in the slots on the door. I marvelled at the genius of this elusive but persistent threat that would keep her in its thrall and felt lucky to be me with different threats and shadows; future unknown.

I left, chastened, and caught a bus. I was learning the bus routes, avoiding taxis, doing my bit. I met Lizzie for lunch and ordered a bottle of San Pellegrino with an avocado wrap.

The waiter hovered with hairy arms in a sleeveless black vest. 'No wine?' he asked, and looked offended.

'No, thank you.'

Lizzie gave me one of her looks as I filled my glass with bubbles.

'Wars are going to be about water when all the oil's gone,' I said.

She stopped dressing her salad. 'Olive oil?'

'No, no, the stuff we put in cars.'

She pushed the cork back in the bottle and added a few grinds of black pepper. 'I suppose that's Tom talking.'

'Not at all...'

'You usually like to talk about sex.'

'I don't only talk about sex.'

'You do when you're not getting any.' She fluttered her eyelashes as she stared back across the table. 'I have never seen you looking so...so pleased with yourself.'

'You always say that.'

'Do I? So he really is a good lover?'

I took a long breath. 'The best,' I said, gasping like I'd just had a tiny orgasm.

'When's he off?'

'Don't ask,' I replied and felt the hollow snatch of *petite mort.* 'What about Ray?'

'Don't ask,' she repeated in a different tone. 'We should get together, the four of us. I can't wait to meet this Tom whatever-his-name-is.'

'Bridge,' I told her. 'It's so poetic. On a bridge you are connected with the two halves of yourself.'

'On a bridge, dear, you are not in touch with anything. You are neither in one place nor the other.'

'In the middle of everything and the middle of nothing,' I said, and she reached for her wine glass.

'How well you describe my feelings.'

She turned away, her expression haunted, and there was something in her look that made me sure she was thinking about the new girl she had met and how Ray's presence would make it difficult to see her. She liked to give the impression that she was in control, but her life was driven by inner conflict disguised by outward calm: destiny's mistress, not its master.

Lizzie was a sybarite, a hedonist, a slave to pleasure. She was curvy, sensual, a pin-up for sex in all its configurations. She was born wearing high heels and claimed to have a rare disorder that prevented her wearing flats. Trainers to Lizzie were as cloven hoofs, an abomination, the work of the devil. She had the softest skin I had ever seen, the result, she said, of hot semen masques and hats with wide brims. Her small waist was emphasized by a tightly-buckled belt and her breasts pressed like tumbling waves over the v of a black cashmere top. Her cleavage, deep and inviting, was ornamented by a green lizard with golden eyes on a silver chain and filigreed silver earrings hung like a pair of Damocles' swords beside her wide cheekbones. Her hair was black from a bottle, shiny as lacquer, her nose strong and she had perfect lips, full and firm, shaped like a bow of the sort Renaissance painters provide angels.

The silence had stretched while we ate.

'How's the new girl?' I then asked, and she shimmied like a cat.

'Lisa. Lisa Lundt.' She took a long breath and sighed. 'She's...divine, white, like a fresh fall of snow, like a wedding cake, with red, red lips and the most amazing hip-bones I have ever seen.'

'I didn't know you had a thing for hip-bones?'

She did that little half-turn of the head and shrugged as if to say there was much I didn't know about her, which was partially true. We had first met at *Pink*, both in masks, and those who wear masks never reveal everything.

'Ray is so needy,' she said. 'He's so rough...'

'I thought you liked rough?'

'What girl in her right mind doesn't enjoy being tied up occasionally, a tanned bum, but, dear, there are limits.'

'I thought the only limit was death.'

'Now you're getting all erotic on me. I am quite content reading de Sade. I don't want to live with him.'

I laughed.

'You're laughing?'

'Why not?'

'You don't usually do that. Laugh, I mean. It must be him.'

I shrugged. 'Does Ray know about Lisa?' I asked her, and she shook her head.

'What we don't know doesn't hurt anyone,' she replied, and took a sip of wine. 'I'm not a bad person, Katie.'

'Bad people always say that.'

'Only when they get caught.'

She broke off a piece of bread and folded it between her lips. The sun had put a pink blush on the tablecloth and I glanced out at the men in black leather promenading in Old Compton Street. Soho was halfway between our respective parts of London, a good place to meet, and Lizzie always felt at home in its aura of decadence. I was overcome suddenly by a rush of happiness, a sense of calm.

'Yes, let's do that,' I said. 'Let's do dinner.'

She placed her knife and fork at an angle across her empty plate.

'My place,' she suggested. 'After a couple of drinks, Ray usually goes off on one of his rants against *everything* – bankers, officers, particularly procurement officers, whatever the hell they are, journalists, politicians, lawyers, Tony Blair, the television, vox pops, talking heads, bishops, supermarkets, taxi drivers...'

'I'm with him there.'

'I thought you liked taxi drivers. You spend half your life in them.'

'I like taxis. Not the drivers. They always talk about the past, and my legs, or if I'm meeting my boyfriend.'

'It must be such a burden being you.'

'Anyway, I'm taking buses now.'

'You told me the other day you spent more money on taxis than rent.'

'That was the other day.'

'Unbelievable. You're so unpredictable.'

'I try.'

She finished her wine. 'I worship taxi drivers. They're so macho the way they turn in front of the other traffic and skirt through the backstreets.'

'That I do like.'

'That's a relief. I thought for a moment I was sitting here with someone I didn't know.' She added some sparkling water to her wine glass. 'I'm not sure what Ray thinks about doctors.'

'Tom can handle it...'

'That's sweet. So unlike you.' She stared at me across the table. 'It sounds as if you have finally fallen.'

I unwrapped the end of my wrap and ate the contents with a fork. 'I don't know what *that* means.'

'I know you don't. I've read your books. Exquisite as they are, love is one area you have studiously avoided.'

'I have never avoided love. It was never pertinent to the plot. My books are about self-discovery...'

'Don't tell me what your books are about, I edited them,' she said. 'I'm happy for you. It doesn't happen very often. It has *never* happened for me.'

'What about Lisa Lundt?'

'Ah, the hip-bones. Her breasts,' she ran her palm over her breast to her throat. 'The hollow here,' she said, 'her eyes, her nose, her tongue...ah, her tongue...'

'Stop. You're making me go all shivery.'

'She does that, I can't tell you...' She paused, and her brow furrowed. 'You never did tell me why he was alone on New Year's Eve. Is there a twist in the tail?'

'There was someone,' I said. 'A French girl, a cellist.'

'Beautiful?'

I shrugged. 'Delicious.'

'What happened?'

'He found her in bed...with her brother.'

'That's absolutely glorious. I'm so jealous.'

'You don't have a brother.'

'It's the idea, it's so literary. You'll use it, of course?'

'I don't know.'

'You must. It's a gift. What's her name?'

'Marie-France.'

'You only write about yourself. It will stretch you.'

She called the waiter and asked for another glass of wine. I was going to say I don't only write about myself, but didn't. We believe what we want to believe.

The waiter came, filled her glass and glanced at me, bottle hovering, a mischievous look in his dark eyes.

'No thank you,' I said, and he gave a little shrug and wiggle as he left the table.

I caught myself wondering what Marie-France would have done that day having lunch with a friend, how the *bonheur verre de vin* glues the different parts of life's mystery together. Lizzie raised her glass.

'Cheers,' she said. 'How's the writing going?'

151

'Oh, you know, slow, depressing. It'd like an endless game of Scrabble.'

'You think so?'

'All the words are there, you just have to keep dipping into you head to find new ways to arrange them. Everything you can think of has been thought of before.'

'There's nothing new under the sun.'

'Beware of Greeks bearing gifts. That's the thing, you see. As soon as you see the word sly, you want to say: as a fox. Cold as ice. At the end of the day. Too many cooks. When all is said and done. On a level playing field...'

'All you need is love?' she said and shook her head. 'Never mind. The Beatles. You're too young.'

'The hardest thing in the world is to be original. It seems like our heads are filled with banalities and clichés. You have to keep digging deeper and deeper to try and find a fresh new seam that hasn't been explored.'

'That's just what you're good at,' she said. 'Great writing requires great courage, great doubt and great confidence.'

'Who said that?'

'I did. You have it.'

'Well, I have the doubt, that's a start.' I paused for a second. 'What if I have no more than a frail talent, one of those little rosebuds that never opens and blooms?'

'Frail talent,' she repeated. 'Don't think about it. Just do what you do and see where it takes you – which I know you're going to do anyway.'

The waiter returned to our table. Did we want coffee? Yes, we did want coffee. And, no, we didn't want dessert. Lizzie decided to order another glass of wine and my phone vibrated.

14
Tunnel of Love

Texts buzzed back and forth, brief and business-like, with occasional kisses. Tom was at a meeting to discuss the refugee situation in Syria, and was going to be late. He had been following the developments and left the papers folded back on articles he wanted me to read. It was all so depressing. War is like the seasons, sunrise and sunset, an endlessly repeating cycle.

We met as the sun dipped behind the trees in Battersea Park, the bare branches moving on the darkening night like the arms of people watching some moving event. There was an old-fashioned funfair with music grinding from tin speakers, the Everly Brothers, Elvis, Buddy Holly, their songs scored with jangling chords and optimism. The air smelled of hot dogs and candy floss.

The sky turned black and the fairy lights created a bubble under which we were a part of London's M&M's bag of humanity, families with bright-eyed concentration as they set out on the quest of pleasure. Children spiralled down the helter-skelter on coconut mats; horses with mournful faces charged at full gallop on the carousel; the big dipper shuddered over silver rails.

We stood at the side of a stall where two couples were throwing bean bags at a pyramid of cans stacked on a shelf trying to win a panda with a cute face. The showman leaned over and pointed at me.

'Come here, come here a minute,' he said. 'I'll tell you what, darling, you've got a lucky face.'

He dropped two sets of three bags in front of us as we took a step closer.

'Don't know about a lucky face,' said Tom. 'You look like the panda.'

'What, an endangered species?'

He glanced back again at the stuffed toy sitting there with its cockeyed smile and legs stretched out. 'What are we going to do with it?' he said.

'That's like asking what you are going to do with your winnings when you buy a lottery ticket.'

'You have to think positive. I'll put it on my cot. Then, I'll think of you when I go to bed at night,' he said, and it reminded me that he would soon be leaving.

'We've been invited to have dinner with Lizzie, a friend of mine,' I told him.

'Best news I've had all day. I've been dying to meet some of your friends.'

'Her boyfriend's something in Special Forces, a sergeant, mad by all accounts.'

'Sounds even more interesting.'

The stallholder butted in. 'Well, Lucky Lady, you going to have a go or what?' he said, and I admired his persistence as I went for my purse.

'I'll get it,' Tom said, and I shook my head.

'No, I'm the lucky one, don't forget.'

'Actually, I think I am.'

It was a moment, just a moment. Our eyes met and I wanted to go home, climb into my big bed, feel his hands on me, his chest holding me still, a dream sequence interrupted by the stallholder.

'Right then,' he said, and the flashback had gone.

'How much is it?' I asked.

'Two pounds, each,' he replied.

'That's robbery.'

'Bank crisis, not me, darling.'

We got serious. We studied the angles, measured the distance, weighed the bean bags.

'The panda's such a great symbol,' Tom said. 'Look. It's half black, half white and comes from Asia.'

'Did you make that up?'

'No.'

'I won't use it then.'

He laughed. I liked his laugh, it was real, natural; it bubbled up like champagne over the top of the bottle.

'How's your finger?' he then asked.

'Up for it,' I replied.

'Are you doing the exercises?'

'Zealously,' I assured him.

He counted down like it was a moon mission, three, two, one...and we launched our greasy cloth bags of beans at separate sets of cans; to use them all on one stack was against the rules. The people before us had, with each attempt, tried to take out the middle can at the base of the six-can pyramid. The strategy scattered the outer cans, leaving two hard shots with only two bags. I went for the wing cans with the objective of clipping the central can by default, not that it worked, the presence of the remaining can always left behind on the shelf siphoning the money from my purse as we had another go, and another, performing the very act I had mentally mocked when I'd observed the two couples before us trying and failing.

'I thought I had a lucky face,' I said to the showman and he threw up his hands.

'You almost had that last one, you should have another go.'

'I don't think my bank manager would approve.'

'Now, they're the real robbers,' he said, and glanced away as he spotted another girl blessed with a lucky face.

We ambled through the crowd. Children fished for ducks and threw hoops over jars to win small stuffed toys. We watched a man bring a mallet down on a wooden block, a metal clanger rose up a numbered scale like a barometer and everyone cheered when a bell rang and he won a stuffed monkey. His girlfriend clapped and looked proud, her silver heels sunk in the mud, her lips drawn back in a delicious smile. The barrel organ ground out a merry melancholic tune, and an older couple wearing grave expressions were waltzing. A white balloon with a candle inside rose into the sky and the girls on the big dipper trembled with secret pleasure.

In the tube, on buses, in the street, if you catch people when they lift their gaze from their smart phones, they mostly look lost, bewildered, unsure about their lives, their relationships, the meaning, not of existence, just their own existence. People live with the vague fear of things over which they have no control, the weather, neighbours, bosses, unemployment, low pay, long hours, gangs, university fees, mortgages, interest rates, wars in far away places. Inside the light dome over the park those things were forgotten. They were happy, we were happy, and happiness is fleeting, it has to be held on to when it comes.

I grabbed Tom's arm.

'I'm starving,' he said.

'You're always starving.'

'It's true.'

We grinned. We were filling in the blanks like a painting by numbers. We held on to each other's eyes another moment and I pulled closer as we stood in line behind an Indian family, dad in a coat and tie, mum in a sari, their children, two girls and a boy in new clothes from Gap and French Connection, a generational disconnect. The eldest of the girls was about fifteen, skinny and chic. Her gaze went over my jacket with the leopard collar and she smiled as our eyes met.

'From Zara,' I said.

'I must get one,' she whispered.

'Yes, you must.'

The line shuffled along like refugees at a soup kitchen, I thought, and of course it wasn't like that at all, the simile springing to mind utter rubbish. I tried to imagine what I would have been doing that night without him in my life. It would never have entered my mind to visit the funfair. I would have been on the other side of the river in one of the clubs on the Kings Road, or in Wardour Street sipping champagne with a stranger prior to the danger rush speeding through the night in the back of a black cab.

With intermittent affairs with actors and photographers, my life was a cycle of research for Greta and Sophie and Milly, the girls who drew breath in my stories, little bits of me cloaked in the mask of words. At that very moment, I was gathering and distilling impressions from the movements of the crowd, the faces animated by the shadows and lights. The girl who had admired my jacket was now a character. She turned her head and smiled as she wandered off with her family, and it struck me that I was a part of London's multihued, polylingual population, not a species apart observing the city with the gloom and distance of the reactionary press, the bigots.

We ate hot dogs dripping ketchup and mustard. He finished mine. I licked the red and yellow smear of war-paint from his cheek and he leapt up on the high step around the dodgems. He pulled me up.

'Come on, I bet you're good at this?'

'I've never tried.'

'If you've never tried you've never lived.'

He was smiling, boyish, the orphans of Sri Lanka forgotten for a moment. We ran across the steel floor and I stepped into a cream dodgem with crimson flames flared along the sides. I heard on the soundtrack *My love is bigger than a Cadillac, something, something, something,* and adored the metaphor, the energy. I jammed my foot down on the pedal and fled. He chased me around the circuit and rammed my car into the barrier. Orange sparks danced over the roof where the long arms at the rear of the dodgems grazed a meshwork of humming current.

A boy dressed from a fifties' film, tight jeans, white tee-shirt, red leather jacket, stepped on the rubber fender at the back of my car, leaned over to guide me in a tactical course and forced Tom's blue and silver charger into a head on collision with a man in a turban who waved his fist as he turned intent on revenge. They swerved and manoeuvred, butted each other like two stags fighting over a doe, and I slid out of reach with my private James Dean guiding the wheel. I could smell sweat and oil, the burnt sugar char of spent electricity. The night was cold but I didn't feel cold. My brow was damp. My fingers prickled with pins and needles and the world beyond the dodgems could have been a hologram.

The funfair appeals to the primitive genes buried in our DNA. It's where girls taste their first kiss and boys scar each other in knife fights. On the wet earth shoes grow muddy and faces gleam. The big wheel releases long shadows as it churns like a giant clock against the velvet night where unknown birds trace patterns on the invisible sky. Beneath the strobe lights and spotlights the people take on the appearance of dream creatures with luminous eyes and immobile faces, flamenco dancers and matadors, and I was transported back suddenly to an Andaluz night, hot as day, on an empty beach with a boy just met. We listened to the waves stealing into the bay and swam naked in the murmuring sea. We listened to the drums in some club along the coast. We listened to the falling stars hissing across the sky. We made love on the sand and never saw each other again. His name was Paco. He had black hair, shiny as a Cadillac, and he was beautiful.

Tom slipped his arm around my waist as we queued for seats on the big dipper. The ghosts of our breath disappeared, fleeing into the night. I gazed up at the vast network of girders and joists, a towering flimsy structure like something built by an ancient civilization, its meaning and purpose lost to time. My heart beat faster as we settled into a metal carriage behind an iron safety bar, our bodies pressed together, the music muted, the lights dimmed as if glowing through mist. The wheels juddered beneath us and my back grew clammy as the train of cars climbed the incline. The night as we rose turned black and I could taste ice in my mouth. The helter-skelter and dodgems below became buildings laid out in a toy town, the people small as ants moving aimlessly in every direction.

We reached the peak, the train shuddered, paused, as divers pause at the end of the diving board, and I screamed as we plunged grinding and screeching over the silver rails. Up we went again, rising into the void, and it felt as if the past had been wiped clean as we dived into the abyss. I buried my head in Tom's arms and he slipped his hand inside my jacket to still the red bird fluttering in my breast.

On the carousel I rode the white horse from my dream. Tom galloped along at my side on a black stallion with a golden mane, up and down, and it's like making love, the same rhythm, the same motion, the continuous rotations making me feel giddy. The wooden saddle slid over my sex and I grew oddly content sitting on the carousel beside this man who had come into my life like a stiff wind on a still day. I hadn't seen him since morning. We hadn't made love since before breakfast and I wanted to go home and make love again.

When you remove love from sex you enter a mansion with many rooms shaded in nuance and excess, an invitation to peel away all conventions and programming. A chance to explore your hidden self. A chance to be wicked. You shed something and clothe yourself in something else. Sex is the greatest of gifts, orgasm a glimpse of perfection. When you add love to sex it feels as if your soul is being drawn from the chains of gravity into the core of the infinite. New feelings come to life, emotions without explanations that we try to name with that perplexing little word we avoid using as if the word is sacred or sacrilegious.

Love is indefinable, a mystery, a distant light in the shadow of death: Romeo and Juliet. Tristan and Isolde. Mickey and Mallory from *Natural Born Killers.* Love is the twin of death, the conqueror of death. Love bends and curves like space and time. When you are in love you are less afraid of death because you would give your life for the object of your love. If love is blind and unconditional it must be because we have no control over it. Like nature. Like the tectonic plates below the earth's surface. Mothers feel that way about their children. But love and being in love are not the same. A woman takes the man she loves into her body and absorbs his oils and essence. A part of him enters her and becomes a part of her.

Love changes the chemical balance in the brain like a drug. It is a drug. Food tastes better. The rain on your face feels warm. When you dance it feels as if the notes of music emerge like an invisible chain that links directly to your moving feet. You smile for no reason. You like people you would not normally like. You forgive them. Love is like being on a small boat in the middle of the sea with no compass and no one to rely on except each other. Falling in love is completion. Falling out of love is a mini-death. I had, as Lizzie said, avoided writing about love and had never sensed that rush and buzz that comes with love, the release into the brain of body chemicals, pheromones and dopamine – the taste of love to which I was becoming addicted, his spearminty tongue when we kissed, his male sweat, the outdoor vanilla tang of his semen.

We bought candy floss, whirls of pink sugar on a stick, impossible to eat. Flags and bunting snapped at the air as we made our way towards the gate that would take us back to the Albert Bridge. We paused midway between the Ghost Train and the Tunnel of Love.

'One last ride?' he said.

'Which one?'

'You chose.'

I shook my head. 'I hate making decisions.'

'Is that true?'

'No, not at all,' I said, and he put his arms around me; he stroked my hair and I felt like one of his orphans gathered up.

'You love being contrary.'

'No I don't,' I replied and we both burst out laughing.

'Well, what's it to be?'

He released me and I looked around.

'Neither, I said. 'Come on.'

159

I led him towards the House of Mirrors. I paid and we snaked through the eerie light, two beautiful creatures from the masquerade, two grotesques from a drawing by William Blake, *tyger, tyger burning bright.* I was tall and short, fat and thin, joyful and sad. All the things that we are, and all the things we imagine we are, appear in the mirrors. I could see again that Andaluz night. I could see myself across the candlelit table with my tutor. I could see myself with Mr Devlin losing my virginity over and over again. The past emerges like the dead rising from their graves. The reflections reflect each other capturing movements and moments, and again I was reminded of *Nude Descending a Staircase,* the genius of it. The placement of each mirror in the maze was juxtaposed against the next, yet isolated, and I got the feeling that I was removed from time, that time wasn't continuous, but omnipresent, not a progression, but a ball of mirrors, that everything that ever was and everything that ever will be were connected by a cycle, by cause and effect.

Just as you have to squeal on the big dipper, you have to laugh in the House of Mirrors. We stood close together, our features elastic in the bowed and bent glass. I saw us as an old couple, withered and sparkly still. We moved on, turned a corner. We had long faces like the figure in Munch's *The Scream* and compressed faces like a half-eaten hamburger. Marie-France appeared and disappeared. I saw myself in Lizzie. And Bella. And Mother. And the Chinese girl in the photograph with Daddy in Singapore. The mask under the mask slips away and in the House of Mirrors the stranger you see is yourself.

15
Death and the Maiden

My tutor's rooms were at the end of a narrow passage lit solely by a leaded window with scratched dimpled glass. The passage led to the back of the building and ended at a wooden door slightly askew in it frame. I gave the door two taps. There was no reply. I knocked again, a little harder, and his voice rang out like Don Giovanni in Mozart's opera.

'Yes, yes. I'm not deaf?'

I turned the handle and entered Professor Masters' den for the first time. It was hot with a gas fire blazing and the winter light filigreed with the curls of blue smoke that rose from the incense burning in a teak holder. He was sitting in the centre of a black leather sofa stabbing the pages of the paper he was reading, a red marker pen gripped in his fingers like a scalpel.

'Just wait a moment,' he said, and waved me towards the alcove on the far side of his study.

Dons' rooms tend to be shabby with ancient dust ground into ancient desks, books ranged like mountains of impregnable knowledge on every surface and two centuries of pipe smoke staining the ceiling. By contrast, Oliver Masters had created from his cloistered space the incongruous feel of a Berber tent with oriental rugs, saffron walls hung with black and white images in miniature frames and no chairs, just beaded cushions marooned around the sofa. The incense smell of dead flowers made me feel giddy and, the longer I stood listening to the scratching sound of the red pen pressing against the paper, the more ill at ease I became.

There was a draught around the window. The garden outside was planted with palms and banana plants wrapped in polythene to protect them from the frost. They appeared in the thin light like a row of beggars below the leaden sky. Like the tropical flora, I was bundled up with just as much care in a grey cashmere v-neck over a blue silk blouse, a grey wool skirt too short for the season, blue tights, black leather boots and a ski-jacket to keep me warm.

The weather was bitter, but it was hot in the room and my back grew damp.

'May I take my jacket off?' I asked.

'I beg your pardon?'

'My jacket, it's...'

'Take off anything you want.'

As he read through the last pages of what I realized was my essay, I studied him in profile. Oliver Masters had a large head with curly dark hair threaded through with silver streaks, a nose like the prow of a Viking ship, and a jutting chin that supported a clipped beard that he fondled as he concentrated, his focus like a snake before it strikes its prey.

I had on various occasions watched him striding across the medieval cobbles of Trinity, but it was the first time I had seen him up close, the first time I had been alone in his presence. I felt like the mouse beguiled by the cobra, terrified and lured as if by a gravity. My tutor was wearing a voluminous white shirt, faded denims with split knees and his bare feet crossed at the ankles seemed inexplicably large and intimate.

He turned back to the first page of the essay and read in a staccato voice.

'Hell Is Other People.'

He looked up. I tried a smile and my shoulders rose in an agreeable shrug. He glanced down again at the pages on his lap.

'You are Catherine Boyd?'

'Yes, I am...'

He looked surprised. 'You have from the two million words penned by Jean-Paul Sartre chosen the most renowned and overused quote as the title for your first assignment. Intriguing,' he said before reading the opening paragraph. 'Jean-Paul Sartre was born on 21 June 1905 and died on 15 April 1980. A novelist, playwright and critic, he is best known as an existentialist philosopher who famously refused to accept the Nobel Prize for Literature in 1964.' He paused. 'Why?'

I felt a moment's reprieve as I reeled off the answer. 'He believed writers should remain independent and awards would make them a part of the establishment.'

He sighed. 'I mean why are you writing this twaddle?'

My mouth turned dry and my voice became a whisper. 'I'm not sure what you mean?'

He shook his head. 'Sit down,' he instructed. I did so, at his feet, and looked up into his brown eyes; they were huge, like two holes in space. 'Where did you attend school, may I ask?'

'Saint Sebastian's...'

'Ah, yes, in Broadstairs,' he continued, as if it confirmed some principle. 'Nuns believe they can beat knowledge into girls, but that's not discipline, it's restraint. It doesn't open the mind. It closes the mind. What you have done with this...this essay, Miss Boyd, is show me what you know. I don't want to know what you know. I want to know what you think.'

He dropped the papers on the floor beside the sofa and shook his hand towards the corner of the room. 'Go and get the blue binder on my desk.'

The leather cushion where I was sitting was soft and low, awkward to rise from. My skirt ran up over my thighs as I scrambled to my feet and a flush bloomed on my neck as I realized that he was staring at my open legs. I found the folder he wanted, he wiggled his fingers, as you might to a waiter unnecessarily refilling a wine glass, and I sat again.

'Are you comfortable?' he asked.

'Yes,' I replied, though comfortable was the last thing I felt. I felt foolish and out of my depth, hair glossy with conditioner, unsuitably chic, all the experiences of that long hot summer wiped clean from my hard drive.

He opened the binder and read in a faintly mocking tone.

'Jean-Paul Sartre was a misogynist fart, an alcoholic faux-Marxist riddled through like Swiss cheese with envy for his lover Simone de Beauvoir and his nemesis Albert Camus, both better writers, and in the case of Camus, also a better goalkeeper.' He took a breath. 'Well.'

'It's...it's interesting...'

He waved away the remark and went back to the text:

'It was Søren Kierkegaard who proposed, fifty years before Sartre's birth, that it is not society or religion, but the individual who is responsible to give meaning to his own life. To achieve this, we must live with sincerity and passion, what Kierkegaard called authenticity. In a classic illustration of style over content, Kierkegaard's themes were so ravaged by Sartre there is a belief that he, Jean-Paul, is the great existentialist, not merely a lumpen farmer furrowing someone else's field.' He sniffed. 'Odd use of the word lumpen, but at least there is something here to amuse me.'

He tossed the essay on the floor, on top of my own, smothering it, and nursed his large hands with a moment's melancholy.

'I'm sorry,' I began, and he held up his palm.

'Here enter no hypocrites or bigots, as Rabelais once remarked. Neither is there room for regret,' he said, and leaned forward. 'Zen adepts sometimes spend decades meditating in an attempt to reach a state of satori.' He paused. 'You know what that means?'

'Yes.'

'Good for you,' he remarked; foolishly, I smiled. 'There are times when a great master creeps up on a novice to bash him over the head with a length of bamboo. At that moment, the novice is stunned in a way that he awakens from the nightmare of the mundane to a state of enlightened bliss. A moment's pain can clear the mind of a lifetime of drivel and dross. As Georges Bataille put it, through pain we find the greatest pleasure. You are aware of his work?'

'No.'

'Then we will have to rectify that omission in your education.' He looked into my eyes. 'Do you believe in discipline?'

'Yes, yes I do.'

He sat back and his tone changed. 'My mother is French, you know. When I was seven, she sent me to the school that her father had attended, and his father before him. It is outside Reims in a Gothic building and maintains a Gothic attitude to corporal punishment. If you misbehave, or write a poor piece of work,' he stressed, 'then you are spanked.'

I had been holding my breath and let it out in a gasp. 'Oh!' I exclaimed, and he leaned forward.

'In my honest opinion, a good spanking is exactly what you need.'

His eyes gleamed and his words hung in the air like a phrase in Latin that means something quite different from what you had previously thought it meant. With his prominent nose and inscrutable expression, Oliver Masters had the appearance of an Arabian sheik in a story from Scheherazade and I felt, squatting cross-legged at his feet, like a slave girl trapped in his saffron kingdom. The silence stretched, and I was conscious, as I had been conscious eight weeks before driving to Black Spires, that my skirt had risen up my thighs.

Of course, I didn't have to stay sitting there. I could have protested. I could have stalked out, slammed the slanted door and reported to a higher authority that Professor Masters had made coarse and potentially violent remarks. But I didn't. I was intrigued as well as shocked, attracted as well as repelled. It is one of my qualities or frailties that I can carry twin emotions at the same time and see both sides of an argument. I am aware as I dress that I am doing so to make an impression, or an entrance, that I make the most of the raw material and accentuate the result with patent indifference. I had dressed in soft clingy fabrics to make sure I made a favourable first impression; a woman in a man's world, which academia remains, must call upon all of her assets, and there was another person, another me, gazing from a future not that far distant thinking: you are being seduced and one day you will write about it.

The flames of the gas fire baked the air. The incense carried a heady perfume on its silvery blue smoke.

'Well?' he asked.

'I'm not sure what to say,' I mumbled.

'You are not sure what to say because you are not sure what to write,' he said. 'At school you were taught to learn facts and regurgitate them in a feat of memory. In this place, if I set an essay on Jean-Paul Sartre, I assume you already know the texts. Your task is to amuse me, as well as to try and interpret and extend our knowledge of the subject. Is that clear?'

'Yes, that's...'

He held up his hand and looked fiercely back at me. 'Don't for heaven's sake say as clear as crystal, or day, or drinking water. We want no clichés here...Catherine, is that what they call you?'

'Katie,' I answered. 'Except when someone's angry with me.'

He smiled for the first time. 'Your education,' he said, pausing, 'begins here.' He tapped the arm of the sofa. 'Do you want to succeed?'

'In what sense?'

He smiled again and again I felt irrationally pleased knowing I had made the right response.

'In every sense,' he said, and carried on. 'Because if you want to, you will.' He tapped the side of his head. 'It is all up here. If you have purpose and perseverance, which I assume you do, you need to combine that with an overwhelming desire to succeed. And what is success? Success is setting goals, making a definite plan and setting out on the journey to accomplish that plan without allowing anything to stop you. Success is finding every facet of yourself and polishing it until it shines.'

He pushed himself up, reached for my hand and pulled me to my feet in such a way that, for a second, our bodies were thrown together. He stared into my eyes.

'Is success that simple? No, it is not. Quite aside from patience and persistence, you require an element of flexibility. It is why the Germans lose wars. When it snows in winter, the willow bends. The oak stands rigid holding the weight of the snow until it's limbs crack and break. Are you an oak or a willow?'

'A willow,' I replied, and he nodded his large head.

'If you do everything that is demanded of you, in twelve months you will be all that you can be.'

I felt breathless, exhausted. My stomach muscles had clenched.

'Thank you,' I whispered.

'Come,' he said.

He kept a grip on my hand as we made our way to the bookcase behind the desk. As he ran his fingers along the spines, my eyes were drawn to the collection of prints that hung in four lines between the bookshelves and alcove. The frames were about the size of a CD case and contained pictures of men and women in pairs and groups entwined in sexual positions that were both acrobatic and so...so carnal, my throat tightened again and the tic in my temple that throbbed when I was nervous began to drill through the skin.

He pulled out the book he was seeking, placed it on the desk, and turned back to me, his eyes glowing in the fleeting burst of sunlight that broke through the clouds and lit the room. He then moved along the row of images so that we could study them together.

'Aren't they wonderful?'

I didn't reply. He stopped as if to urge me to respond, and I looked away, back at the gallery of sexual couplings, each drawing showing how the human form, particularly the female form, can twist and open to be skewered and lanced in endless positions. The further we moved along the four lines of prints, the more prurient they became until, finally, not only humans in mounting numbers, but animals, demons and mythical creatures joined the spectacle in one astonishing and implausible orgy.

'They are copies of illustrations from an edition of the *Kama Sutra* dating back to the 14th century,' he explained. 'Remarkable, no?'

'Yes, yes, remarkable.'

'You are not embarrassed, Katie?'

'No.'

'Your cheeks are red.'

'Are they?'

His eyebrows went up. 'There is nothing that pleases me more than reddened cheeks,' he said and changed the subject, pointing at the book he had placed on the desk. 'Possessions possess, don't you agree?'

It felt as if I had swam across the Rubicon and was safely on shore again. 'Yes, I do.'

'Do you mean that? Or are you trying to please me?'

'No, I mean it.'

'I don't want you to please me if it is against your will.'

'I won't.'

'That has to be clear. Free Will Rules, OK?' he said oddly, and waited for me to respond.

'OK,' I repeated.

He took a grip on my upper arms and spoke with sudden passion. 'If the existentialists are right, that life is meaningless, and if we acknowledge that, we are better equipped to find pleasure in small things.' He looked at me beseechingly.

'Yes, I see that.'

He let go of my arms. 'I imagine at your school you went to chapel most days?'

'Every single day.'

'And you are a believer?'

I shook my head. 'No. Not really.'

'Intelligent people who claim to believe are either dissemblers, or have some sexual or psychological flaw they disguise behind a mask.' His expression changed. 'Our responsibility is to shed the shackles of our bourgeois inhibitions, live with authenticity and let go of attachments.'

He retrieved the book from the table and gave it to me.

'Thank you.'

'I must now admit to an inconsistency,' he confessed. 'This book is precious to me. It is a signed first edition that I rarely lend out. It is for your next assignment. Your Jean-Paul Sartre is neatly presented with adequate references, a case of care over content, and barely worth a D. Let's see if we can do better next time.'

'Yes, I will,' I replied, his use of the word 'we' buzzing in my ear.

'You will remember everything I have said today?'

'You can be sure of that, Professor Masters.'

'Oliver,' he said, and showed perfect, large white teeth in his smile.

He crossed the room and I followed, the book in one hand, my jacket in the other. He stopped at the door, turned the handle and stared at me with that look people have when they study themselves in the mirror wearing something new. As I made my way out, he tapped my bottom. It wasn't a smack or a slap, just a tap, entirely inappropriate, but I thought of it at that moment as a cerebral rather than physical gesture, a sign that he had invited me on to the high ground where we would both gaze upon the same broad intellectual horizons.

I had bought a black, narrow-lined notebook from Ryman's to jot down quotes and ideas separate from the notes I made for my course work. On the first page I had written: Knowing others is intelligence; knowing yourself is true wisdom. Mastering others is strength; mastering yourself is true power. If you realize that you have enough, you are truly rich.

The words are from the *Tao Te Ching,* a collection of aphorisms by the Chinese philosopher Lao Tzu written 500 years BC, a work I had grown to admire. Asked by the Emperor how he should rule the kingdom, Lao Tzu tells him that he should rule the kingdom as he would cook a small fish. Lao Tzu was quick, canny, brusque and famously did not easily suffer fools. After meeting Lao Tzu for the first time, Confucius is supposed to have said: I would rather be thrown into a pit of vipers than spend thirty minutes in discourse with Lao Tzu.

I felt a bit like that after thirty minutes with Professor Masters, my guide through the first year philosophy module that was part of my degree. I had taken the course at the suggestion of Alicia Pym, an Old Basher who had gone up to Cambridge a year before me. 'Oliver Masters is just so...masterful,' she'd cooed. As the only girl from Saint Sebastian's at my college, I felt obliged to take her advice.

When I made my way back along the passage from his rooms that day, my head was spinning and I had a stabbing sensation in my right pupil, the sign of a coming migraine. I couldn't work out if my tutor's remarks were tiered in subtext, or if such implications were the product of my imagination. What with the heat, the peculiarity of sitting at his feet and those singular ink drawings, all that I had seen and all that he had said were spiralling through my brain like the pale smoke from the smouldering incense.

Rushing back to my room, I slipped on the frosty stones crossing Nevile's Court, cut my knee and tore a hole in my new tights.

'Bugger,' I said.

'Bless you,' came the unexpected response of a thin young cleric who passed at that moment and didn't pause to help me up. I wondered what sexual-psychological flaw was hidden behind the mask of his white collar and realised as the thought drifted through my head that I was already intoxicated by the influence of Oliver Masters.

A statue, of whom I had no idea, was peering down at me with the look of an ancient member of a gentlemen's club still riled that women were allowed in for lunch Sundays. I heard the clock in the medieval tower strike four times, it did it twice, first on a low note, then on a much higher one, a variation from a piece of classical music I knew but couldn't place.

In halls, I swallowed two Nurofen Plus and stared at my gaunt reflection in the mirror. My skin was grey and my cheek bones seemed to be breaking through the flesh.

In my honest opinion, a good spanking is exactly what you need.

I said the words aloud to myself.

Did he mean this in the literal sense, or was this some intellectual reference I didn't know or understand? He had called my essay 'twaddle,' then said: 'A moment's pain clears the mind of a lifetime of drivel and dross.'

Pain, yes, but in what sense?

He asked me. 'Do you believe in discipline?'

I do, I told him. But by that I meant the discipline required in study. I don't often agree with Mother's glib maxims, but that time when she discovered the maid had stacked up numerous bags of ironing *para mañana,* she told her, 'You don't get ahead by falling behind,' which I thought was both witty and true, not that Golo had any idea what she was talking about.

Ah, yes, si, gracias, Misses Boiled.

Professor Masters had declared that 'nothing pleases me more than reddened cheeks,' an image that may conjure up the gaudy makeup highlighting the cheeks of a dancer swirling her petticoats at the Folies Bergère, but I felt confident it was something quite different in his mind.

Or was it in my mind?

Not at all. I had thought of university as an extension of school. It wasn't like that. I was no longer a child sheltered behind convent walls, but a woman familiar with the ways of the world; at least to my own immature perceptions. Before that hot summer of 2003 turned into a golden autumn, I had been introduced to *Pink* by Bella and Tara. I had walked near naked across the club's pastel-lit dance floor in the mask that had found me in a little basement in Old Compton Street. I had entered dim nooks and niches with women likewise masked to discover, as Bella famously said, it's fun being a girl. I had felt liberated after that day at Black Spires and wasn't sure why I was so shocked to find my tutor setting the stage in much the same way as Roger Devlin when he asked me to remove my shoes and walk barefoot on the grass.

I turned the book Professor Masters had given me through my hands as if it were a religious relic.

'Eroticism,' I said, and said it again. *'Eroticism.'*

It was by Georges Bataille, the writer he had mentioned, the writer of whom I knew nothing and would end up knowing everything. His book was first published by Les Editions de Minuit in 1957. What I clutched in my damp palms was the first English translation by Mary Dalwood, published in 1962 by Calder and Boyars. I make a point of reading the copyrights and small print before reading a book and see it as a courtesy, like watching film credits before leaving the cinema and coming away knowing that the best boy was Bill *Sparky* Baker.

The book's single word title *Eroticism* immediately evoked everything louche and vulgar that I could think of, and I was relieved to discover as I skimmed the Introduction that it was not a raunchy novelette, but a history of erotica, taboo, mysticism and transgression through the ages, a study of human urges, passions and the impulses that, according to Bataille, exist in the night of our subconscious like creatures in darkness seeking the light.

He opens his study with this sentence: 'Eroticism, it may be said, is assenting to life up to the point of death.'

I found this baffling and enthralling. I drank a glass of water. My headache had dulled to a faint throb. I read the book from cover to cover without taking notes and was about to start reading it again when I realized I was hungry. My room with its high fluted ceiling and dormer window had turned inky with shadows. More than three hours had gone by and the Nurofen had turned to acid in my stomach.

The sky was black and clear, though starless, and my breath drifted from my lips in feathery coils. The walls of Trinity loomed up like Mount Doom from *The Lord of the Rings,* and I realized as I reached for the simile how it belonged to who I had been in my scarlet blazer sitting exams in the spring, not who I was and might become. My leg hurt from the fall, but the cold was an anaesthetic and I was wearing the same blue stockings, the hole in the knee buttoned by a bloody scab.

I was still learning my way around Cambridge and wandered the winding streets clutching my book like a simulacrum of every scholar who had walked those same streets across the vagaries of the last five hundred years. I was conscious, too, that I was a beneficiary of the college's current updates, a young woman bearing a copy of *Eroticism* after centuries of bent men nursing the Bible, including those, like Oliver Masters, whose intention was to subvert its contents – Bertrand Russell, Francis Bacon, Wittgenstein, they had all pressed the leather of their soles on those ancient cobbles.

The sign *Slice of Melon* over the entrance to a wine bar drew me into a warm expanse of green leather banquettes in raised booths and Madonna whispering about sex over hidden speakers.

There were few customers and I found a seat in the corner below a yellow light bright enough for me to return to my book.

The waiter was young, good-looking, off-hand and had an accent from the north of England I was unable to place. In a moment of madness, I ordered a hamburger with bacon and blue cheese, a side of chips and a large white wine.

'How do you want the burger?'

'Five seconds after bloody,' I said.

'Haven't seen you in here before. You a fresher?'

'Yes,' I replied and he turned away.

'One more thing, a bottle of sparkling water, please,' I added, and he waved over his shoulder.

'Right you are.'

I ran once more through all the things my tutor had said and the same phrase kept coming back at me like an echo from the mirror: a good spanking is exactly what you need. What he was actually saying is: a good spanking is what I intend to give you, which was shocking, and all the more so that I wasn't more shocked. I was aware from reading Bataille, and perhaps that was the point of loaning me the book – the precious first edition – that I had been invited into an erotic, as much as a cerebral game, a surreal piece of theatre. On the stage he had constructed, in the scene he was setting, Professor Masters would play the role of the seer with cryptic knowledge, a contemporary Lao Tzu. I was cast as the desirable young woman, or 'privileged object of desire,' to use Bataille's phrase, the acolyte who had more to gain from conceding than resisting the inevitable course of the drama.

According to *Eroticism*, the pursuit of the erotic is to break down *all* barriers – to live so fully, even death loses its grip.

How do you do that, make that leap of faith? How fully is fully? Is sex erotic or passionate, and I wasn't even sure of the difference, the highest goal; the greatest attainment? A lot of girls at my school must have thought so. From the moment their breasts began to grow and their bottoms became rounder, they talked about little else. Like the rats and cats and orang-utans, is our prime motivation reproduction? Bataille says humans are uniquely graced with choice. Once you take reproduction out of the equation, what remains, he says, is bourgeois coupling doomed to ennui, or the uncovering of sexuality as if it were a

Spanish onion with endless gossamer thin layers of piquant potential.

The way Oliver Masters had arranged his study with the *Kama Sutra* prints, the burning joss sticks and distinct lack of chairs had hauled me like a little mouse in the talons of an eagle away from my old world of uniforms and Holy Sisters and dropped me like carrion on the far edge of my imagination. He had in his suite of rooms set out to seduce me intellectually as foreplay to a physical offensive, which I now anticipated and would be prepared for when it came.

The sulky waiter returned with the wine and water. He glanced at my book.

'What are you reading?'

I showed him.

'Never heard of it,' he said, shaking his head, and I felt a need to explain.

'It's a philosophical study.'

'Like the title,' he remarked, and I realized he was likewise a student, probably a bright grammar school boy juggling time working his way through college.

Mother had planned the same agenda for me. Like politicians who have never seen war and blithely send others into battle, she believed work would widen my horizons and, In one respect, at least, she was right: my four weeks as an intern with Drew Butler had not been entirely wasted.

My father was home the first two weeks of September. He was delighted that I was going to his old college and chatted wistfully about his time at Cambridge, years that had shaped his life, although not entirely in the shape he had imagined. Mother had entered his circle like a brightly burning flame in a red dress and they walked down the aisle at the Norman church at St Nicholas in Kent before knowing anything about each other beyond their backgrounds and class, those qualities that had once mattered so much and matter less now that it is solely money that matters. Father only came to realise when they were alone on their ten day honeymoon in Venice that they seldom saw things the same way, but avoided confrontation and set about fine-tuning Mother's decisions, the shapeshifter behind the scenes in marriage as in his career.

One morning, while I was bronzing in the garden, he slipped a book on the edge of my sunbed.

'Lovely day,' he whispered, and continued along the path to the rose arbour.

The book was *The Glass Bead Game* by Hermann Hesse, a sky-blue cheque like a bookmark tucked between the pages.

'I'm so dying to read it,' I called, and he turned with a bow, his long fingers revolving in a swirl like Raleigh with Elizabeth I.

He was inspecting the carnage left by the gardener and became Charlie Chaplin as he hacked his way through the overhanging roses with an invisible umbrella. I laughed until tears ran down my cheeks and it brings a tear to my eye even now as I recall those rare times when my quiet courteous father let go and became himself. Daddy had been briefly in the Footlights, classics paved the road to the Foreign Office, but he had secretly dreamed of the BBC.

The waiter had returned to his place behind the bar where two other young men sat on high stools nursing bottles of lager. It was obvious by the way in which the waiter leaned forward to whisper replies in answer to their questions that they were talking about me. Their eyes kept flicking in my direction and I stared back over my shoulder until they looked away. That night I realized that a girl alone with a book is always an object of fascination.

According to Bataille, corporal punishment is intrinsic to erotica as a corruptor of established patterns. Being dressed is civilized. Stripping naked, especially where it is inappropriate to do so, is a direct challenge to civilisation. Ultimately, the purpose of eroticism is to break down traditional thinking and attitudes in preparation for living life free of rules.

I had been subjected to those patterns of traditional thinking at my strict school and it seemed odd to me that parents and educators are not aware that the firmer the discipline the greater the desire to transgress. Within weeks of leaving school, I was performing a striptease for a complete stranger. From Black Spires to Pink had been a tiny step. I had been funnelled into one pattern and was freewheeling relentlessly into another.

My food came. I asked for another glass of wine and some mayonnaise to which I mixed a splash of ketchup, the marriage a guilty secret for dunking hot salty chips. I ignored the two boys at the bar with their furtive glances. The hamburger dripped, and I can see myself sitting beneath the yellow light with a hole in my stockings in that wine bar ten years ago reading Georges Bataille.

'As often as not, it seems to be assumed that man has his being independently of his passions. I affirm, on the other hand, that we must never imagine existence except in terms of these passions.'

I read the sentence a second time. I wiped my fingers on the paper napkin, and my mind slipped back once more to those weeks in September when Daddy was home. Mother had her bridge and tennis. Matt had formed a band among the rowers they'd called Rowlocks, and was constantly locked in his room with an electric guitar he was hopelessly learning to play. It was immediately after I had danced for Roger Devlin, and it occurred to me that there had been an oedipal element to that sudden urge to shed my virginity with an older man, a metaphorical passion to break the incest taboo, as Georges Bataille would have it. Fast forward ten years and I see myself in the skin of Marie-France floating on the surface of a moonlit swimming pool with the eyes of Kamarovsky watching. As Hesse explores in *The Glass Bead Game*, there is an invisible thread that runs through all things we can't understand and call destiny.

My father never went anywhere without a book tucked in his pocket and it was moving the way he led me those weeks a decade ago through his library as if Hesse, Kundera, Kazantzakis and John le Carré were stepping stones leading to his secret world. He said reading releases you from the limits of yourself, and I came to see that my father had always limited himself in pursuit of some ideal he wasn't entirely sure of, that England, his England, had become, in his lifetime, a country he no longer knew.

When I had finished reading *The Glass Bead Game,* we discussed Magister Ludi's quest for the key to perfect knowledge, his awareness in his final hours that death comes before the key is in your hand, that if life has meaning it is found in simple things, in what's happening now, today, that it is the journey not the destination that's important, a maxim so well known it is easily forgotten.

Father then gave me the darker, more abstract *Steppenwolf,* which I devoured, and it was curious that he should introduce me to Hesse's self-doubting cast of characters as I was about to start university. He left me to fathom his intentions, and I began to see that it is not the amassing of knowledge that's difficult, it is dealing with doubt and uncertainty, the curse and goad of the writer, the artist, the fresher flushed from convent into the rosy delights of Cambridge.

I sipped my wine. I was young, naïve, oddly content and suddenly excited to be the maiden from the medieval dance with death, the symbolic sacrifice to my tutor's unheavenly desires. In primitive times, when crops failed, or a volcano erupted, our ancestors placated the gods with human sacrifice, a girl stepping from childhood and, logically, the prettiest in the tribe. As Mother had said, speaking of herself, I'm sure, beauty is a burden, as well as a gift. Beauty puts less desirable women on edge and torments men. The smiling pink lips of a cute girl suggest that unsullied part of her that men want most. The fact that only one man is going to seize the prize provides logic to her slaughter and, paradoxically, while man is born appreciating beauty, just below the surface he carries a predisposition, a gut feeling that beauty should be profaned, scarred, destroyed. There is no more conclusive way to obliterate beauty than in human sacrifice, as Joan of Arc discovered at the hands of the heathen English.

Georges Bataille infers that there is an innate gratification in falling from grace, that the supreme pleasure of love is illicit love, a feeling that you are doing wrong. Add existentialism to eroticism and what do you get? I wasn't sure. But it was something I imagine Oliver Masters understood.

16
The Messenger

I cupped my breasts beneath the quilt and listened to the bells in the tower chime the hours. I was tingling, electric, and my head throbbed from cheap white wine. I would learn one day that life is too short.

Pearls of pale light slid over the walls, oblong fragments shaped by the window. It was the start of my drift to insomnia, stealthy as a cat, it creeps up on you like an addiction. At midnight, I got up, opened my notebook and began to write without thinking about what it was I was writing. At school, words for me had been iron bars that imprisoned thought. Suddenly, it felt as if the pen in my hand was a key to a secret box.

Day was breaking when I turned on my computer. I transferred the notes into my essay. Over the coming days and weeks, I phrased and rephrased; cut and slashed. I thought of Georges Bataille as my lover. I was subservient to his tender dominance, his thoughts in my head like a plangent hymn I couldn't stop singing. In the bullring, the terrified bull always returns to the same spot as if it is a place of safety. It is called the querencia. In writing, I had found my querencia. My place, my passion.

My next tutorial wasn't until the middle of November and I felt crushed when it was cancelled. Professor Masters was in London recording a radio programme on how Flaubert had created the first misery-memoir with his novel *Madame Bovary*. The next time I made my way down the corridor to his rooms was two weeks later. He opened the door the moment I knocked. He was wearing a green corduroy suit and an open-necked white shirt, a raincoat thrown over his shoulder. He had an unscheduled meeting he had to attend and was obliged to cancel again. He took my essay, tossed the blue folder I had brought it in on the sofa, and I followed him back down the stairs.

'Bataille?' he said

'Amazing.'

'Amazing,' he repeated. 'Yes, I suppose he is. Of course, the book's a lot more profound in the original. I didn't know if your French was up to it.'

'It isn't,' I admitted.

'Just as well, then.' He paused. 'Home for the holidays?'

'Yes.'

'Jolly good. Try not to do anything too pagan.'

'I won't...'

'And read for fun, not...information.'

I wanted to say more, but I wasn't sure what and the moment passed. He gave a sort of shrugging smile, slid his arms into his raincoat and I watched him march off down Trinity Street. The clock chimed three times, the low and high notes in urgent progression. I had been listening to the bells all night without being able to place the melody and a chill ran up my spine as I recalled the variation from Schubert's *Death and the Maiden*, the title I had given to my essay. The striker chimed, the bells rang out and I was struck by a revelation: it wasn't me who had sat up that night writing my own *Death and the Maiden*, but something outside of me. I wasn't a fount of creative thought, merely a messenger.

Professor Masters had just turned towards Green Street and I set out to follow him. He had a long stride and his pace was so fast I had to run down Trinity to catch up. I slowed as I rounded the corner. I watched him cross into Sidney Street and vanish into the wan light of Hobson's Passage. I lost sight of him as he cut through the crowds. I looked left and right as I left the passage, and caught a glimpse of his broad back in his raincoat as he made his way towards Christ College. From there, he entered the backstreets of the old town and I shadowed him through the maze.

I wasn't totally surprised when he entered the same wine bar where I had sat that night reading Bataille. I waited for a few minutes to catch my breath. I took a woolly hat from my bag to hide my hair, wrapped my scarf to cover the lower half of my face and felt like my father's daughter as I ambled past the bar. My tutor was sitting in a window seat with his back to me facing a woman I instantly recognised.

178

Ruth Raphael had been at Trinity ten years before me. An expert on everything, she had been on the same radio show as Oliver Masters and her face was familiar from staring out of *The Sunday Times* every week above her regular column about her brilliant life and other matters. In the photograph she has her hair pulled back and stares over half-moon glasses with that faintly raised-eye expression of people who know secrets. In the wine bar window, her wavy hair fell in dark curls to her shoulders and her brown eyes sparkled as she stared back across the table.

My breath misted through my scarf. I stood there for a long time and felt a stab of envy like a sharp knife which lasted through Christmas and was still smarting when I arrived back at college in January.

Two days after I had settled back, I received an email – Please call me. OM. I did so, on my new BlackBerry.

'I am so pleased you're back. We have to discuss Bataille. When are you free?'

It was rather a silly question, as I was free all the time. 'Whenever it's suitable,' I replied.

'Tonight,' he said. 'Meet me at the Great Gate, seven-thirty sharp. There's a little French place along the river. We can talk over dinner.'

'Dinner?'

'You do eat?'

'Yes, yes, of course, I...'

'Seven-thirty, then. Oh, yes, you can return Bataille if you're finished with him.'

'Yes, wait. What shall I wear?'

He laughed. 'My dear, you must be beau, chic, elegant. Always.'

He hung up and I sat in my room with a feeling that I had found something I didn't even know was lost. I felt breathless and light. One puff of wind and I would have floated away. I laid on my back staring at the map of Italy on the water-stained ceiling. I stretched out my arms and legs as if they were connected to elastic and I was being pulled in two directions. I took deep breaths until the little bird in my chest settled. Beau, chic, elegant. Like Ruth Raphael.

*

179

I am a Capricorn – organized, pessimistic, good at climbing walls. December had completed the 12-month cycle of the planets and I wasn't ready for the next one. I had enjoyed being eighteen. Eighteen straddles the threshold between being young and grown up. The figure 8 is aesthetic, infinity on its feet. I saw the 9 in nineteen on my birthday cards as a tadpole, a dark sperm carrying alien DNA, the word – nine – in tune with the grating sound Matt made grinding out broken chords on his new Fender.

Daddy was home for Christmas. Uncle Douglas was drinking the wine cellar dry with Mother, and Mother was so sparky and pleasant it occurred to me that of the two brothers she probably thought she had married the wrong one.

I should have been happy, but I wasn't. The Black Dwarf was in my brain and in my bed. I dreamed I was drowning and what flashed before my eyes wasn't all the things that I had done in my life but all the things that I had wanted to do and had not yet done. I put on a false face, a mask, and didn't go to Midnight Mass with the rest of the family. *Try not to do anything too pagan.*

Christmas passed with presents and there was that dead time that takes you to New Year's Eve with its cracker of false promises. Douglas, a writer, famous in a small way, observant as a nun, caught me one morning coming down to breakfast as he was climbing the stairs.

'Ah, there you are. What have you been up to?'

'Just reading.'

'You can read with that racket going on?'

Matt was already practising. Douglas looked at his watch. It was about eleven o'clock.

'Come here a moment, I've got something for you.'

I followed him into his bedroom. He opened a drawer, removed a little wedge of £50 notes from his wallet and folded them into my dressing gown pocket.

'Go and buy something wicked, it'll cheer you up.'

'I can't take this,' I said. I held £300 in my hand to give back to him. 'You've already given me a present.'

'A bunch of books. What good are they?' He slipped the money back into my pocket and lowered his voice as if to relay a secret. 'When money goes it comes. When money stays death comes.'

'I like that.'

'It may even be original. I've got to the stage when I can't remember what I've written and what I've pinched.' He sighed. 'How's Cambridge, by the way?'

'Quite hard, actually. It's easier at school when they tell you what to do. Now, you have to decide everything for yourself.'

'That's the thing with decisions, you decide one thing and never know what might have happened if you'd tried something else. Now,' he said, 'go and do something frivolous.'

He gave me a hug and the Black Dwarf loosened his grip on my throat.

I was about to leave his room and stopped. 'Douglas, how did you decide to become a writer?' I asked, and he laughed.

'I didn't decide. I can't do anything else.'

'That's not true.'

'My dear, it is. Your father got the brains. Now, go on, and bloody cheer up.'

I waved the cash. 'Thank you.'

'A mere bagatelle.'

A smile slipped about my cheeks. I skipped breakfast. I showered, pulled on a pair of jeans, caught the 19 bus that Mother takes to Peter Jones and got off at Shaftesbury Avenue. I had no plans. But when you are not looking for anything you always find something you didn't know you needed.

My blue trainers with red laces led me down Old Compton Street and into the shop where I had made my first acquaintance with the mask. I descended the stairs to the basement and was drawn to the mannequin in the corner wearing a white lace uplift bra, tiny briefs tied at the sides with bows and white stockings with elastic tops and matching bows like garters. I tried the set on and my black mood lifted as I stared at myself in the mirror. There's nothing like white to clear away the black.

I went to Selfridge's in Oxford Street where I bought a sleeveless white dress that fitted snugly over my hips and buttoned up the front to a high collar threaded through with red ribbon to match the red buttons. I found a pair of red patent medium-heels and when I studied myself in the mirror at home I

181

wondered when I would ever wear anything quite so chic, quite so elegant, quite so beautiful?

Oliver Masters obviously knew the answer to the question before I did. That day of our dinner I laid out the costume on my bed, the dress to one side, the underwear like a figure beside it. I went for a long walk and my feet felt as if they were barely touching the ground. The day was cold but I didn't feel cold. I felt numb. I watched a couple kissing under a bare tree. I read for pleasure in the afternoon and fell into a strange sleep over the pages.

There was no shower, which I missed. I took a bath, washed and blow-dried my hair and gazed at the clothes laid out on the bed, pure, white, according to Bataille, an invitation to be sullied. I dressed slowly, as if I were being watched. I smoothed the lace panties up my legs, snapped into the bra, the stockings with bows, the red shoes shiny as jewels. I paraded around the tiny space in the empty room with that wanton feeling you get when you are doing something illicit. It was the beginning of my romance with pretty underwear and dressing with the curtains open.

There wasn't a long mirror and I could only see sections of myself by standing back and twisting at odd angles. I leaned forward over the sink to paint my lips in a shade of red that complimented the ribbon in the dress. There was a look in my eyes I didn't recognize and I watched my reflection as I pushed the cap back on the lipstick. I cleaned my teeth, dried the toothbrush and dropped it in my bag where it took on the look of a cuckoo's egg in a blackbird's nest.

He was waiting at the Great Gate. We climbed into a black Jaguar with a wooden steering wheel. It had belonged to his father. I sunk into the leather seat, knees together, cherry red lips unsmiling. The girl in the mirror. Life has patterns. Each act is another pebble thrown in the pool and the ripples spread and join, grow and diminish. Everything is linked by cause and effect. You are what you think, and what you think, if you think about it long enough, becomes real.

The car revved and the gears grated. The lights picked out trees and signs and silhouettes. I would like to say that I felt like Marie-France when she rode through the country lanes beside Kamarovsky, but that would be a slip in time.

We arrived at an old farmhouse converted into a restaurant that stood on the edge of the river. I watched a shooting star cross the sky and explode into dust. It could just as easily have been Earth, I thought. Life is short and fragile. We sat in an alcove beside lattice windows like cracked mirrors. There were two red candles in silver holders on the table, a white linen cloth, silver condiments and cutlery.

I had been carrying *Eroticism* and gave it to him now.

'Bataille,' he said. 'A whole new world.'

'Yes.'

'We live in a lukewarm bath of complacency and tedium. There other realities we can reach for. Don't you agree?'

'Yes, I do.'

'Are you agreeing to be agreeable?'

'I am agreeing because I agree.'

'So wise for one so young. Then,' he said, 'perhaps you have an old soul.'

He was seducing my mind. But I had known that was going to happen. The mind is just another organ fixed to the whole landscape of the body, the red lipstick, the white tights with garter bows. I had been...not afraid, not nervous. I wasn't sure. I was wrapped in a moment of madness. His eyes strayed down to the book and an odd, twisted smile crossed his features. He tilted the cover towards the light.

'A little accident?' he said.

'I was in that wine bar, *Slice of Melon.* Do you know it?'

'It looks like fingerprints,' he said without answering my question; I recalled Mother's rule to never to explain nor apologise, but the words slipped out.

'I'm awfully sorry.'

'So, the Katie Boyd imprimatur will remain in my library and I will think of you every time I reach for the book. Was that your plan?'

'If it was, it was subliminal. Sometimes we do things without knowing the reason,' I said.

He placed the book on the shelf in the alcove and I was saved by the waiter.

'Monsieur, Mademoiselle?'

183

'I am going to order for us both, is that acceptable?' Oliver said and did so before I replied, a volley of French I could barely follow.

We clinked glasses and sipped white wine. It wasn't cheap. I could taste the difference. He asked me about Christmas and I didn't avoid the truth. I said I had been depressed.

'Christmas provides that promise.'

'I usually enjoy Christmas. My father is always home...'

'Your father?'

'He's stationed in Singapore at present.'

'Military?'

'Civil Service.'

'One of those keeping us safe from unknown threats and dangers,' he said. I didn't respond. 'Is it a new dress?'

'Yes.'

'It suits you. You must always dress simply. Nothing showy.' He laughed. 'I could say the same about your prose.'

'You have read my essay?'

'We will come to that later.'

'You liked it?'

He smiled. 'You are looking for compliments. Don't be vain, Katie,' he said and my name sounded strange as it left his tongue, like it belonged to someone else.

We ate soup with bits of fish floating on the surface. The waiter kept refilling our glasses, buzzing back and forth like a fly, archetypal with a moustache and dinner suit. The restaurant was half-full, or half-empty, the conversation in the background like a rippling pool below the beams of the low ceiling. He had been in France, visiting his mother during the holidays and had used the time to do some research. He was working on a book about Napoleon's fiction. During his conquests, Napoleon kept a mobile office pulled by four horses. At night, while his soldiers slept, he entered the office, sat at his Louis XV desk on a padded chair and wrote unspectacular novels. He ruled half of Europe, but dreamed of being a great writer.

'He had passion without gift and no understanding of the gulf between literature and philosophy.' He paused. 'Literature is the question without the answer. Philosophy is the answer without the question.'

The waiter slid into view with the main course. Stuffed pigeon in burgundy with small bones. I pushed the food around my plate and drank with inexplicable thirst. Philosophy, writers, thinkers, painters. My head was spinning; no, not spinning, it was an open closet filling with new accessories. He admired Duchamp, thought Richard Hamilton under-valued and Picasso over-rated. He enjoyed French writers, and considered the only good writers in English to be Indian. He rained salt over his food.

'I'm trying to harden my arteries,' he said.

'Why?'

'I have a bet with a scientist who abhors salt. Whoever lives longest will win £20.'

'How will they collect their winnings?'

'It is a surrealist bet.'

His eyes flicked from his food to me and back again. 'How very droll that you should plaster your DNA over my Bataille.'

The candle flames danced. The waiter loitered. I felt like an actress in a play. I knew, I had known since the first time I was alone in his office, how the plot would unwind to the dénouement and had done everything to stay in character.

'My essay?'

He ran his hand through his curls. 'The writing's competent, a few too many run on sentences. The comma is a sign of hesitancy. The full stop shows clear thinking. He who hesitates...' He broke off, then asked: 'Tell me, Katie, are you the maiden?'

'Yes,' I replied.

He smiled. He finished the wine in his glass. 'You understand her role?'

'I understand the role as Bataille sets it out.'

'We shall drink to that.'

We tapped the rims of our glasses. I felt a wave of contentment, not happiness, exactly, but an insight into my own stupidity. It is never wise to fret over the past or the inevitable. I had been fretting over both.

He waved away the menu when the waiter returned and ordered coffee. He stood, went to the coat rack and returned with a parcel wrapped in newspaper.

'Here,' he said.

He dropped the parcel on the table. It was book-sized. I picked it up and gave it a shake.

185

'A tennis racket?'
He laughed. 'Do you play?'
'Sometimes.'
'Be careful. If you play against me, you'll get a thrashing?'
'I didn't get anything for you. Was I supposed to?'
'You are not supposed to do anything except be yourself.'
The newspaper wrapping the parcel was a page from *Le Monde*. Inside was *A Spy in the House of Love*, a novel by Anaïs Nin.

'In English,' he said.
'Thank you.'
'It is not a course work. It is for your education. You can fingerprint this one as much as you like.'

We drank coffee. I was aware of the other diners watching us as we left the restaurant. The night was black, icy, the view hazy through the windscreen. The engine throbbed beneath me. It was like entering the future, my gaze focused on the light ahead not the darkness behind. I felt a moment of giddiness, as if I were fleeing a crime, but that was probably just the burgundy.

We crossed Nevile's Court, climbed the stairs, went Indian file along the corridor. The rows of prints gleamed like eyes as we passed through the Berber tent to his bedroom with its big four-poster bed and oak furniture. He lit the table lamp, peeled off my coat and I stood passively as he slowly worked his way down the column of red buttons at the front of my dress.

17
Truth & Lies

The music from the funfair followed us on the wind as we crossed Albert Bridge and found a cab on the Embankment. We could see the strings of lights across the river, the big wheel like a giant clock, the silent chimneys of Battersea Power Station. We sat close, and I felt a terrible impatience every time we stopped at a red light.

We shed our clothes on the living room floor as we hurried for the bedroom and made love with the tree branch drumming the window. Our bodies were growing to know each other, they knew things our minds were still processing, and slid together like oil on oil. He kissed my brow, my nose, my lips, the hollow of my throat, kiss after kiss as if he were unzipping a tent flap before climbing inside. We made love again, and tears welled into my eyes.

'You're crying,' he said and I smiled.

He licked away my tears. I rolled flat on my back, my head resting on his arm. The light from the lamp in the next room created a feeling of space and distance. I could hear the pulse of a heartbeat and wasn't sure if it were his or mine.

In the House of Mirrors I had caught a glimpse of the girl I had been that night in the restaurant with Oliver Masters, candles reflecting in the windows, a finger-stained book. I remembered the car beams flashing in the trees, my knees together, pale as pearls below my coat, and I remembered Sibylle Durfort hanging her last show before driving off the road and breaking her neck. I watched his fingers run through the red buttons on my dress. It fell to the floor and I stepped forward as he took my hands. His eyes ran over my lace underwear, white stockings with bows; a Christmas gift.

Like the stillness before the storm, there was a pause, a theatrical moment, the last chance to turn back. He then sat on the stool at the end of the bed and bent me like a folding lamp over his knees. He slipped his fingers under the elastic and drew my panties over my bottom. His hand thundered down on the soft flesh and I felt a pain like no pain I had ever felt before, a searing burn threaded through with shame and humiliation. He hit me again, a second time, and a third, a fourth and a fifth, and just as Georges Bataille had described in *Eroticism*, the pain warmed my sex and became an inexplicable pleasure. As his hand came down one more time, my insides melted and my entire body went into spasm. I gasped for air. My heart exploded like a flower. I squirmed on his broad knees and he stroked my bottom as if I were a small bird that had been trapped and was now ready to be released.

How much of my story was false-memory, embroidery, a confession? It's hard to know. There is a kind of truth in a well-told lie. When we look back, we don't see things as they were but how we would like them to have been. Every mother's son was particularly bright at school. The past has a knack of rearranging itself. Was I casting a stone into the lake of the future? Was I testing him? Was I competing with Marie-France?

We had made cheese on toast and sat in the living room drinking tea from big white mugs. I was wearing his sweater.

'I suppose you got an A for the essay?'

'C, actually,' I said. 'It only happened that once. Oliver's a fan of Duchamp. He doesn't repeat himself.'

'And you still use his first name.' It was a statement, not a question. He put his plate on the floor. 'It was a typical display of power over weakness.'

'That's not entirely true.'

'What part of it isn't true?'

'I always knew where it was going. I wanted to go there.'

'That's because you were nineteen, you're five minutes out of boarding school, you want to gulp down new experiences. Having fantasies is natural. Your teacher taking advantage of that is abuse, whatever way you look at it. He was treating you like...like an object.'

'The female contradiction,' I said. 'We've got two forces in our heads. Half the time, we splash on the war paint and dress like objects. We want to be desired. And sometimes, we want to put on an old pair of jeans and be left alone. Wasn't I adorable in my little red kilt?'

'It was the damaged finger that really got me,' he replied. 'You are doing the exercises?'

'I always do as I'm told, well, nearly always,' I said, and was glad to see his smile.

'What you say about contradictions,' he went on, serious again. 'You've come to that conclusion as a woman, not when you were nineteen.'

I heard the ping of an email arriving and thought what an evocative sound Apple had found for their laptops, sly and intrusive. I looked back into his eyes.

'Don't they say you should try everything once?'

'Everything except hurting people,' he replied; he started counting on his fingers. 'Everything except making arms, selling arms, putting arms in the hands of warlords, making wars because it's good for the corporations...good for the banks.' He paused. 'Don't you have a job in a couple of days?'

'A hedge fund seminar.'

'A what?

'I'll have to iron my black suit.'

'Black suit. Why do you think they build their banks to look like temples? Money's the new religion. They want you in black like nuns.'

'Nuns in short skirts, and they like a bit of cleavage...'

'Disgusting. Don't go.'

'I have to pay the rent. My bank hates me as it is.'

'Cancel it, Katie. Write an article. Do something else. Don't take their blood money. You're too good for that.'

He stood and crossed the room. I was sitting at my narrow desk below the window and rose into his arms.

'You know I'm off in a few days.'

'Don't go.'

'I have to...'

'I have to earn money waitressing.'

'It's different.'

'Why?'

'People are relying on me,' he said.

We kissed. I clung on tightly and felt bereft. I had watched birds in the park walking on the thin ice and felt the same, shaky, cautious, the ground cracking beneath me.

'You're not angry?' I said.

'About what?'

'My moment of dissolution.'

'At university?' he asked and I nodded. 'Bloody angry. I want to know how come it's always the wrong people who get into power? The narcissists, the psychopaths, the abusers – blokes who make a fortune in business and swing round the revolving door into politics for the hell of it?'

'It's the way it is. It's always been the same. What can we do?'

'What we can. You know what the Buddha said, you can't change the world, only yourself.'

'Is that what you're doing?'

He shrugged. 'I don't know what I'm doing half the time,' he said, an odd admission, or a concession, I wasn't sure. He kissed my nose and changed the subject. 'Now I know why you write erotic books, and so well. They get you off balance. You think they're about one thing, but there's a lot more going on. You have real talent.'

'Thank you.'

'I mean it. You make the characters so real, I can't help thinking they are all you.'

'They're not me, they're reflections of me.'

'That's why you wanted to go to the House of Mirrors, to look for yourself?'

'Tom Bridge, you are getting to know me too well, and you know what happens when that happens?'

'No, what happens?'

'People get bored.'

'We won't let it.' He stood back, holding my hands. 'Have you ever thought about writing other kinds of books?'

'Now you sound like my mother,' I told him and he laughed.

We were quiet for a moment. I could hear the heat pipes humming, the wind in the eaves.

'Do you want more tea?' I asked, and he shook his head.

'No. I want to go back to bed.'

Reading Bataille had opened my vocabulary to words like taboo, transgression, orgy, lust, temptation. My tutor had introduced me to Anaïs Nin with that Christmas gift wrapped in *Le Monde,* and at the spring break I had a tattoo inscribed on the back of my neck. It intrigued him. He ran the tip of his tongue over the spirals. I was a girl who had learned how to let go and Tom, with all his passion and energy, was able to let go, too. We made love recklessly, continually, as if time were running out.

Days clicked by like snapping fingers. Were the skies as blue as I remember? Did Mr Patel really keep up his New Year optimism? I recall seeing unlikely smiles on my face in shop windows, and realised that after my shower each morning I had neglected to clear the steam from the mirror. I had forgotten to check to see if I were too fat or too thin. I grabbed things from the closet without worrying if this shade of that colour went with that shade of another colour. We played what I call boutiques. I cat-walked my clothes and Tom helped me decide what to keep and what to take to Oxfam.

'A documentary team's going to turn up at some poor African village,' he said, 'and all the girls are going to be dressed for the Kings Road.'

'Kingsland Road,' I reminded him.

'You live here, but you belong there.'

'So I'm frivolous and a bit snobby, am I?'

He laughed and held his hands up defensively. 'No, I'm joking, I take it back.'

'You do know my cupboards are bare?'

'Doesn't it feel good?'

'No, I feel naked.'

'We're going to take a look at the shoes next.'

'Not in this lifetime,' I said, and he opened the wardrobe door.

He then stretched out on the bed. I cat-walked in low heels, medium heels, sandals, pumps, boots, espadrilles.

'I can't really tell when you're dressed, take everything off.'

We made love in the closet, on my swivel chair with the laptop pinging on the desk, in the bathroom with bankers watching from their glass temples. We made love with the clock ticking and the sun pallid in the winter sky.

We went to clubs, restaurants, bars, plays. We stood in the spooky light of the Rothko show at the Tate Modern and walked over the Millennium Bridge to see if it swayed. We climbed the 528 steps to the dome of St. Paul's and tried the acoustic trick of the Whispering Gallery. You mumble words against the wall, they rise up the dome, and you can hear them clearly across the other side of the gallery. He waved across the vacant space, turned away and cupped his lips.

'Katie Boyd, you're beautiful.'

'Tom Bridge, you're a flatterer.'

'Katie Boyd doesn't like compliments.'

'Oh, yes she does.'

'I love you, Katie Boyd.'

'Does that mean I'm paying for lunch?'

'Yes, and I'm hungrier than a pigeon.'

I laughed. There was a lot of laughter. Tears and laughter. We ran around the gallery into each other's arms like movie lovers. I led the way down the stone stairs worn thin by the long tromp of humanity, and I thought about those three words wondering what they implied. In Spanish you say *Te quiero,* which means both I love you and I want you, a safety valve. The French say *j'adore,* sensual, sexy, evasive. I love you is a carving on an old tree, like something made of plaster standing in the rain; girls kiss and squeal *love you* to their friends when they hate each other.

He gave me a sea shell from Sri Lanka and I could hear the waves slipping over the beach when I held it to my ear. The shell was patterned like a tortoise with two rows of blunt shiny teeth. I kept it in my bag with my iPhone and lip gloss. I called and cancelled my waitressing job, though Tom most mornings took the tube to the Médecins Sans Frontières offices in Saffron Hill. There was an Ebola epidemic in West Africa. Syria and Iraq were disintegrating. In South Sudan, 25,000 people in a refugee camp were sitting in floods of water from the monsoons. Blistering heat and biblical rains. Tom thought God weird to keep punishing the same region over and over again, but then, he didn't believe in God.

When we met at his office he had aching shoulders from carrying the weight of the world and I watched his spine grow straighter as we continued our pilgrimage. Another play, a Helmut Newton show of erotic images from the sixties. Like a camel taking on water before crossing the desert, he was filling up on culture, on London life, fusion food, strong beer from new breweries. At night we made love and slept and made love again, the moon peeping through the blinds, the sun rising with an X to stamp on the calendar.

*

Lizzie wore red. Her colour. Ray was long and gangly hauling himself out of the chair to shake hands. He looked awkward, hesitant, a sergeant dining with a doctor, a rank thing, the omnipresent whiff of class. We carried two bottles of wine, some red tulips flown in from warmer places.

'I hate it when people bring flowers. You have to stop what you're doing and go and find a vase.'

'They match your dress,' I said, as she turned away.

Ray got busy with the corkscrew.

'White to start?'

The cork popped and he poured the wine, filling the glasses on the coffee table. I admired the simplicity of Lizzie's flat, white cabinets free of photographs, a solitary abstract covering one wall. There was a narrow shelf containing two white china elephants supporting a modest row of books; once read Lizzie gave them away because authors, she believed, want to be read not lined up to gather dust like tombstones.

I left the men and went through to the kitchen with two glasses of wine.

'What are you doing in here?'

'I came to help.'

'That's a first.' She glanced at the boxes of lasagne from Marks and Spencer's ready to go in the oven, then back at me. 'Now I know why my number's been wiped from your phone.'

'Have I been remiss.'

'Remiss. I'm going to write that down.' She filled a vase with water and peeled the cellophane from the flowers. She turned. 'He's cute,' she added.

'How are things with Ray?'

'He's still a good fuck, if that's what you're asking.'

'Lisa?' I queried.

She sighed. 'Agh, Lisa. She reminds me of you, in a way, when you were young.'

'And innocent.'

'Katie, were you ever innocent?' She stopped what she was doing and gave me a long stare. 'You look different,' she said.

'You usually say I looked pleased with myself.'

'That's because you usually do.' She looked me up and down. 'You're wearing jeans and flat shoes. You look like the proverbial woman who's just got out of bed and can't wait to get back in again.'

'It's true.'

'There, done,' she said, and adjusted the flowers. 'How's the writing?'

'Like a bicycle with a puncture.'

'You must write every day, every single day, even if it's just a few paragraphs. Write a blog or something. They're usually amusing.'

'You're right. I will. I've been...'

'Don't tell me what you've been doing. I know what you've been doing.'

'And you?'

'I'm turning you into a novel, you know that.'

'I'll get my agent to sue.'

'You don't have an agent.'

'That's not going to stop me.'

'Nothing's going to stop you, Katie. Not when you know what you want.'

Lizzie placed the lasagne in the oven, set the timer, and I thought about what she'd said as we joined the men. It is, I'm convinced, the secret of life: knowing what you want and then setting about getting it.

I sat on the arm of the sofa beside Tom. There was music in the background, Arabian, mournful; Lizzie had obscure tastes. I watched Ray top up the glasses, an intense look in his washed out blue eyes. The skin stretched over his cheekbones, hair prison short, a scar on his jaw. The reserve he'd shown when we'd arrived had gone, diluted by the alcohol. He leaned forward with an unnerving expression and took a breath. It's fucked. Everything's fucked. There's nothing we can do about it. No point trying. The enemy's not over there in Iraq and Afghanistan. It's behind our backs in Whitehall, in Washington.

'The real war starts when the boys come home without legs and arms and eyes. And the Ministry of Defence spends years fucking them. No psychological care, rundown houses full of rats, pensions they can't live on. All these poor fuckers are going to have to rely on the National Health for the rest of their lives, and

194

what are they doing with the National Health, fucking that as well?'

Ray was a paratrooper with special forces. They went in first, readied the terrain for occupation, or tidied up some mess before scarpering and denying they were ever there. He spoke quickly in spurts, as if his words were stuffed in a paper bag and were bursting to come out. He was a proselytizer, a man hurt and obsessed.

There was a silence. 'Sorry,' Ray added.

'No need,' said Tom. 'I don't disagree. I just don't think we should give up.'

'You're not on the front line, mate.'

'There's more than one front line.'

Ray sniffed thoughtfully.

'I'll give you that,' he agreed and finished his wine. 'I'll tell you something, the boys coming out are fucking angry, and fucking embarrassed. Why do you think we fucked up in Basra? It wasn't the fault of the men. It was the lack of equipment, vehicles without armour, not enough safety vests, officers who come out for three months to get their war medal and sit on their backsides doing fuck all and knowing fuck all...'

'If that's true,' Tom said, and Ray waved his hand.

'You think I'm sitting here making it all up? Thing is, no one gives a shit. The Americans had to come in and clean up after us in Basra. Same in Helmand. We like to think we're punching above our weight. What a joke. Two wars, thousands dead, and what have we achieved? Fuck all. The Taliban's back in Afghanistan and there's a civil war in Iraq. How do you think the mums and dads feel knowing their boys got fucked for nothing?'

'But you're going back?' I said.

'Can't do nothing else, can I? Eighteen down, two years to go.' He took another long breath. 'Then what?'

He shrugged, offered the bottle.

'Thanks,' I said, and knew as he refilled my glass that I was going to be taking Nurofen in the morning, but you do it anyway.

'The blokes who aren't injured when they get out don't want to sit on their arses, they want jobs,' he said. 'What do they do? What can they do? Go into security so they can get paid decent money to piss on all the poor fuckers in the Middle East, in Africa. Or they join the police force. I'm not joking. Half of them are fucked up here,' he tapped the side of his head, 'and they're out there patrolling our streets. And, I'll tell you something else: you see a beggar with dead eyes and ten to one he's an army boy.'

'I thought they were usually heroin addicts,' I said. 'I always feel guilty when I don't give them any money and feel stupid when I do.'

'Course they're addicts. After going to hell and back they want to escape from reality. Drugs help.' He held up his glass. 'You can see it when someone's lost their legs from an IED, you can't see it when they've got so much stress their brains have turned to shit. They can't put plating under our vehicles, but when it comes to talking bollocks, those cunts at the MoD are the best.'

'Why don't they put plating under vehicles?' I asked him and he shrugged his big shoulders.

'Because money's more important than lives, that's why. This country's been stolen from under our noses. We're owned by big business. London's a tax free zone for the mega-rich, the oligarchs, the oil barons.'

Ray had joined up because he was proud of being British and would come out in two years ashamed of being British. He was impassioned, convincing, he knew his subject, and it went through my mind like a lost piece of music that I wanted to write everything down, check the facts, write his story.

'It's hard to believe,' I said.

'That's what we're up against.'

The oven pinged. I helped serve the lasagne. Lizzie had made a bowl of salad with pine nuts. We sat around the table in the corner of the kitchen. Tom talked about Sri Lanka, South Sudan, and Ray was a good listener as well as a good talker.

'When you leave the forces, there's always work in the voluntary sector,' Tom said.

'I know that. One thing I really hate is land mines. They kill the women working in the fields. They kill children, not the enemy. Whoever the fucking enemy is? I'll go back to Afghanistan for a month every year, help the engineers clear the fuckers.'

'That's only a month, Ray,' Tom said. 'If you want to give me a call, I can find plenty of things for you to do.'

'I'm not a medic. I know how to kill people, not cure them.'

Tom put his fork down and sat back. 'Tell me something: have you ever built a temporary bridge?'

'Yeah, course, fucking hundreds.'

'Ever put in a water pump?'

'What's your point?'

Tom was doing his finger counting thing. 'Do you know how to wire up a bomb?'

'Yeah, and it's a lot easier than dismantling them.'

'Is there a difference from wiring a bomb and wiring a house? I don't think so. When you get out, you're not going to go and start killing bankers, are you?'

'When I've finished with those fuckers at the Ministry of Defence.'

'I'm going to put you on Médecins' mailing list.'

'You can do that. Don't promise I'm going to read them, though.'

'We've got four hundred kids, really bright most of them, they pick up English a lot faster than I can learn their language. We need people who can do things, make things, build things. We pay expenses, though a lot of volunteers pay their own. They come out for three months, six months, live in barracks, muck in, and almost every single one comes back for another tour. They see they're making a difference, and it makes a difference to their own lives.'

Lizzie cleared the plates. I helped. She cut up some pears with goat's cheese.

'I did warn you. He can't stop beating the same drum,' she said.

'What he's saying is interesting. It needs to be said.'

'Not when you've heard it all a thousand times.'

'It makes me feel as if I'm living in a bubble.'

'Course you are, Katie. But you know that.'

18
La Bohème

Tom produced a pair of tickets for the Royal Opera House and I wasn't sure whether to be moved or furious as I watched Rodolfo first seduce and then cast Mimi aside in *La bohème*. A tic pulsed in my neck as we walked through Covent Garden after the final love duet. The Opera House had been packed and I couldn't imagine how Tom had found eighth row seats at the last minute. He put his arm around my shoulders.

'You okay?'

'Yes...No. I'm angry with Rodolfo.'

'Rodolfo. What's he done?'

'When Mimi's ill, he doesn't want to know. He tells his friends she's *fickle,* that she's having an affair. Which she isn't. When he finds out she's actually dying, he's all over her.'

'It's just a story.'

I stopped. 'Yes, and you learn more from stories than you ever will from an encyclopaedia.'

'You should write that down.'

'No, you should,' I said and he laughed.

'You are so smart...'

I waved that away.

'Rodolfo dresses like a poet, but he's got the heart of a hedge fund manager. We never see him finish a piece of work. His best friend pawns his winter coat for food when Mimi's dying, Musetta sells her gold earrings to buy medicine. *La bohème* isn't a love story, it's a warning. What Puccini's saying is fall for a poet and he'll rip open your chest and eat your heart.'

'You really saw all that?'

'He didn't spend however long he spent writing the opera without thinking about the characters and what he wanted to say through them. That's what drove him to get up every morning.'

'Is that what drives you to get up in the morning?'

'No, it's the alarm on your phone.'

He laughed. He kissed me. People streamed around us like we were a rock in a river and we carried on, keeping pace with the crowds on Long Acre, girls in big shoes and bare shoulders, men with knotted scarves. Motionless cranes loomed over the new buildings going up on every free space, and I thought one day London will look like New York and will lose what makes it London.

We headed towards Shaftesbury Avenue and turned into Old Compton Street. The snow in the air melted as it fell, sheening every surface. People spilled out of restaurants and theatres. I stopped at a shop with magazines and porn videos in the window.

'That's where I bought my mask, downstairs,' I said.

'You don't need it anymore.'

'I thought it rather turned you on?'

'It does, but you don't *need* it.'

Had I ever really needed it? What had I been hiding from if it wasn't myself? I caught the slight change in my voice as I looked back at him.

'How did you manage to get the tickets?'

He was about to answer, then stopped himself. His eyes glowed in the red neon from the shop sign.

'Katie, where do you think I got them?'

'I don't know.' My shoulders went up. 'Last minute, great seats. I suppose you must know someone.'

'Someone like who?'

'I don't know?'

'It's over. Dead. Buried. Relationships don't last in my world. People spend too much time apart. It takes over your life.'

I bit my lips. 'I'm such an idiot.'

'Very smart most of the time, very stupid some of the time, and rather beautiful all of the time.' He didn't smile. He shook his head. 'Jamie Doyle, you met him at the office. Poor bugger got the tickets for his wife, for their wedding anniversary, then she walked out. He was on a plane to Nigeria yesterday. He wouldn't even let me pay for them.'

'That's so generous.'

'He's going up to the border with Cameroon, where Boko Haram's operating. There's poverty and conflict...'

'People are killing each other?'

He thought for a moment. He knew what I was asking. Tom now seemed to know far more about me than I knew about myself.

'We're safe. Someone gets shot or slashed by a machete and we stitch them back together again, doesn't matter what God they believe in. You work in these places and your priorities change. Opera tickets are just...opera tickets.'

'Okay, tomorrow I'll work on my shoes.' I kissed his cheek. 'Come on, let's go and eat something. I know the perfect place.'

'One of your old hangouts?'

'That would be telling.'

My tummy was in tangles. I picked at a salad, abandoned my New Year Resolution and drank too much. Just one glass usually means two. Two always turns to three. Time was going faster. We made love slower, as if it would trick the inevitable. But making love has its own rhythm and time never cared about anyone. I wanted more of him, all of him, and it was like trying to hold on to that nice dream at the moment of waking. Marie-France was a flash of paranoia, a photograph in my head deleted from his phone.

He left early for the office: emergency meetings, recruitment, fund raising, and what it conjured up for me was a misty portrait of King Canute setting up his throne on the beach and daring the waves to defy him. The tide was rising with the flotsam of disaster and I couldn't help agreeing with Ray Fowles: everything was fucked.

I made a pot of Starbucks and went back to our warm sheets with a mug of coffee and my laptop. Taking Lizzie's advice, as I secretly do, I wrote a blog on Rodolfo's shallow love in *La bohème* and posted it on my website the way Bradley had shown me. I sent an update to my little band of subscribers, and checked back at Google Analytics every five minutes to count the hits. In the UK, a million people were using food banks, the Tamil orphans were growing older, and I felt an absurd stab of pleasure when the first comment appeared on my blog from a furious poet defending poets.

I clicked on Facebook; 53 messages. A man in New Delhi had invited me to be his friend. BarbaraLoveAuthor from Alberta wanted me to review the first part of her trilogy 'set in the black heart of the Athabasca tar sands.' There was a photograph of Matt falling out of a taxi at a stag night in Budapest and baby pictures of babies who appeared so alike they may all have been the same baby old Bashers were sharing. Facebook creates a universe where past and present connect as if our lives are an unending wall of mirrors in which we see limitless, indiscriminate reflections, a cello in the arms of an anonymous girl, Hemingway standing with a typewriter on a high shelf, a face that looked familiar illustrating a post about striking teachers.

When I made the image bigger, I recognized Bridget McKinley, another girl from school, and it struck me how fresh and young she looked with disorderly hair and a tee-shirt with the slogan *Free Schools Are Not Free.* She had a defiant expression as she stared at the camera and brown eyes in a face I recalled being thin and formless but had grown sculpted and intense. I had gone out of my way to be friendly with Bridget, I made an effort to like everyone so everyone would like me. But she was one of those girls who continually seemed as if she disapproved of something and, rationally or otherwise, I had the feeling that what she disapproved of was me.

While the other girls were checking to see if their breasts had grown bigger and nattering about boys, Bridget had become a vegetarian and joined Greenpeace. That year when we started our A-levels, in 2002, she became an object of envy and suspicion when she sneaked out of the back gate, got the train to London and joined the march against the War on Iraq. War was a good time for the church, it provided a reminder of its purpose, and a Bishop came one Sunday to preach a sermon on the bombing of Baghdad as 'a necessary evil.' I stared at the shapely carved thighs of Saint Sebastian and Bella sat at my side behind a pillar reading *Vogue.*

We were only allowed out of school for three hours on Saturday afternoons. One time, I walked back from Broadstairs with Bridget when I had just bought a new pair of shoes, which I promptly showed her.

'How many pairs of shoes do you have now, Kate?' she asked.

'Not many. Not more than twenty.'

'If you have more than two pairs of shoes it means someone else is going barefoot.'

I put the shoes back in the bag. 'That's not true,' I said.

'It's not a mathematical equation. It's true as a concept.'

'So, how many pairs of shoes do you have?'

'Far too many,' she replied.

'Well, then...'

'The thing is to realise it, to think about it. We're lucky. Most people in the world are the opposite.'

'We can't help that. We haven't done anything...'

'No, we haven't. But that doesn't mean we can't.'

'I don't see how my shoes are going to make any difference.'

'It's like I said, Kate, it's just a concept, an idea.'

'I think you're just trying to be different.'

'Is that really what you think?'

'Yes, it is,' I said, but deep down I didn't think that at all.

I don't recall that we spoke again, but I always tuned in when she was talking to someone else. Bridget studied law. She now worked for the teacher's union, and her face in the photo that morning had a similar look to those friends with babies, the contentment that comes, I imagine, when you have chosen your path and are happy to be following it.

I quit Facebook and opened the closet. I was relieved when I counted my shoes that there were less than 100 pairs. I lined them up like aircraft in three squadrons, ready for combat. The kamikazes in the vanguard were ready for the Oxfam shop. In the second chevron were the old favourites with heels worn down in the cause, their future in the balance. In the rear, with medal ribbons and fancy tooling, the Jimmy Choos and Manolo Blahniks went back in the velvet bags and boxes they had come in.

There, Bridget, are you happy now?

My phone buzzed with a text. A double xx. Two kisses. No message. I flicked through my clothes, it was easier now the closet was half empty. I chose with more care than usual, usual in those last few days, hung the outfit in a suit bag and went to the gym. I sprinted on the walker, swam in the pool, showered and brushed my hair under the dryer. It was a white underwear day. I zipped myself into the fitted green dress that matched my eyes, a green satin jacket embroidered with silver dragons and spiky green heels that had survived the clear out. I read the *Guardian*, phone at my aside. It was something I'd sworn I would never do: hang around waiting for a man. But this was different. It felt different. It felt acceptable.

Another message came just before midday and I rushed out to search for a taxi. The winter sun over the New Year had gone. The sky was pale with rain not falling but in the air like mist. Christmas trees, like a felled forest, littered the street with an air of spent good will. He was leaving in a couple of days and it wasn't enough time to look back to see where we had come from or forward to where we were going. It was like a piece of music ended half way through. A taxi did a U-turn. The wind whipped my hair about my face and I bundled into the pack as if escaping from something.

Tom was waiting outside his office.

'The Hurlingham Club, please,' I said to the driver as we settled into the back.

'Now it's my turn to be inspected,' he said. 'You look great.'

'It's not for you' I replied. 'Don't take any notice if Mother's rude, she says things to sound fascinating.'

'Perhaps she is.'

'To herself she is.'

'You've already made her sound interesting and I haven't even met her.'

I glanced out the window. It had started to rain, a kept promise.

'I hate this weather,' I said.

We were holding hands and I couldn't work out how this had happened. Had I reached for his hand? Or had he reached for my hand? Or had our hands reached for each other?

'How's your finger?' he asked; I had stopped binding it in tape.

'Better,' I said.

The traffic parted. The taxi whizzed along the Fulham Road.

Daddy had booked a table for four. Matt would join us if he could for coffee; people with little to do are always busy. His rowing obsession had turned to music, but his band never moved beyond the local pubs in Canterbury, where he'd quit uni in the second year. He now mixed cocktails in a hotel and was taking acting classes.

The taxi slowed as we entered open gates watched over by two men in uniform. The road narrowed through bare wintry trees clutching handfuls of frost and The Hurlingham rose up like a colonial outpost on the banks of the Thames. Everything was clipped, neat, painted, the open patio facing the lawns with an air of waiting for spring when the daffodils edged the path and waiters in white jackets curved among tables pinned with umbrellas.

The bar was full, glittery with the lights over the optics, the burnished brass and wood, strident with the sound of laughter. It crossed my mind that I'd got the day wrong when I didn't immediately see my parents. Then I spotted Father where I should have looked to begin with. He was in the corner hunched over a book, frameless round glasses perched on the end of his nose, the gin and tonic at his side like an ironic gesture. He stood as we approached his table.

'Katie, darling,' he said, kissing my cheek before turning and stretching out his hand. 'You must be Tom. I am so pleased to meet you.'

'Mr Boyd, my pleasure,' Tom said as they shook hands.

'Edward, please. Or just Ed,' Daddy added, not that I had ever heard anyone call him Ed.

'Where's Mother?' I asked him.

'Tennis tournament, doubles, a big match. She'll be here in a moment.'

I looked at the cover of the book Daddy had closed with a bookmark, it was *Zoo Time,* by Howard Jacobson.

'Any good?' I asked.

'Quite funny,' he replied. 'It's about a novelist who hates being a novelist and feels the need to explain himself when he starts writing a new book.'

'I rather know how he feels.'

'It is the burden of talent,' he said diplomatically, but then, he would. He stood back, holding my two hands. 'Christmas has just flown by. I've seen nothing of you.'

'It's his fault,' I said, glancing at Tom. 'He's so demanding.'

'It's true,' Tom said.

'Well, you're looking very well on it.'

The things people say. We all smiled. The two men were sizing each other up, as men do, as women do. It struck me how similar they were, the same height with the same inquisitive eyes in narrow faces, soberly dressed. Daddy was in pale tawny corduroys, a blazer with brass buttons, a shirt with a faint check and a knitted-wool tie, holiday clothes. Tom was in a tweed jacket from the same storage case as his fisherman sweater, chosen, I assumed, for the occasion. I looked from one to the other and felt as content as the prisoner in *One Day in the Life of Ivan Denisovich,* when he finds an extra potato.

We ordered drinks, sparkling water for me. Tom had a beer. English people don't talk until they have a drink in front of them, and it usually takes more than one before they find anything to say. Traffic: dismal; weather, yes, dismal.

A man with a red face in salmon trousers and a striped shirt bellowed with laughter. I glanced towards the bar. He was standing with a man in a kilt who I recognized as the MC at the tartan ball, his appearance like a loose thread in the fabric of New Year.

Daddy was swishing the ice about his glass. He took a sip from his drink and turned to Tom.

'Katie tells me you're working in Sri Lanka,' he said.

'Yes, with the Tamils. I sort of run an orphanage.'

'Bad business, the war. Things improving, I trust?'

'Slowly. If we could get our hands on more money we could do so much more, and much more quickly.'

'That's the problem. The same small group of people always seem to get their hands on everything and they won't let go,' Daddy said as if the thought had just occurred to him.

'The same here, wouldn't you say, in this country?'

'Absolutely. That's what I meant.'

They paused, two swimmers who have finished the first length of the pool and take a breath before setting out again.

'Then it's the system that's wrong,' said Tom. 'That's what needs to change.'

'Those in charge are extremely dexterous. When they recognize that there is a demand for change, they make small concessions, a few pennies off the price of a pint, an addition to the minimum wage.' My father shrugged as if he had said too much, but went on, talking as a hungry man eats. 'Power becomes entrenched. We can see that clearly in the developing world, but it's really no different here. We are just much cleverer at hiding it.'

Tom smiled at me across the table. 'That's what I was saying to Katie. We put bribes in brown envelopes to get people to do

206

things they shouldn't do. In Sri Lanka, you bribe people to do things they are being paid to do.'

'Making the most of situations for yourself is human nature. It's how we survive. Helping a friend or a relative to get a job or a home or a chance isn't nepotism, it's normal. What isn't normal, or at least it wasn't until recently, is politicians colluding with corporations and milking the system for all it's worth.'

'But how do they get away with it?'

'Successive governments over thirty years have arranged the tax and welfare system in a way that divides the pie to the advantage of the rich. Remember trickle-down economics? It was quite brilliant and totally false. As they say in the Mafia, the money always flows up. I have benefited myself with my own modest investments.'

'Katie said you're with the Foreign Office?' Tom said.

'Ah, you have spotted the hypocrisy. Yes, indeed.' Father removed his glasses, polished them and put them back on again as if they were a mask, a disguise. 'I thought I could do something useful, but I'm just an extraneous cog in that machine of entrenchment.'

'A double-agent,' I said flippantly, and immediately wished I hadn't.

We attended to our drinks. We had become reflective, serious, and I realised how rare that was, how men instinctively find things that matter to talk about and how, in the presence of women, they yield to froth, to gossip.

'That was silly. I didn't mean that,' I said, and my father took my hand across the table.

'Not at all, darling. I was being far too solemn for lunchtime.'

'Stop being the diplomat, Daddy. I was just thinking, there is so much trivia in our lives it's like a fog, we can't see through it.'

'Trivia?' Tom said.

'Yes. Celebrity gossip. Football. Erotic novels...'

'Come, come, I must object on that last point. Erotica is the oil of revolution,' Daddy said and our brief laughter came to an end as Mother strode across the bar in a yellow dress like a memory of summer.

'Everyone laughing. You must be drunk. How marvellous.'

The men leapt up, Father slightly bent, Mother studying Tom as if he were bric-a-brac, or livestock.

'This is Tom,' I said and Mother nodded.

'I'm glad you told me, I thought you may have picked up another stray on your way here.' We laughed politely. 'I understand you're a doctor?'

'Yes...'

'I've been having a terrible pain in my back, right here.' She rubbed her side.

'Perhaps it's a strain. I could take a look,' he said and she burst out laughing.

'My dear, how very sweet. I have a friend who always says that when she meets a doctor, it must be so irritating.'

'Occupational hazard,' he said.

'Really?'

She took his arm. Mother was radiant with a lingering tan from five days skiing in Gstaad and must have spent an age on her hair and makeup. She turned to me, her eyes going up and down over the green dress and jacket.

'You look very pretty, dear, is this his influence?' she inquired, taking in Tom's seen-better-days jacket over a denim shirt.

'Thank you,' I said, dodging the question. Pretty for Mother didn't mean pretty, it meant not quite right. 'How was the tennis?' I asked, and she glanced at my father.

'Don't we have a table booked?'

'Yes, we're a bit late.'

'Well, come on then,' she said, and spoke over her shoulder. 'We beat Sylvie and Milly Dupont, they've won the doubles more times than you can count. It bodes well. Is that the right word, Kate?'

'Yes,' I said, but she wasn't listening.

Mother smiled and waved at friends. She stopped to kiss the cheeks of the man in salmon-coloured trousers. People called out Happy New Year and I remembered the Christmas trees left in the street.

The table was waiting for us, starched linen, shiny silverware. Mother gave us a blow by blow account of the tennis doubles as an agonizingly thin waiter waited with a pad, pencil poised, a blank expression. Mother had seen herself in the dominatrix from one of my books. I must have drawn subliminally on her character, punished her in fiction for some injustice, real or imagined, for which she still had not forgiven me.

The laughing man from the bar joined a table occupied by friends with the same leaning to the red side of the spectrum in trousers, men with amplified belly laughs issuing from ample bellies, minor public school rowers, good drinkers, doubles of Dylan Thomas. I always felt on these occasions like an outsider. But the feeling was at odds with the reality. I was, from the cradle, an insider. I had never quite shaken off the shadows of the past and father, with his round glasses shiny in the overhead lights and paperback in his jacket pocket, was the same, a minor cog in the machine of entrenchment. I am sure he tossed handfuls of sand in that machine when he could, as did I with my feeble writing. But the machine was like the tide, like the turning of the universe, inescapable, unstoppable. There was a long tradition of men going from Cambridge into the Foreign Office to change the world and failing utterly. We had never spoken about his beliefs, his politics, but by giving me Hesse, Camus, Orwell, he had opened the window to a view I was only now beginning to see with any clarity.

Mother finished her tennis tale on a self-effacing note. We ordered. I drank a glass of white wine and listened as Tom provided an abridged version of his life in Sri Lanka. Mother asked questions, but her eyes glazed as he answered. She found it difficult, or absurd, to be curious about things outside her own interests.

'You're returning soon?' she said to Tom but glanced at me.

'Yes, in a few days,' he replied and a little barb scratched inside my chest.

'There,' she continued. 'We are in the same boat, Kate. Your father has already packed his bags for China.'

'Singapore,' he corrected, and she turned in her seat.

'You know what I mean,' she said. 'Aren't they all Chinese?'

'Yes, that's true.'

'When are you leaving, Daddy?' I asked, and he did that thing, removing his glasses for a polish.

'Tomorrow afternoon,' he replied.

'That's so soon.'

'Not soon enough for your father.'

He put his glasses back on and glanced around the room as if seeing it for the first time. Did Mother know he had a lover in Singapore? Did she care? She had her own life. They stitched a veil of deception from each other, from themselves, and I wondered if love was like the earth's resources, doomed eventually to run out.

I ate asparagus with vinaigrette and parmesan shavings, roast cod with sticky rice, a spoonful of Black Forest gateau. The men at the next table laughed their big laughs, and Matt appeared, looking about the dining room as if for a seat on a full train. He was wearing a white shirt, the collar twisted, a short jacket, and red skinnies. He was beautiful like a new puppy with green eyes peeping through a hedge of hair. Matt had the air of being a rich man's son without being one, and Mother adored him for his small failures, his similarity to her, his dependence on her. She stared up with an impatience that revealed more than concealed her love and he bent down to whisper something that I didn't hear.

After the handshaking and kissing, the thin waiter appeared with a chair and we shuffled around to widen the circle before ordering coffee.

'You look like you've just got out of bed,' Mother remarked, and Matt pushed back his hair with his two palms.

'It's my hairdresser, he's such a prima donna,' he said.

We laughed. Matt ordered a glass of red wine. My little world was around one table in a moment of happiness, something you have to grab hold of and hang on to, something that comes when it comes and can't be chased or hunted or pinned down or imprisoned.

19
Everyone is Waiting for Something

Darkness was lifting. A dull green glow touched the horizon. Aircraft lay everywhere, like my shoes on the day of the great cull, and I imagined girls wearing them in the broken streets of crowded cities in Africa and Asia.

A plane sped along a corridor of amber lights and took off, sliding through the haze before vanishing from view. I stood with a blanket around my shoulders, my forehead resting against the thick panes of glass. I could smell him on my flesh, on the sheets in the hotel bed where countless couples must have spent restless nights waiting for the alarm.

The control towers became more defined against the rising light. Vehicles moved like busy ants on a landscape fragmented by wire fences. There were no trees, just steppes of cement with buildings the same colour. Another plane rolled into position ready for take-off. The room was muggy, airless, but a chill ran through me. I pulled the blanket closer. It was hard to imagine a place on earth more grey and mournful than Heathrow on a bitter January morning.

There was a knock on the door, a double tap that made me jump.

'Breakfast, please.'

I pushed my arms into a robe and opened the door to an Asian man with a white splash of teeth between shiny black cheeks and a white jacket a size too big for him.

'Thank you very much,' he said.

He placed on the table a tray containing two glasses of orange juice, two cups, a pot of coffee, milk and two croissants wrapped in paper napkins.

'Wait,' I said.

I gave him a £10 note, his smile broadened and his head pivoted from side to side like it was on a spring.

'Thank you very much. Thank you very much.'
I poured coffee and warmed my hands on the cup as the plane on the runway took off. Another rolled into position, people coming and going, our nomadic genes replayed in this endless shift of humanity, that sense that there is a place where we should be and we spend our entire lives searching for that place.

From The Hurlingham we had rushed home and made love, the sand hurrying through the hourglass making the vacant space seem all the more empty. He held me so tight I felt like a tiny creature in a cocoon.

'I wish you weren't going.'
'So do I.'
'You have to?'
'I have to.'
'People are relying on you?'
'I'll be back. It won't be so long.'
He ran his hand down my thigh. We were whispering as if what we were saying was unformed; secret. His hand was warm. I could feel each one of his spread fingers like lines of sunlight.

'Don't stop,' I said, and he carried on stroking my leg. Then he paused.

'You must finish your book.'
'Yes.' The light was fading, the shadows growing longer. 'I will wrap it in a reed basket and float it down the river.'

He kissed my eye-sockets. 'Then start another,' he said, and my shoulders went up in a shrug.

'Who knows.'
'I love your collar bones,' he said and paused. 'You have to, it's who you are.'

'Or who I was? Everything that begins must end.'
'Not everything,' he said. 'They never finished the Great Wall of China.'

'That's because they forgot why they started building it.'
He stretched and straddled my waist between his knees. 'You know something, I think I detect a faint smile on those beautiful lips.'

'That's because you always have an answer for everything.'
'You're one to talk.'
He reached under the bed where the mask had remained out of sight. He pulled the elastic over the back of his head.

212

'Who do I remind you of?'

I shook my head. 'Give me a clue.'

He cupped my face in his two palms. We kissed and the feel of the fascia against my skin was cool as he slithered down my body. He drew my legs apart like curtains, hooked my thighs over his thighs and dipped into the pool of our juices. The tip of his tongue stroked my clitoris, my eyes pressed shut. For a moment the grains of sand in the hourglass slowed in their race. I was about to climax and he stopped, he always knew when to slow, slow and gradually cease, how to suspend orgasm. He must have had a superb teacher.

'I'd like to take this little part with me,' he said, and I could see myself in the mask as I opened my eyes.

I was panting for breath, floating.

'Just one part?'

He kissed my pubis, my belly, my breasts. 'This part and this part and this part.' He took my right hand and kissed the little finger. 'And this part.'

He slid up inside me and we rowed down the river to the sea.

Next morning, he went to the office for a couple of hours. I met him there and he led me around the corner to a store where he bought a video camera. He asked the assistant to show me how it worked and didn't part with his credit card until he was sure I'd got the hang of it. I held the bag containing the box containing the camera as if it were a talisman, a curl of hair in a locket, a fetish gone digital.

'Thank you,' I said.

'I couldn't think of anything else.'

'You didn't have to buy anything.'

We wound our way through the windy canyons of tall buildings to the Millennium Bridge and crossed to the Tate, a new exhibition, I can't recall what, one last dip in London culture before he entered the desert.

The Thames was gun metal grey. We walked without talking. We lunched without eating. We made love in front of the mirror, watching our reflections as if they were movie stills and I locked him inside me as if I never wanted to let go. His body on me was a second skin pressing down in such a way that it was impossible to find a gap between us. Love is possession, a sort of vanity. I remembered the nuns at school with their neat nails and sour

213

expressions. They loved God because they were unable to open themselves up to let love in. They compelled us to believe and we came away from five years behind the convent walls believing in nothing.

My breath had misted the window. I had never before stayed at an airport hotel to stretch the seconds and it made the seconds after the last kiss last longer. The clock on the TV read 5.41. The sealed room was colour consistent, functional, containing everything and nothing. I showered and tubed back to Hackney, ninety minutes in which a kaleidoscope of morning workers passed through the hissing doors with coffee cups and Kindles, coats smelling of charity shops. A black woman in a nurse's uniform leaned across the narrow space between us.

'Here, take this, dear,' she whispered, and gave me a Kleenex.

Tears rolled down my cheeks.

'Thank you.'

She smiled, and I felt ashamed of my lack of spleen, of purpose, of what I wasn't entirely sure. I had never been tested.

The carriage sucked in passengers and pushed them out again like a bellows. I was normally sleeping at this time of day. I never saw the nurses and cleaners, the teachers and tradesmen, the call centre girls, the office boys in cheap suits who churned through the revolving doors in the glass-walled buildings that reflected each other with sly narcissism, the oil that greased the wheels and kept everything running. I changed at South Kensington on to the District Line, racing east underground as he was flying east into the sun.

He'd stayed every night and his presence remained like someone who has died. The camera he'd bought was on the table, still in the box, and one of his shirts was balled up in my laundry basket. I changed, made fresh coffee, took two Nurofen and opened my laptop.

I went back to the beginning of the novel I'd been writing with a sense that it had been composed by someone else. I usually work at night and surprising the manuscript when it wasn't expecting me uncovered the flaws and excesses inscribed by the person I had been with last year's genes and bulging closets. I watched the word count recede and felt lighter and ready for lunch.

Rain was in the air like spray from an atomiser. The plastic sheet over the newspapers was sheened in damp. I reached for *The Guardian* and the bell rang as I entered the shop with its towers of magazines like a shrine to consumer society. Mrs Patel was on her knees, adding fresh offerings, and her daughter was breaking open a carton with the word Cadbury's along the side. Mr Patel grinned red-stained teeth.

'Filthy weather. On your own?' he asked.

'Yes,' I replied. 'Tom's gone back to Sri Lanka.'

'Ah, yes, very sensible. He is a wise and clever man.'

I found the café in the street lined with horse posts and ordered avocado salad. I read about a woman in Norwich who had raised her mentally handicapped son of fourteen alone. The council had provided respite care four hours a week, allowing her to go out, have her hair done, buy a new skirt. Austerity cuts had brought the care package to an end. The woman felt unable to cope and was considering having her son taken into care. The cost of respite visits four hours a week was £100, which she could not pay herself. The cost of residential care was £500 a week, which the council would be obliged to pay if she did place her child under their protection.

An experiment in Cambridge showed that when numerous metronomes were placed on a stage and set off at different times, they quickly lost their individuality to connect to the rhythms of those around them. I paused and was struck by a blend of grief and relief that I felt no nostalgia for my university years. Golden ages always belong to other times. The past isn't another country, it is Atlantis, sunk beneath the sea. There is nothing beyond now. Rain pattering the windows. The newspaper folded. Warm air from hidden vectors.

The waitress came to the table with bread on a tray. I hovered over the warm slices of wholemeal made on the premises and plucked up a chunk of white bread instead. The couple by the window waved their arms about as they talked. The girl was young, early twenties, with strong features and a wide mouth. The boy was wearing a fur hat with flaps over the ears and a grubby white fisherman's sweater. Syria, Pakistan, a car bomb in Baghdad, another in Kabul. It all seemed so hopeless.

My hand froze as I turned to the arts pages. In the bottom right hand corner there was an advertisement with the heading

215

'Marie-France Durfort Live in Concert' above a photograph of her playing the cello, face drawn, intense. I studied the picture as if it might contain a message, then called to book.

'How many?'

'Two, please,' I heard myself say.

'Centre of the balcony? They're excellent seats.'

'Perfect. Thank you.'

I scrolled down my list of contacts, paused at Julian Rhodes, as you may tarry on the climb up a long flight of stairs, and went on to Lizzie Elmwood.

'I've got two tickets for a concert Friday. Will you come?'

'Has he gone?'

'At daybreak.'

'How fitting. Perhaps you'll get back to normal.'

'Will you?'

'Me? Get back to normal?'

'No, will you come?'

'What kind of concert? Rock, pop, jazz, classical, choral, bagpipes...'

'A cello recital...'

'A what?' she said, and her tone changed. 'It's not the French tart, is it? The one he was screwing before you broke your finger?'

'Yes, actually.'

'You are in a state. Katie Boyd loved to fuck, fucked by love.'

'Very clever.'

'Where? When? What time?'

'Cadogan Hall. I told you, Friday, half past seven. I've already got the tickets. My treat. I can book a table at Colbert for after.'

'French cellist. French food. I'd better wear Yves Saint-Laurent.'

When you are expecting a call and the call that comes is someone else it feels like a practical joke, an intrusion. Evelyn Talbot at Evelyn Events wanted to know if I was 'still resting' or whether I would deign to make myself free on Saturday.

'At the Shard,' she added. 'Close to where you live.'

'Bankers?'

'Does it make any difference? And, no, architects, developers, that lot.'

'Why not?'

216

'Black skirt, white top. You know the drill.'
'Tight skirt, plenty of cleavage?'
'If you've got it, dear, flaunt it, and if you haven't, buy a Wonderbra. I'll text the details.'
Friday concert. Saturday, Team Talbot. Things to look forward to. This is what patience looks like, I thought, and placed the phone beside the man smoking as he waited beneath the Victorian lamppost. I had a zero-hour contract with Evelyn. No obligations appealed to me, although I knew it didn't suit girls who needed regular hours, a reliable income. The men at these events, it was mainly men, behaved with a bullying sense of entitlement that would have been amusing if they weren't pulling the strings of those who had created zero-hour contracts in the first place.

I remembered Daddy at the Hurlingham saying the same group of people always get their hands on everything and won't let go. He was a chameleon, a shapeshifter. Whenever I thought I knew him he surprised me and became someone else. I had been trying to work out the similarities between my father and Tom and perhaps that was it, nothing to do with appearance, nothing incestuous or clichéd, just two men aware that the spirit level had tipped too far in one direction and were quietly doing what they could to rebalance it.

It was 2.30, 7.00 pm in Sri Lanka, an odd four-and-a-half hours difference. He would have had his swim and would be sitting down with a beer and some almonds. I tried him on Skype and a xylophone of clangs and jangles ground into silence. The bleak afternoon light gathered around the glass buildings. It started to rain. I read for an hour and fell asleep. When I tried calling again, the lines were down. It was normal, high summer. Stormy. Singing palms. Lazuline skies.

We didn't speak until the following day. He needed a shave and his head appeared huge on the small screen, hair spiking out at all angles, stripes of sunlight through shuttered windows. Yes, he'd just been swimming. Yes, I was working on my book. I didn't mention the concert, I'm not sure why, and we paused to look, actually look at each other. There had always been so much to say. Now, there was nothing to say, because there was nothing to say. He leaned forward. 'Kiss,' he said, and we grazed screens in a hum of static and dust. I heard a voice behind him.

'Doctor Tom. Look. Doctor Tom.'

He turned away. 'Not now, Darshan, let me finish my call.'

'Is broke.'

'I don't think so.'

'Hurt. Is broke.'

'Sorry, Katie, I'll just be a moment.'

He pushed away on his chair and I could see the rest of the room on my screen, wooden walls, bookshelves, shutters. Behind him, a boy of about nine with Gandhi eyes in a grey shirt and blue shorts was balancing his left wrist in his right palm.

'Let's have a look. What happened? Tom asked him.

'Fell...' The boy shrugged as he searched for the word.

'You fell?'

He nodded his head swiftly up and down. 'Corridor,' he said, rolling the rrs.

'You fell over in the corridor?'

'I fell in corridor.'

'That's because you're always running about, Darshan.'

'In corridor.'

'Go to the kitchen and ask someone to give you a bowl of ice-water.' Tom waggled his finger. 'It's not broken. You have a sprain.'

'Is broke.'

'No. Put your wrist in icy water and it will get better. You understand?'

The boy nodded. 'In the kitchen?'

Tom mimed. 'Put your hand in the icy water. I'll come in a jiffy.' He held up his finger again. 'And don't run.'

The boy grinned and I remembered the man at the airport hotel with his tray of coffee and croissants, two of everything.

'Thank you very much.'

Tom glided on the typing chair back to the computer. 'If he can stop falling over, he's going to be a formidable batsman.'

'Cricket?'

'It's like a religion. We managed to get one of the players on the national side to visit the orphanage and they're still talking about it,' he said. 'It's the sort of thing that helps them bury the past and live in the present.'

'Perhaps we all need to do that?'
'I've got friends ruining their health working to become rich and when they get rich they spend their money trying to get their health back. It makes no sense.' He smiled and leaned forward. 'Listen to me, going on, I'm sorry.'
'Tom, go and make sure the boy's alright. You don't want him his ruin his career.'
'That's true. Kiss,' he said, and we kissed screens again. 'Let's try and speak every day...'

We met in the foyer. Confident voices, undercurrents of French, eddies of Russian. Chandeliers and silvered mirrors. The music crowd, different from the theatre crowd, the film crowd, more intellectual, less arty. We sipped our drinks. Lizzie's eyes ran over me like one of those electronic sensors at the airport.
'Very soigné.'
'Classical music's always a bit posh.'
'You came to my flat last time looking like a hippie who'd just burned her bra.' She paused for another scan and smiled. 'Of course, the competition does have an edge.'
'You always have an edge. Especially in Yves Saint-Laurent.'
'Not me. You know exactly what I'm talking about.'
'If only.'
Lizzie waved her programme with Marie-France on the front.
'Oh, really!'
'If you start looking for motives you're going to find them,' I said.
She thought about that for a moment. 'You're writing again?'
'Yes. And you?'
'*Drabbling*. Teaching and writing are like fish and vinegar. Only the English put them together.' She waved her programme towards two women who stood at the bar as if posing for a magazine shoot. 'Can you imagine them eating chips from newspaper?'
'Friends of you know who?'
'You're obsessed. Look at the one on the right. The pale green heel on her shoes is exactly the same shade as her necklace. I bet she fucks like an angel.'
I laughed and caught a glimpse of myself laughing in the glass front of a picture of Benjamin Britten. I had made an effort to

dress up without being sure why. I had talked to Tom. He'd shaved. His hair was turning bronze and his eyes were the same colour as the sky framed by the window. Darshan had a sprain. It wasn't serious. He'd been swaggering around like a hero in his crepe bandage and sling, Tom said.

A bell rang. We climbed three flights of stairs and looked down from our seats at the stage with its silent piano and a cello on a stand. I studied the programme, it seemed eclectic, not that I knew anything about cello recitals: Richard Rodney Bennett, *Dream Sequence;* Tchaikovsky, *Alone Again, As Before;* Jean-Louis Duport, *Romance;* Bach's Concerto in C Minor, the so-called Casadesus forgery, 'for which Marie-France Durfort has become famous,' as I had read in Wiki along with a mangled version of her mother's career and death.

People moved between the seats to take their places. I glanced from face to face. I had never seen a photograph of Kamarovsky, but felt certain I would know him if I saw him. My palms were sticky. A man in tails came on stage and made an introduction. The pianist appeared and was applauded. He sat in the shadows and the audience rose clapping as Marie-France floated from the wings in a sleeveless black dress, shiny stilettos, a double string of pearls at her throat, the combination simple but erotic, the bow she carried like a cane or whip. She sat, gripped the cello between her thighs and held the bow motionless on the strings. She remained still for what seemed like eternity. There was a muffled cough, the shufflers grew silent, and she bowed off into *Dream Sequence* like a fencer in a duel.

Her performance was moving, spirited, emotional. The music got into your head, humming like a bee in a jar. Her skirt rode over her knees revealing shapely legs. She was intense, sensual, complex. Behind my closed eyes I saw flickering images as if from a mirror ball, Tom rising over her, his white bottom like a moon, his waist gripped by her strong thighs, her mouth stretched in a rictus. He was the bow. She was the cello. Richard Rodney Bennett poured from her pink lips.

Applause. A wolf whistle. She stood, turned and directed her hand towards the pianist. She sat again, flicked over the sheet on the music stand, paused for the shufflers unwrapping their cough sweets and closed her eyes. The bow once more wove its spell. Waves of sound slipped from the feminine curves of the cello's thorax as Marie-France unveiled Tchaikovsky in a melancholy mood. I glanced about the auditorium for Kamarovsky as if he were Svengali and she his protégée. They had been lovers when she was a girl. It was clear to me now. Like a novel, each life is a puzzle that can be pieced together. The Russian had seduced her, inspired her. He lit the match that had fired her genius and I remembered a sultry hot day at Black Spires dancing to the silence of butterflies.

My heart raced. Lizzie knitted her fingers in mine. I took a momentary glance. She was wearing glasses with green frames and I didn't recall ever having seen her in glasses before. I had dreamed of Marie-France. I had dreamed of Tom making love to Marie-France. I had dreamed of making love with Tom while Marie-France watched. Envy is a terrible thing. Envy is the ghost that can only be exorcized once seen in the light. My heart rate dropped. Lizzie had lowered her glasses and looked at me over the rims. She leaned closer.

'He made a smart choice, Minnie.'

I whispered back. 'I hate being called Minnie.'

We drank champagne during the interval. After the standing ovation following the Bach Concerto in C Minor, we slipped up the aisle in front of the crowd and crossed the road to Colbert.

After two flutes of champagne, whatever your resolve, you hear yourself asking for a third and order sparkling water to top up the glass. We are more similar than we are different. Colbert was half-full with reserved signs on the empty tables. I enjoyed the ambience, the smell of old brass and savoury sauces, so different from the cafés I had grown fond of in East London. The waiter placed four breadsticks and a bowl of butter on the table. Lizzie ordered eggs benedict.

'I'll have the same,' I said.

She closed her glasses into a slim silver case.

'I didn't know you wore glasses,' I observed.

'An affectation, dear. Like a mask.' She sat back. 'Are you feeling better now?'

'Yes,' I replied.

'She's not my taste, not at all,' she continued.

'Beauty is everyone's taste.'

'Beauty has to be interesting; interesting without being intimidating. A little country church can be beautiful. You look at most cathedrals and you think, if God walked down the street he'd throw up his breakfast.' She sipped from her glass. I could see the bubbles bursting in the light. 'I've never seen you like this.'

'Like what?'

'Irrational,' she replied.

'I've always been irrational.'

'Yes, but not in an irrational way.'

Two couples from the concert were edging into the room with that look people have after an emotional experience. The women wore long dresses; the men were in dinner suits.

'I saw you doing that in the concert, looking about all the time. Who are you looking for?'

'Kamarovsky.'

'Who?'

'Her stepfather.'

'I didn't know you'd met him?'

'I haven't. You know what it's like when you create a character. They have this tendency to come to life.'

'Has he come to life?'

'I do believe he has, lived and died like someone in an Agatha Christie mystery.'

'There's nothing wrong with a touch of jealousy, you know. It's good for the soul. You could say it's a sign of love.'

'You could say it's pretty pathetic, too.'

'That's up to you to decide.'

'Thank you for coming tonight. I feel, I'm not sure...'

'You feel great, that's how you feel. She's just a French tart who plays the cello. So what? You're an English tart who writes books and will write better books. This is what you've been waiting for.'

'I didn't know I'd been waiting for anything.'

'Everyone's waiting for something.'

20
London

Everyone's waiting for something. If that's true, we have to make sure we know what we are waiting for, or we won't see it when it comes.

If it comes.

Lights flash. A bus groans as it curves around Sloane Square. Lizzie leaves the table for the loo and comes back with her lips repainted. She has the knowing look of the femme fatale, striking more than beautiful. At Colbert they maintain an old-world ambience, the décor, the food, the waiter leading us out with an umbrella and waving down a cab.

London flows by in its suit of lights. Hyde Park Corner. Piccadilly. Romilly Street. We step out into the smog drifting from the chop suey stands on the south side of Shaftesbury Avenue, slanting rain, the sizzle of neon. Boys with pony tails pedal by on rickshaws. Men in sleeveless shirts. Runaways. The anonymous theatre fans setting off for the suburbs with another programme for their collection.

Soho is a stage set, a place apart. Another country. At night, while the visitors journey home, creatures allergic to sunlight surface to feed, male, female, girl-boy, boy-girl; femdoms, trannies, drag queens; the schizophrenics enjoying care in the community; pimps and gangsters; drug pushers with baggies of smack, crack, scag, and one guy selling his dreams. Lizzie doesn't break step.

'Been there. Lost my map,' she says.

'Cool,' he calls as we hurry towards Dean Street below my yellow umbrella with the cold rising under our coats.

Prostitutes, too young to be sour, gather in doorways feeling free, unaware in their tiny clothes that they are already in captivity. Greasy paving stones underfoot, a bitch in heels. The smell of kebabs outside the mini-cab office where drivers who know the broken streets of Iraq and Afghanistan wait for a fare. Girls in jean shorts and bras shiver under red lights at the entrances to strip joints owned by Albanians, and I wonder how they got to London, how they had replaced the local villains.

A man roasts chestnuts on a brazier. Porn shops, BDSM suppliers, the *French House*, where writers will be talking about the books they plan to write; *Groucho's,* where I had listened to actors talking about the roles they just missed, missed by a whisker; *Jacques,* where the shadow of a girl sits at the bar with legs crossed scribbling in a notebook.

We tap-tap-tap along the wet street, the phosphorescent sign *'Pink'* hanging in the cold air like a memory. The hat-check girl displays long cylindrical breasts like weapons in red latex. She takes our coats.

'Raining still?'

'In gilded showers,' Lizzie says, and the girl's breasts wobble as she laughs.

'God hates us.'

'God is dead,' says Lizzie.

I run my fingers through my hair and turn with dog-like familiarity into a silver-walled tunnel. Tables lit by candles stand at one end in nests of red armchairs, the shifting flames, like orange sails, mirrored on the shiny surface of the back wall. The music is loud, the usual, pounding mix of KD Lang, Melissa Etheridge, Tribe 8.

There are no men, just women looking pretty, women looking butch in neck ties and Brylcreemed hair, women half-naked, women in fetish clothes, piercings, inked flesh, a forlorn pursuit of the anarchic, the extraordinary, when the arrangement of lines and colour on canvas or walls or bodies can only be a rearrangement of all that has gone before. They dance, kiss, stroke each other, their shadows rising over the sloping roof. My head spins; too much champagne. Or, too little. The dance floor sways and I feel as if I am on the deck of the Santa María, sailing into the unknown.

Lisa Lundt is shell-white as if there is a light behind the surface of her skin, eyes the colour of summer fjords, her red dress tight as a tango dancer's. Her voice tinkles, like hand bells playing a tune.

'You are Katie. I have heard so much about you.'

'Nice things?'

'Lizzie only says nice things.'

We kiss.

Lizzie's eyes are on me.

Lisa obviously doesn't know you, I thought. Ray is an addiction. The masochist in her craves his attention.

They touch cheeks. They are happy.

We enter a passage lined with Helmut Newton photographs of languid women with aloof expressions, and pass under a low arch into another tunnel with saffron walls, the colour of my bedsheets. The air is sweet with the perfume of candles that burn on pyramids of wax melting at the centre of long narrow tables. Hundreds of candles had been sacrificed to create surreal sculptures like stalagmites in an ancient cave.

The music has grown soft, repetitive, a bass and drums. The couples on the oval dance floor move as if making love. A naked girl in a cat mask puffs on an electronic cigarette. They'll ban those, too, eventually, I thought. Egg-shaped niches with curved banquettes are inset along each side of the cave, those furthest from the dance floor a sanctuary for couples ready to become more intimate.

As you sit inside the egg, it's like returning to the womb, the helixes of your DNA still forming. In *Pink* you can open doors like shutters on an Advent calendar and find aspects of yourself that may have remained hidden. I can't imagine it is possible to describe a journey across the Sahara desert by camel without doing it, feeling the heat of the sun, the sway of the beast, the taste of grit in your mouth, the smell of baked air, a sense that time has lost its urgency and meaning. I knew when I wrote my second essay at Cambridge that I was going to write and to write, you must open the shutters and let the light in.

Lizzie catches the eye of a waitress, a girl in black suspenders with a tiny waist, breasts like fruit cupped in a bra, one strap off her shoulder. I watch the flirting couples, women who carry their sexuality with confidence, indifference. Images of the images by Helmut Newton. It is de rigeur to drink pink champagne. The tunnels are hot, the bubbly freezing.

The waitress emerges through the candle smoke with an ice-bucket and glasses. She smiles with her eyes, not her lips, and reminds me of me when I was eighteen, soft-edged, two steps from Saint Sebastian. The girl has green eyes, dark hair, pink lips, white teeth many in that room of women would have enjoyed being sunk into their necks and drawing blood.

After setting down the bucket with champagne, she juggles the glasses like a gunslinger as she transfers them from the tray to the table.

'Bravo,' says Lizzie, applauding. Lisa joins in.

The naked girl releases a jet of vapour from her e-cigarette and laughs, her voice shrill, a nail on a blackboard. A woman in white on wings wearing a mask floats across the room with a woman in black, a zip tattooed in loops from her ears to the corners of her lips.

Pink is a dream. A fantasy. It was where I had first met Lizzie.

She turned with a bewildered expression as I placed one of the glasses back on the tray.

'I should go,' I said.

'We've just got here.'

'I have a lot to do tomorrow.'

'Katie, it's barely gone midnight. Have a drink, for heaven's sake.'

'No, I really do have to go.' I stood and bent to kiss Lisa's cheeks. 'It was so nice to meet you. We will see each other again.'

She shook her head. 'Do you think so?' she said.

'We shall see.'

Lizzie eased herself out of the egg. She took a deep breath as if the effort was exhausting. I could see by her rapid eye movement that her brain was clicking and calculating.

She put her arms around my waist.

'You know I love you,' she said.

'Of course I do.'

'Send me your novel when it's finished.'

'That's going to be a while...'

'I'll wait.' She paused. 'You do know I know you better than anyone else in the world, better than you know yourself.'

'Probably,' I said, and we laughed.

She squeezed me tight and I felt, as she let go, like a soap bubble being blown out through a metal ring.

I made my way back along the passage, through the pounding beat inside the silver tube and out into the snow-grey night. I turned right and left into Wardour Street. I passed the girls in doorways, the girls with gooseflesh outside the strip joints, the dispossessed men sipping from bottles of meths, and turned towards Piccadilly where I could catch the night bus back to Hackney.

In Regent Street a man in a ragged tee-shirt with dead eyes approached selling the *Big Issue*. He was shivering, my age, perhaps younger, the streets are aging.

'Please,' he said. 'Please. I just need to sell two more and I can get a hostel for the night.'

'I've heard that one before,' I said.

He bounced along at my side. 'It's true, darling, honest. I'm freezing.'

'What happened to your clothes?'

'Robbed, weren't I? At knifepoint. Talk about scary.'

We reached the bus stop. I was going to save £20 getting the bus instead of a taxi. I took the money from my purse and his dead eyes lit up when I gave it to him.

'Twenty quid, amazing. Listen, there's an all-night burger bar round the corner. Want to have some nosh, you know, the two of us?'

'I thought you were going to a hostel?'

'It's alright, I'll stay at your place,' he said.

'You've got an answer for everything.'

'Got to try it on, darling. One day my luck's going to change.'

'I think it already has.'

'Does that mean you're going to take me home with you?'

'Sorry, boyfriend,' I told him; the word sounded silly to me.

'What you doing on your own then?'

'He's abroad, working.'

'And you're gallivanting around the West End. I dunno.'

The white light from a sign that said English Classes gave him the bleached look of someone needing a blood transfusion. He gave me a copy of the magazine and I watched him wander off. He had invented himself as a man robbed of his clothes at knifepoint. Even beggars need a business plan.

I sat at the front upstairs on the bus and watched the lights grow dimmer as we moved west to east. Like the Underground early mornings, I had never used buses at night and felt the sort of weariness I imagine refugees feel as they cross borders with their belongings on their backs.

I flicked through the *Big Issue*. There was an article about an actress who loved smoking; her picture reminded me of Bella, the same engaging smile, the same wilful look in her eyes. The first time I had gone to *Pink* was with Bella and Tara Scott-Wallace ten years ago. Ten years that had melted like Salvador Dali's soft clock. I had remained in the same skin, the same costumes, reordered the same doubts and desires in my novels. The book I was redrafting was flat, tired, insipid. Art is about breaking down internal structures and presenting the world from a different angle. Artists have to remake themselves or their work becomes formulaic, a product.

The cold when I stepped off the bus bit into my cheeks. I struggled with the door key, the wood had swelled, and ran up the stairs as if being pursued. I warmed my hands on the iron radiator, then opened my laptop. It was my writing time, but I didn't feel like writing. Emails tumbled in from the ether. I didn't feel like reading emails. White light pulsed in my head, the beginnings of migraine. I clicked on the *Dancer* file, keyed cmd+a and, without a pause, pressed delete. I glanced at the smoking man.

'Bet you didn't think I'd do it.'

He peered back with a weary look in his porcelain eyes. He was tired of waiting.

In an ironed black skirt, fitted blouse and low heels, I stepped into The Shard and rose interminably floor after floor to a bland open area with round tables and a view of the sun sinking into the outcrops of lower building. Of all the tall glass Towers of Babel in London, the elongated, pyramid-shaped Shard was the tallest with the most glass.

I could see in the lift's shiny fittings that my eyes had that hurt look that comes from lack of sleep and appeals to some men, those same men who like prostitutes, and for the same reason, I suppose. I had slept badly, my dreams twisted images of the night before, Lisa ice-white with blood running down the insides of her legs, Lizzie in a surgeon's mask; the pianist at the Cadogan Hall staring from the shadows like the Phantom of the Opera. The tree branch tapped out the rhythm of Bach's Concerto in C Minor as Marie-France sliced through the strings of her cello with the scalpel she had taken from the hand of a surgeon who I realised on second glance was Lizzie. I was looking round for something lost. My laptop, on the seat beside me, was covered in ants, and Ray Fowles was in the distance, the man under the lamppost lighting a cigarette.

When I woke, the first thing that popped into my head was Lizzie sitting across the table at Colbert: There's nothing wrong with a touch of jealousy, she says. You could say it's a sign of love. Jealousy and love. They were emotions I had avoided and considered irrational, another word that had passed across the table as we drank champagne. My big bed felt like a wasteland, a cold empty tundra, the wind moving through the window frames and shaking the blinds. The tree branch was building to a crescendo. I had a thought on the edge of my mind, like a word on the tip of your tongue, a funfair balloon that flew away before I could reach it. I slept again and woke restlessly from another dream where I was standing naked before a large mirror ironing a black skirt.

Evelyn was in full flow, a general reminding the other ranks how important it is to be 'on your toes as if you are wearing six-inch heels.' Always say yes, whatever the question. 'Remember we are in a service industry. The people who come to our events expect the best service.' She raised her fist.

'Team Talbot,' she cried.

'Team Talbot,' the girls echoed.

She had noticed me coming in, Evelyn noticed everything, and approached when the team talk was over.

'Late, Katie?' she said, and I shrugged. 'You'll be late for your own funeral if you're not careful.'

Evelyn was skeletal with streaked blonde hair in a French pleat, heels too high, a tad too much make-up, lipstick too far along the curve from pink to scarlet, a case of if a little of something is good, then a lot must be better.

'What would you like me to do?' I said, and she pointed at the table set slightly apart in a semi-circle of floor to ceiling glass.

'That's the power table. The booking came from the architects.'

'What are they building?'

'Does it matter?'

229

'Everything matters, Evelyn.'

Her hair remained immobile as she shook her head. 'Some buildings in Mayfair, two crescents that will make a circle. Something unique.'

'Until the next unique thing comes along.'

'I really want to get in with these people. Just be, you know,' she did a little shimmy. 'Just be great, Kate. We can really go places.'

'We?' I asked her.

'It's there if you want it. You've always known that.'

She tottered off in small steps. Evelyn didn't particularly like me, but must have thought I added something to Team Talbot.

We unpacked crystal glasses. The three men on the team, moonlighting actors, were in charge of opening the champagne, not something you could leave to girls, not on their own. Evelyn watched from below arched eyebrows, and the first guests began to wander in just as were finishing.

A man of indeterminate age, with gold in the bands of his turban, robes and dark glasses, entered with his court. Everyone grew silent before putting their hands together in a round of applause. Evelyn led the party to the money table and the sheikh sat between two younger Arabs, his sons, probably, polished young men in shiny suits with thick moustaches. The sheikh turned as if bored and gazed out into the mystery of the universe, the skyline hidden by low cloud. Helicopters glided by, the sound through the glass like the buzz of mosquitoes in the bedroom at night.

The names of the guests were embossed in gold on grey place cards and we girls in our tight skirts flapped about giggling as we helped the men find their places. There were almost a hundred guests, just two women, the party divided on twelve tables of eight. A four-girl string quartet in floor-length dresses played Vivaldi and Mozart.

When everyone was seated, we hurried to the kitchen where sombre chefs served soup in bowls with gold rims and gold crowns glazed into the china. We watched Evelyn until she gave us the nod and exited in a file with trays containing eight bowls of soup, breasts pushed forward, spines pulled back against the strain, and I thought for some reason of girls carrying water jugs on their heads in far away places.

The sons of the sheikh had moved to new positions. A tall, dapper man in a blue velvet jacket and bow tie now sat on the sheikh's right. On his left was a muscular, square-jawed ex-rugger player with a mane of flowing gold hair, wide shoulders and a wide knot in his gold tie. I drew the conclusion that the bow tie was the architect, the gold tie the main constructor.

As I placed the soup in front of him, he leaned round and gave my backside two soft slaps.

'Don't spill any, there's a good girl,' he said.

'You can be certain of that. I'm very careful,' I replied, and turned away.

The light had gone. The sky was leaden, vast as the sea. The quartet slipped through their repertoire. After collecting the bowls from the soup course, one of the new girls dropped her tray as she returned to the kitchen. Evelyn took deep breaths and gripped her fists. I helped the girl pick up the broken pieces. Like the sky, the colour had drained from her face and her hands trembled.

'It doesn't matter,' I whispered.

'It does,' she said, and I could see panic in her eyes.

The chefs were filling plates with roast lamb and vegetables, typically English, or typically Arabic. My stomach turned queasy seeing the vast quantities of meat, so much food that we would remove again from the tables and scrape into black bins. While we girls carried laden trays, the actors served a Côte d'Or Grand Cru; £800 a case wholesale, Evelyn whispered. The sheikh indicated that he would take a small measure of wine, and the rugby prop with the gold tie threw up his two hands as I placed a plate in front of him.

'Look, no hands,' he said.

'You'll need them for your knife and fork,' I replied, and he laughed.

'So, what's your name, honey?'

I paused. 'Kate,' I replied.

'Kate. That's nice. That's pretty. Hey, everyone, this is Kate. She's *very* careful.'

The two young Arabs studied me with eagle eyes and I thought perhaps they weren't the sheikh's sons but bodyguards. All over London that winter I had noticed vigilant men in black suits standing beside polished parked cars with black windows outside hotels, boutiques, night clubs, casinos, building sites.

We served treacle pudding. More wine that loosened their tongues. The noise level rose, drowning out the quartet. An MC in a white jacket tapped a microphone and fiddled with the electrics, preparing for the speeches.

The builder beckoned.

'Hey, Kate, Kate. Come here a minute. Come, come.'

The eyes of the men at the table were on me as I approached. 'Yes.'

He placed his hand on my bare arm – anchoring; I knew all about anchoring.

'I wanted to give you my card.'

He removed a card from his top pocket and gave it to me.

'Thank you,' I replied.

He ran his hand up my arm and down again. 'I thought you might like to give me a call.'

'You should speak to Evelyn.'

'Evelyn? Who?'

'If you need a waitress.'

'A waitress? That's the last thing I need.'

He swept his hand through his golden hair and laughed. He was handsome, sure of himself. The others laughed. The sheikh had made a spire with his fingers. His dark glasses were on me. This was a game. I imagined there was a wager at stake.

'No, nothing like that,' the builder added. 'I thought we could have a drink?'

'A drink?'

'Yes, you know, meet up, go somewhere nice. Anywhere you like. Have a drink?'

'A drink?' I said again.

'Yes. The two of us.'

'But why?'

'Why? Why not, Kate? Kate. You know, I love that name. Don't you think that's a great name?' he said, and glanced around the table. Everyone loved Kate. He looked back with a smile. 'See,' he added, as if some point had been proven.

'You want to have a drink with me?' I said.

'You got it.'

'Why?' I said again.

'Well, why not?'

'Because I don't know if you really want to have a drink with me, or whether you just want to go to bed with me?'

Now there was silence. The men at the closest tables had stopped talking and were listening.

'No, no, not exactly.'

'Then what?' I prompted.

'Well, yeah, if you want to put it like that.'

'Then this is a business arrangement?'

'How do you mean, Kate?'

'You don't want to know me. You don't want to go traipsing round the bars drinking. You want to take me to bed.'

He held up his palms in the same surrender gesture.

'Okay, you win. What do you say?'

The silence stretched. We were playing tennis. Maybe I'd broken his serve.

'I just thought, as a businessman, you understand everything is business. Politics is business. Sex is business.'

He smiled and did that thing, stroking my arm.

'You know something? I like a girl who's direct.'

'I've got your card. I'll text you my bank details.'

He sat back, grinning. 'You what?'

'I thought we'd agreed. This is business.'

'You're something else. OK, baby. You do that.'

'When you get my text, set a time and date and wire me £200,000.'

'You what?'

'I'll send my bank details.'

'Are you out of your mind? You want £200,000 for a fuck?'

'You don't think I'm worth it?'

'Nobody's worth that.'

'Yes, you're right.'

I glanced at the sheikh. The lights reflected in his dark glasses. The two young Arabs stroked their moustaches. Those men at the table by the window were used to getting whatever they wanted.

Evelyn, who missed nothing, appeared like Death in a play.

'Is everything alright?' she asked and the builder pushed his chair back before replying.

'This waitress of yours is soliciting,' he said.

'She's...What's that? What...'

'That's right,' he looked around the table. 'She wants me to wire her money, a lot of money.' He smiled at the sheikh. 'And in sterling, not dollars.'

Evelyn was shaking. She looked at me as I placed the business card down on the table. Evidence.

'Get your coat. You will leave this instant,' she said. I noticed her apologetic shrug as she turned to the architect. 'Nothing, nothing like this has happened before, I promise you.' She looked back at me. 'Go. For heaven's sake go. You are more trouble than you're worth.'

The round room of glass had grown quiet except for the quartet. They played on like the band on the Titanic and the other waitresses remained motionless like pillars of salt.

21
Sunrise to Sunrise

I walked home through the grey streets beneath my yellow umbrella with a feeling that I had taken on the world of bankers and builders. Not that I had. Those men at the money table were sitting back at that moment listening to speeches applauding their vision. The crescent buildings would rise over Mayfair and the woman in Norwich denied respite care would still be looking after her handicapped son. In the end, you have to decide who you are, take sides. There's no future sitting on the fence. Eventually, you fall off.

Since I had ironed my skirt that morning, an unformed thought had been playing through my head like a jingle, like a word in a foreign language you know you know but can't bring to mind. I stepped off the kerb into a puddle. My soaked shoe made sucking noises as I crossed the road. I told myself I would have to go out and buy another pair and, the same second, it occurred to me that I didn't have to do anything of the sort. I would dry the shoes, polish them, make do with the shoes I already had, that these small frustrations are like mist drifting in from the sea and concealing everything solid and tangible. On the corner, the scribble of white neon above the windows of a shop reminded me for some reason of meeting the man in the torn tee-shirt in Regent Street.

I took a shower, changed into my pyjamas and made scrambled eggs on toast. I sat at my desk with a mug of spice dragon chai, gave the yellow exercise ball a few squeezes, then watched my fingers type 'English School' into Google without being entirely sure why.

There are hundreds of schools where you can learn English and almost as many where you can study for the TEFL certificate you need to teach English. I sat back with that feeling you get when you're following a map and suddenly see a sign that makes sense. I remembered that night when Tom told Ray to contact him when he came out of the army. 'We need people who can do things,' he said.

I found a school a few stops down the tube line at Kings Cross with an intensive four-week course starting Monday, in two days. I emailed, apologising for being late applying. I explained that I would arrive at the school early Monday with the full fees and prepared to start immediately. I paused before adding that I had a degree in English and French Literature, and the opportunity of a job.

Sunday. Lunch with Mother. I needed a loan. Just a loan. I had withdrawn as much as I could from the ATM machines, I explained, but needed to top up what I had to pay the fees for the TEFL course.

'TEFL,' she said. 'Isn't that the black stuff they put on saucepans and it always comes off?'

'Teaching English as a Foreign Language. I'm going to become a teacher.'

'A teacher? Teaching what?'

'English.'

'I can't see much future in that, dear. Everyone we know speaks English.'

'Yes, Mother. I am going to teach people who do not speak English.'

'But why?'

'I'm going to Sri Lanka. I'm going to teach children at Tom's orphanage.'

'You are going to teach English to orphans?'

'Yes.'

She sat back and shook her head. 'You like this one, don't you.'

I nodded. 'I don't know why,' I said.

'There is no why, dear. It's that thing, you know, chemistry. Now hang on to him for heaven's sake. Don't go and sleep with all his friends, or whatever it is you do.'

'Mother, what are you saying?'

'You know what I'm saying. You're my daughter.' She paused. 'Not too tightly, mind you. They hate it if they feel suffocated.'

236

I wasn't drinking, I'd told her that, but she added a sip of white wine to my sparkling water for form's sake. She raised her glass and I followed suit.

'Good luck, darling,' she said.

We clinked glasses.

'Thank you,' I replied.

'You know I love you, don't you?'

'Of course I do.'

'Matt's weak. Don't think I don't know that. You're strong, Katie. I admire you for that.'

'I don't know what to say.'

'That's certainly a first.' We both laughed. 'You, teaching English. Who'd have thought it.'

I poured some wine in a wine glass.

'To you,' I said.

'To me,' she replied.

Piers Ashton, head of the Winston School of English, wore a beard, brown leather brogues and a white shirt with a top pocket bulging with pens and a spiral notebook. It would not normally have been acceptable to begin a course before completing the foundation work, but due to the extenuating circumstances, and incidental to the £1,200 on his desk, I was provided with a course book and a timetable printed on plastic. At nine, together with eleven other would-be teachers, I took my place in a classroom with whiteboards, chairs with writing trays that levered over your lap, and posters with grammar rules illustrated by cartoon ants with studious expressions and oversized heads.

I had thought it was going to be easy. It wasn't. Teaching English in a way that people who do not know the language will learn and understand is not the same as writing English for an English-reading audience. I had spent ten years bending and breaking rules, projecting my ideas beyond the obvious. Now I had to climb right back inside the box.

At lunchtime, I read my books while I had a sandwich and carrot juice at Pret. I called Tom immediately I got home each evening. It was a little after six my time, just before his bedtime. I was tempted when he asked me what I had been doing to tell him, but I didn't for reasons that were still not entirely clear to myself. I read up on Sri Lanka and asked him about the orphanage, the children, his work. We skyped good night kisses and I went back to my books.

Saturday, heart drumming, I booked a ticket from Heathrow to Kankesanturai in Jaffna. I adored the taste of the word on my tongue: Kankesanturai, its foreignness, its spicy flavour, its colour, the hard k and soft vowel ending. I reserved a room at the hotel where I had stayed that bleak night before Tom left on the same journey, the two bookings – and the promise of financial loss for cancellation – more a show of positivity than excessive confidence about the upcoming exams.

I worried myself sick, the same as when I was at school. I studied every night and the TEFL certificate presented to me by Piers Ashton at the end of the course took on the status of a passport to a new immigrant. It only occurred to me why I hadn't told Tom that I was taking the course when I had the qualification in my hand. To have failed would have been too much to bear, and now that I was 'one of those people who can do things,' and could prove it, it struck me that perhaps the last thing they needed at that moment was teachers. We skyped. We kissed. I would present myself as a fait accompli, and I finally removed the video camera from the box to pack in my luggage.

Lunch Sunday with Mother and Matt. He was starting a course in film editing and was going to borrow my flat while I was away. I spoke to Father, kissed the smoking man on the cheek and caught the tube to Heathrow.

Airports at night are a sort of Purgatory, neither heaven nor hell but an interval in life, a mini-death. The cold hand of hotel bedsheets. The half sleep. The roar of the alarm call. The long walk down dimly-lit tunnels, the wheels on the suitcase echoing behind me. The exhausting wait for the flight to be called. More tunnels. Sparky girls in pressed uniforms. A window seat with a glimpse of green light rising over the horizon. The assertive voice of the pilot with his weather report and expectations, the wheels folding beneath the undercarriage as London scatters behind us.

Jaffna sits on the edge of a lagoon surrounded by fan-palms and oleander. I could pick out the temples dotting the shoreline, the cluster of modern buildings, the dark presence of Jaffna Fort. The plane banked through low cloud, the engine roared and the runway slid beneath the skidding wheels. We create in our minds high walls and barriers, reasons for not doing things. When we do them, the walls we thought so high aren't there at all, they are just figments of our own self-doubt. Perhaps Tom had changed his mind; perhaps he doesn't like girls with murky pasts and broken fingers after all. If that's the case, it won't matter. Once the walls have come down, we can move on.

From Kankesanturai Airport, the taxi raced down the new roads of the commercial centre before twisting through a patchwork of colonial bungalows that emerged like polished teeth from the mature foliage. The driver wanted to practise his English; he was with the right person, a teacher with a new certificate. I glanced out at the places I had read about as he told me that he was married now and his wife was having a baby; he hoped it was going to be a boy and he was saving to buy their own house.

'Now tell me, madam, how is my English?'

'It is very good.'

'A gold star?'

'Two gold stars,' I said and he blasted the horn exuberantly.

The journey, with stop-overs, delays and the time change, had taken 24 hours. I had left at sunrise and, as we circled Jaffna Fort, I watched the labourers climb the scaffolding ready to start work on restoration. I had seen photographs of the 17th century stronghold, read the history, the arrival of the Portuguese, the Dutch, the British, 400 years of battles, exploitation, promises lit by the morning sun.

We curved down a winding unsurfaced road overhung by trees and the sea came into view. The sun was warm when I stepped out of the taxi and entered a low prefabricated building carrying my luggage. A woman in a yellow sari was mopping the floor. She was thin, dark, her smile lighting her tiny features.

'Good morning,' I said.

'Good morning. Good morning.'

'I'm looking for Tom.'

'Tom?' She looked puzzled.

'The doctor.'

She smiled again. 'Am. Am. Yes. Yes. Not here.'

'He's gone,' I said, and she seemed to understand my disappointment.

She went to the door and pointed to a track between the trees.

'Swim. Doctor Tom, he swim.'

She took my luggage without my having to ask, stood the suitcase and bag in the corner, then continued mopping the floor.

I set off down the track listening to the morning birdsong. It was sandy underfoot and I carried my shoes. I saw him chopping overarm through the sea, a tiny figure vanishing and emerging through the waves. There was a towel and a pair of size 10 thongs close to the shoreline where I sat and continued to watch as he swam away from me, turned, and swam back.

He ran up the wet sand and stopped when he saw me. He had a puzzled look, a look of such disbelief I thought at first he was angry. I stood. We approached each other slowly, like two animals meeting by chance and testing for danger. I stopped. He smiled and hurried the last few steps. He held me tight and kissed my hair, my cheeks, my lips.

'You came.'

'You don't mind?'

'I wondered how long it was going to be.' He paused. 'Mind?' he then said. 'I told you, if you didn't come, I was coming back.'

'I don't remember that?'

'On camera.'

'On camera?' I repeated.

'I left a message on the camera, the camera I bought.'

'I never looked at it. I'm sorry. I've been so busy.'

He smiled. 'Of course, you've finished your book.'

I shook my head. 'No. I took an English course, for teachers, I can teach English.'

'What? That's amazing. You never told me. You never looked at the message I left for you.'

'I'm sorry.'

'Sorry? Katie, you never need to say sorry. It was stupid, and cowardly. I should have just told you to your face.'

'Told me?'

'You know very well,' he said and I smiled.

'Yes, Tom Bridge, I do.'

We made love, hidden by a fold in the dunes. We swam and, later, we sat in his room staring at the small screen on the camera as Tom in his fisherman's sweater on a grey morning five weeks before said, in that mumbling English way, those things I had wanted to hear.

From the Author

Katie in Love is my sixth novel. The others came out with mainstream publishers Xcite and Random House. This time, I decided to go it alone and join the proud army of indie self-publishers – ten times the work but strangely satisfying.

If you love Katie in Love and would like to continue reading the Chloe oeuvre, may I suggest you begin where it all began with The Secret Life of Girls.

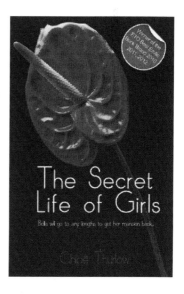

Poor Bella gets cheated out of her inheritance by her mother and wicked stepfather. With her good looks and awakening sexuality, she sets out on the path of revenge.

Available on Amazon.

During the 12 months I spent writing Katie in Love, I also started a blog at www.chloethurlow.com. If you are not a subscriber, do sign on and once a week you will find in your inbox a delicious slice of saucy erotica with a serious subtext and a tang of humour. Read one of the blogs on the diary page and you'll get the idea.

People often ask writers what they are going to do when they have published a new novel. The answer for me is quite simple. Start writing another one. That's what I am doing.

Made in the USA
San Bernardino, CA
10 December 2015